Monday Lunch in Fairyland
And other stories

Angela Huth

For a friend of Mrs Jones

Acknowledgments

The author wishes to make acknowledgment to the fact that some of the stories contained in this book have previously appeared in the following publications:

MONDAY LUNCH IN FAIRYLAND, MATERNITY and UP-STATE NEW JERSEY in *Cosmopolitan*; CONSEQUENCES, LOVING GOURMETS and THE FALL in *Harpers and Queen*; LOAF and THE OUTING in *London Magazine*; THINNEST ICE and DIRTY OLD MAN in *Over 21*; THE FRIEND in *Woman's Journal*.

Contents

Perdita, Twice

Lawrence made an emphatic decision, in February, never to see Perdita again. In May he decided, with equal determination, to put an end to the whole absurd plan.

He rang her one afternoon. She wouldn't be doing anything, he thought. Just frittering away the hours, as she always did after lunch. She was hopeless at afternoons. They weren't her time of day. They depressed her. He was positive she'd be there. She was.

'Hello, Panther.'

'Oh, hello.' Not for anything would she let herself sound surprised, Lawrence realised, with some admiration. 'Hang on. I'm eating something.' He hung on. 'I thought you weren't going to ring any more.'

'I wasn't.'

'Oh, well, now you have.'

Lawrence paused. Then he asked her what she was eating.

'A biscuit thing made out of sesame seeds. I found them in a health shop last week. Not fattening. Much better for you than ordinary sweets. Was it February we last spoke?'

'Yes. The seventeenth.'

'So it was.' She was silent again. Lawrence asked her what she was wearing. Before, this had been a sign between them that if one asked the other on the telephone what he was wearing, it showed that the asker wasn't cross any more.

'Purple boots and an old skirt. You don't know them.' She laughed slightly.

'Is your hair the same?'

'Longer. Where are you?'

'At the office.'

'Work going all right?'

'Fine. Fantastic.'

'Eugenie all right?' She pronounced the name very carefully.

9

'Fine, too.'

'That's good.'

Lawrence's secretary came in and reminded him by signs that he should be at a meeting.

'When shall I see you?' he asked Perdita. Punctilious about time, the thought of the meeting confused him. Instead of thinking up a good way to put the question to her, he bungled it in his hurry.

'Meet?' She sounded genuinely surprised.

'Why not?'

'Do you really want to?'

'Of course. Otherwise I wouldn't be ringing.'

'You won't get at me, will you?'

'I won't get at you.'

'All right, then. Saturday afternoon. How would that be?'

He loved her for that. Once she'd made up her mind about anything, she got on with the practicalities. He thought about Saturday afternoon.

'That should be all right. Eugenie's doing something with the children. I don't think I'm expected.'

'Two-thirty, then. Usual place.'

'Wait in the car for me.' For a split second he hesitated, trying not to ask the next question. But he couldn't resist. 'I forgot to ask : how's Oliver?'

'You didn't forget. He's *very* well, working like the devil. Expanding.'

She laughed again and put down the telephone. She never had learnt to say goodbye.

Saturday afternoon : drizzle but a bright sky. The leaves on the trees seemed frizzy in the rain, almost a vulgar green against the clouds. Lawrence, half an hour early, stopped by the familiar pillar box, turned on the sports news and began the *Times* crossword.

Perdita arrived ten minutes late, parked her red Mini two feet away from the opposite kerb, and ran to Lawrence's car. He let her in quickly. Even in the short dash across the street her hair was misted with raindrops, and her cheeks shone.

Lawrence kissed one of them, smudging the wet as he did so.

'You smell of Irish stew and bittermints,' he said.

'You know it's the only thing I can cook.'

'Oliver like it?'

'Very much, luckily.' They both laughed. Lawrence started up the engine without asking her where they should go. Perdita crossed her hands on her knees and looked at his profile. 'Why did you ring me?' she asked.

'I don't know. I thought we might as well remain friendly.'

'Quite.'

Ten minutes later he said :

'I've found a very good new wholesale place for wine.'

'What, you mean better than that place, what was its name, where we used – ?'

'Much better. I'll give you the address, if you'd like me to.'

'That would be useful. Although, actually, Oliver gets all our wine from Christie's. I think he enjoys the sales.' Our wine, she said.

'Does he, indeed? I wouldn't have thought he had the time.'

'Well, he makes it.'

'But you said he was expanding.'

'He is.'

'In which direction?'

'Oh Lawrence, shut up.' She giggled.

'I'll keep the wine place to myself, then.'

He stopped the car in a clearing in the park reserved especially for cars. Before them was a litter bin, the mild slopes of grey grass, and shaggy trees smudgy as fingerprints, dull in the rain.

'We may as well get out,' Lawrence said.

'What, in this?' She was already half out of the car, eager to please, to show that small things like rain didn't finally matter when it came to the test. Lawrence took her arm.

'It's terrible, this sort of place, on a Saturday. I liked Saturdays at Oxnead.' They'd once had a cottage at Oxnead.

'So did I. All that cow parsley in the garden, about this time of year. It was lovely, even when you came down so late on Fridays.'

'Actually, you hated it.'

'I didn't.'

'You did, you know. At the time.'

'Well, anyway, in retrospect I liked it more than I didn't like it. Don't let's argue.'

Lawrence kicked at a bit of tinfoil shining in the grass.

'The mess. I'm going to join some anti-litter committee. Eugenie does a lot for the pollution people.'

'Does she?' Perdita smiled a little to herself. 'And does she help you out at all with your work?'

'Well, she couldn't really, could she? She doesn't know anything about it.'

'What does she do?'

'She has a very full life. She's very efficient. Looks after me bloody well. Cooks beautifully, runs everything, thinks up surprises . . .'

'How nice for you,' said Perdita, quietly, without sarcasm. Then she added, 'Luckily for me, Oliver loves me for all the things I can't do as well as the things I can. I no longer surprise him in any way. He just accepts me. Sometimes, it's almost as irritating to be accepted by him as it was always to be queried by you.'

'I'm sorry. But I expect it's better that way.'

'I expect so.'

They held hands and began to run, Perdita a little behind Lawrence, puffing, complaining of a stitch; Lawrence saying nonsense, she shouldn't be so unfit; the rain slanting blearily across their eyes. He stopped at last under a tree, let Perdita cling to him, laughing, her head on his shoulder, while he kissed her damp hair, saying you silly fat one and all the things he used to say. But soon she was drawing back and looking at her watch.

'I must go. Oliver'll be back. I have to get tea for the children.'

'As a matter of fact,' said Lawrence, 'Eugenie will be getting back too, expecting me.' He took Perdita's arm and they began to retrace their steps. 'Now if it had been you and me, Panther, we could have relied on the other one to make our own toast.'

'Of course.' She laughed : once she had started laughing almost anything he said she would respond to with this familiar, infectious laugh which he had first loved her for.

He drove fast back to London – this was the only difference, this not having all the time in the world – and back at the pillar box, in the steamy car, he said :

'That rocking horse we bought in Bath – it's still in my attic. I must arrange to get it over to you.'

'So you must,' said Perdita.

'We could meet and discuss it.'

'Breakfast Wednesday, then. The Connaught.'

'That's as good a place as any,' he said, 'to discuss a rocking horse.'

He rang her up every day after that, missing her, suddenly. Once, one afternoon, she rang him. She'd never admit she missed anyone. She merely said she wanted someone to make her laugh. Any of their old jokes would do. And they did.

At breakfast, though, they got off on the wrong foot from the start. Lawrence was late because he overslept – having stayed awake most of the night in order not to over-sleep – and Perdita hated to be kept waiting. She snapped at him and wasn't amused by his excuses, nor mellowed by his apologies. She was an unfeeling bitch, sometimes, Lawrence remembered. This sort of scene brought it back to him. Funny how, remembering her, this side of her character always evaporated. It was the laugh, the gayness, the slightly wicked observations, the warmth of her that remained.

But halfway through the kippers an elderly man they both knew came into the restaurant. He nodded as he passed them by a look of happy conspiracy in his baggy old eyes.

'Think he'll say anything?' whispered Perdita. She loved illicit, or semi-illicit situations.

'I think not,' said Lawrence. 'He's known to be discreet. Any-how, why should we hide? What's there to be ashamed of?'

'Only the past,' said Perdita.

The presence of the old man brought them together again. They mentioned neither Oliver nor Eugenie, and talked gaily only of themselves. They didn't leave till ten, elated, springily, laughingly wondering whether it was wise to meet again, and knowing that they would.

That very afternoon Perdita rang Lawrence at the office. He knew something had happened. She was using her flat voice.

'It's Oliver's divorce,' she said, after a few irrelevant preliminaries. 'It's suddenly come through much quicker than we expected.'

'That's good,' Lawrence heard himself saying. 'Funnily enough, Eugenie's should be through fairly shortly, too.'

A long silence. Then Perdita said, at last :

'So I suppose that means we should get on and do something about ours.'

'Of course,' said Lawrence. 'I'm afraid my solicitor hasn't been hurrying.' He paused for a while, then went on : 'It's funny about timing, Panther, isn't it? I mean, we knew the divorces were coming up, all three of them. We were sticking to what we'd decided to do, happy about it and all that. It's just that, well, I was rather enjoying having an affair with my wife.' With a very sharp pencil he dug a pattern of dots on to his clean blotting paper. He heard Perdita sniff, or choke or something. 'Don't be silly,' he said.

'Sorry,' she said at last, absolutely controlled, ludicrously gay, even managing a laugh. Then, for the first time he could ever remember, she said goodbye.

Loaf

Afternoons like this, Loaf hated. Afternoons like this he'd like to be up in the hills with his stick, bashing at the brambles or lying in the shade chewing a bit of gum. A man shouldn't have to work in this heat. Especially as there wasn't even any sun: just grey, dull, sultry heat so you could almost touch the stickiness in the air, and there was nowhere you could get away from it, no shady places.

Loaf sat on a bale of straw in the barn. His big legs in their khaki dungarees were slung apart to support a saddle. He polished its dark leather with an almost defiant feebleness, his big head hanging to one side, small strange eyes staring at the shining reflections that emerged, as he rubbed, from the dull surface. At his feet a couple of brown hens scratched at clumps of clover. Their silly clucking annoyed Loaf, a little, as it always did. Though once when his mother had taken him into the town for the day, a dreadful day with a tie round his neck and carrying paper bags of women's shopping, he'd said on the train coming back, 'I missed those bloody hens.' Now he said, 'Mind out, you pretty buggers,' and gave them a kick with one of his big, slow feet.

He didn't hit them but they squawked in their daft fashion and raised their wings, as if any such pathetic gesture could help lift their plump bodies out of Loaf's way. He looked up to see Gracie standing up at the barn door, lolling as usual, still in her school uniform.

'You hurt them and Pa'll go out of his mind,' she said.

'Ah,' said Loaf. Gracie with her airs and graces – he'd teach her one day.

'Tea's on,' Gracie added. 'But I should finish that saddle if I was you.'

"Tis finished.' Loaf put the saddle on the ground and stood up, newly conscious, as he was many times a day, of his own massive height. He looked far down at Gracie. She was small for fourteen, but had lovely breasts beneath her schoolgirl shirt, anyone could see that, and spindly legs under her short skirt. She gave him a funny look, challenging, like she often did, and pouted her pretty mouth.

'Come on, then,' she said, 'you got to have a bath tonight.'

Loaf followed her to the house, remembering. It was tonight he'd promised to go with her – well, been forced to promise by his parents. The thought of it made him roll his shoulders, and feel the huge wet patches under the arms of his shirt. He'd give anything, anything not to have to go. But there was no getting out of it now. For a week, since the suggestion had been made, he'd been wracking his brain for some idea that would release him from the ordeal. But nothing had come to him and all the thinking had made him slow and clumsy. Pa had been sharp with him several times, and threatened to send him to work on a neighbouring farm.

At tea Gracie was all excitement but still managed to get through a large amount. Loaf pushed his own plate of eggs and sausages away. He felt sick enough already.

'Eat up,' said his mother. 'I've no patience with poor eaters wasting good food.' She was skinny as wire herself, never ate a thing.

'Be glad when tonight's over and Loaf's back to his normal brilliant self,' said Pa. 'Done a good job on the saddle, have you?'

'Done a good job, Pa.'

'Hung it up?' There was a long silence.

'Well, I was going to,' said Loaf.

'It's on the floor,' said Gracie. 'Quite safe,' she added. Another silence.

'There's no call for tell-tales,' snapped her mother, taking away Loaf's plate of unfinished food. Gracie pouted.

'I only said because I knew Pa'd do his nut if it stayed there all night, and Loaf might forget, all the excitement.'

'You'll hang it up right after tea, Loaf,' said Pa.

'He's got to have his bath,' said his wife.

'He'll have his bath after he's hung up that saddle or he'll not be going to the dance.'

New hope leapt within Loaf. Gracie wailed.

'Shut up that noise,' snapped her mother. 'Loaf'll hang the saddle up *then* have his bath.' In the end, Mother always had the final word. She ran her hand through her son's short hair.

'And get that hay out of your head and put on some of Pa's grease.'

Loaf knew better than to protest. When his family wanted to do something they had their ways and means. They had quick tongues and a flow of words that always beat him. In his head, he could argue against them : in his head he was just as brilliant as they were, full of convincing arguments on his own behalf which, had he been able to articulate them, would no doubt have won them over. But getting over his own point of view was the trouble : translating thoughts to words was not a talent he possessed. All his life the easy spinning of words had eluded him, leaving him stranded, unable even to shout for help. And other people, even his family, in all their busy going back and forth, had little time for his predicament.

He had a bath and dressed himself in his only suit of baggy grey flannel. With it he put on a white nylon shirt and a plain blue tie, and greased down all but the most impossible spokes of his hair. Then he hung about in the kitchen, feeling more enormous than usual, waiting for Gracie.

When at last she arrived he understood why she'd been so long. She'd done something to herself, all right. She looked terrific, pirouetting about, aware in every fibre of her body of her own attraction.

'Like it?' She looked down at the bouncy pink skirt jumping about her legs as she moved, the neck of the jersey scooped out so that her breasts bulged above it. Her hair moved and shone : she had thickened her long eyelashes with black mascara and greased her pouty lips. Only her legs seemed frail and child-like : almost sad, their spindliness, Loaf thought. Weren't the ugly clumpy shoes too heavy for them?

'Oh yes,' he said, dully, because he was still thinking of her poor legs having to bear the weight of those shoes.

'Smashing,' said Pa, smiling. Gracie could always make Pa smile.

'And do hold your head *up*, Loaf,' said Gracie.

'Yes, chin up, Loaf,' said Pa. 'You've a sister to be proud of tonight.'

Loaf raised his head. His hair touched the beams of the ceiling. He tried to smile at Gracie, but she was frowning at him now.

'Couldn't you have worn anything more – you know?' she asked.

Loaf felt his heart quicken. He didn't much like Gracie, most of the time, but he didn't like to disappoint her, either. He didn't understand. Mother had gone to great pains to choose his clothes for the evening : she'd been pressing and brushing all afternoon.

'All this and I'm wearing the wrong things?' he said.

'Of course not,' said his mother, quickly. 'You're lovely and smart, Loaf, take it from me.'

'But all the others'll be in jeans and tee-shirts,' said Gracie.

'Then Loaf will be much better turned out,' replied her mother. 'Now, you'd better be getting along.'

Pa drove them in his old car. Loaf sat in the back, brushing the seat with his hand before he got in. He didn't speak, but loosened his tie a little. Gracie chattered excitedly to Pa. When they arrived at the village hall, and got out, Loaf remembered about his head and held it up for a while.

Inside the hall an explosion of sound unleashed the sweat glands in his body. The wetness he had been dreading arrived with startling suddenness : with each new blast from the band the dampness spread, from arms to feet, to face to spine; it even trickled down his legs. Unnerved, Loaf put his big hands to his ears, then caught someone looking at him, so smeared his gesture into one of casualness, as if he was merely rubbing them.

He looked round for Gracie. She was already gone. He couldn't see her.

'Excuse me, you're blocking the door.' Someone had pushed him. There seemed to be so much room. It puzzled him he could be in the way. He moved.

18

Loaf

As he walked away to a row of empty chairs by a wall he felt his head jerk in time to the music : he couldn't control it. When he sat down, he gave in and let it loll to one side. Sideways, he looked about him. The hall had been decorated for the occasion. A solitary string of coloured lights was strung across the ceiling. Paper roses were pinned to the glittery curtains drawn across the high-up windows, and posters of pop-stars were stuck here and there on the shabby green walls. Loaf thought it looked very nice.

He turned his head to the band on the stage. It consisted of four very small, thin young men with long hair and scarlet hearts painted on their cheeks. They wore identical pink satin shirts, and winced and swayed as they clutched at their instruments, as if the wood and strings were hurting them. One of them was singing. Loaf couldn't catch the words. The voice was a shrieking groan that struggled to surmount the music. But the frenzy of their massive sound was successfully transmitted to the dancers. Forty or fifty young things, all in bright clothes and no ties, were springing about with a wild rhythm, their eyes rolled up to the coloured lights, every part of their bodies rippling with the music. Loaf watched their fast, skilful feet for a long time, then shuffled one of his own, so gently no one would notice, under the chair.

He caught sight of Gracie. She was the prettiest and best dancer in the room, definitely. People were looking in her direction. The man opposite her, to whom she seemed to be directing her sinuous movements, was the only one who had his eyes shut. He looked a decent enough sort of guy, Loaf thought, but with his eyes screwed up like that and his head thrown back, he, too, might have been in pain. Then Loaf noticed a message on the man's tee-shirt. *F**k me*, it said. Loaf felt the hot dampness beneath his heavy clothes again. He stood up, head jerking. He'd have to rescue Gracie somehow, or he'd never hear the end of it from Pa.

He walked round the edge of the room, careful not to get in anyone's way, to a point where he thought Gracie, if she looked, would see him. For a moment she glanced in his direction.

'Gracie,' he said. But perhaps she didn't notice him, because she didn't stop dancing. Obviously she couldn't hear him. Loaf lifted one of his hands, looked at it, then waved it at her. She still didn't see. She was laughing at the man with the shut eyes, and stamping her skinny legs so that her skirt flew high. There was nothing left for Loaf to do, other than go over and drag her off the floor, and he'd never do that, not for anything. Maybe she'd be all right so long as he kept watching her. So long as he didn't let her out of his sight. If anyone tried to lay a finger on Gracie he'd bash them over the head, in the stomach, everywhere, till they were unconscious.

He bought himself a Coke and a cheese sandwich from a long table covered with drinks and food. He took them back to another empty chair, further from the band, and settled himself to watch Gracie. As the music ripped painfully through his head, and the dancers confused his eyes, he thought how nice it would be to be able to go home and say to Mother and Pa in the morning how much he'd enjoyed it all. How much he'd liked the music and the dancing. How nice it would be, too, he thought, if they really were Mother and Pa, if he was their real son like Gracie was their real daughter. He didn't have such thoughts very often, just sometimes when things went badly, when Pa shouted at him and he forgot to do something he'd meant to do for Mother. Then, for a few days, he'd find himself looking about more carefully : looking out for a very tall old man who just might be his real father, and a woman with very whitish hair, like his own, who could be his mother.

Gracie was coming towards him, her body still wriggling with the music, followed by the man whose eyes were half-open now.

'Stop staring, can't you?' she shouted. 'Your eyes always on me gives me the creeps.'

Loaf blinked. He wanted to say he was unaware he'd been staring and he was sorry if he'd annoyed her. But the man put his hand on her shoulder and pushed her away. They went towards the food table. Loaf stood up, watching them. He felt himself shaking. He saw Gracie point to the gin. The man poured her a glass and added orange. Gracie wasn't allowed gin. If Pa knew Gracie was drinking gin there'd be a row all right. He moved towards the table and almost at once got in the way of some dancer.

'Mind out, Loaf the oaf,' shouted the swaying girl, and laughed at the hirsute man dancing opposite her.

Loaf dodged out of her way, looking at her. Familiar face. Chemist shop – that was it, the girl in the chemist shop who'd made a rude joke when his mother had sent him to buy a laxative. Remembering, he blushed.

He sat down again, nearest chair he could find, gripping on to his empty Coke bottle with both hands. With a jerk of his head he saw Gracie and her man leave the hall, carrying their drinks. He swallowed, searching for moisture in his mouth, and looked at his watch.

He looked at his watch again two hours later when Gracie returned, alone. By now the evening was almost over. The satin shirts were packing up their instruments. The new quietness of the place had left Loaf feeling weak, and still he sweated. Gracie came up to him, perky as anything.

'We off, then?' Gracie was flushed, pleased with herself.

'Oh yes, if you want.' He didn't want to be any further nuisance to her. He wanted her to have her own way now, to make up for his staring.

'Come on, then. Derek's gone. He offered me a lift on his bike, but I said no, Pa'd do his nut.' Swing, swing, swing she went, towards the door in front of Loaf.

Outside it was still warm and airless, a faded summer night with a cloudy moon. Bikes revved up, white arms shuddering on handle-bars, shiny girls on the back seats squealing to each other.

'Wish I could have gone with Derek,' Gracie said.

'Sorry,' said Loaf.

They walked down the quiet road between tall black hedges. Soon as they were out of sight of the hall Gracie took Loaf's arm. He couldn't remember her ever having touched him before.

'Quite gives me the spooks, the dark,' she said. 'Doesn't it you?'

'No,' said Loaf.

'The spooks . . .' She drew out the word, then gave a shriek. 'Ooh my God, there's a shadow moved, Loaf.' Her hand tightened on his arm.

'It's nothing, really.' Loaf was pleased to be able to reassure her. He looked down at her. He smelt gin. She seemed a little unsteady on his arm.

'You been drinking?'

'We had a couple. Gin and orange, my favourite drink. The gin brings out the taste of the orange, Derek says. He's right, mind.' She giggled. 'Did you notice Derek? I think he's smashing. Very gentle.' She was quiet for a while. 'He kissed me, you know. He wanted to go on, but I said no. I said you mustn't do that Derek, or we'll go too far.' Loaf felt her small body stiffen.

'God, I wanted to go too far,' she said.

'Did you?' said Loaf.

They were walking very slowly now. The farm buildings were in sight. They walked the rest of the way in silence. There was a quiet stir of animals in the farmyard, the sudden darting flight of a bat, a smell of warm manure, and tobacco plants that grew by the barn. An owl hooted.

'Jesus, that scared me,' said Gracie. She stopped, forcing Loaf to do the same. 'You're brave,' she said. 'So brave you'd dare come with me into the barn for a fag.'

'A fag?'

'Derek slipped me one. You wouldn't tell Mother and Pa, would you? But Christ, I'm dying for it. I daren't smoke it in my room. Pa'd smell it out and do his nut.'

'We wouldn't want to set the barn on fire,' said Loaf, slowly.

'We wouldn't do that, silly.' Gracie broke away impatiently from Loaf and started towards the barn. 'We'll take great care.'

Loaf followed her, half flattered, half afraid.

The barn rustled, full of dark shadows and warm musty smells of clover hay. They sat on a bale of straw. Gracie lit her cigarette and puffed smoke at the doorway, a dim square of sky in which the moon floated halfway up.

'Wouldn't like to spend a night in here alone,' she said. 'I'd be dead scared.' She passed Loaf her cigarette. 'Have a drag.'

Loaf shook his head. 'Go on, be a devil.' Loaf shook his head again.

Gracie sighed. 'I don't know what you *do* like,' she said. 'I sometimes wonder what goes on in your head, what turns you on.' She shifted herself a little. One of her legs touched his. He didn't move, frightened of annoying her. 'What really gets you?' she asked.

'I like going up the hills with my stick,' said Loaf. 'I like beating the bushes so's the butterflies come out.'

Gracie gave a small laugh. 'Big deal,' she said, eventually.

'Probably sounds silly,' said Loaf, 'but you did ask.'

Gracie leaned back, supporting herself on the bale behind them. She took another long draw at her cigarette, carefully watched the smoke filter up into the darkness. 'And mind the ash, for Pete's sake,' Loaf added. His limbs felt suddenly tight.

'I'm not a fool, Loaf.' Gracie sounded languid, slow. Not at all her normal pert self. 'D'you like sex?' she asked.

'Sex?' Just saying the word sent a quiver down Loaf's back. 'What d'you think of it?'

Loaf hesitated. 'I'm not sure.'

'Go on.' Grace laughed again, kindly. 'Have you ever had it?'

'Had sex?' The quiver again.

'You're being awfully dumb. You can tell me. Go on.'

'Well, I suppose, not exactly *with* anyone.'

Gracie sat up, interested. 'That way it must be awfully boring.' She nudged him. 'Aren't you dying for it with someone?'

Loaf looked at her.

'I am,' she said.

In the deep brown light her pinkness was mottled with shadows. She was warm and smelt of gin. Her lips shiny, her hair tangled prettily. Loaf was unable to move. Ever since she had been a small child Gracie had been able to exercise a carotic effect upon him, though never so strong as now.

'Yes,' he said, after a while.

Gracie shifted again. Her leg was touching his on purpose now.

'D'you think I'm sexy, Loaf? Derek does. He said he knew what he'd like to do to me all right.'

A strange havoc raged in Loaf's loins.

'If you've finished your cigarette, I think we'd better go in.' He felt his voice to be unsteady.

'Here. Your responsibility.' Gracie handed him the stub. He flicked it out of the door, glad to have something positive to do. Hand very weak.

'You ever seen a girl undressed?' Gracie was lying back again now, legs a little apart. Loaf studied her small sharp child's knee. He clasped his hands together to protect himself from touching them.

'No,' he said. He paused. 'Did you hear me? I said I thought we should go in.' He felt her hand on the back of his neck.

'Wait a tic, Loafy. I'll show you.'

Loaf tried to get up. Instead he turned to her.

She had pulled her jersey out of the skirt. It was gathered up under the chin, leaving her breasts triumphantly bare : firm, pale, two perfect round shadows at their centre, quite still, while the barn shadows trembled around them. Loaf looked, and looked.

'Go on, touch them. Do you good.'

'I'm your brother, silly. Gracie . . . come on.'

Gracie put a hand on his arm. 'Brother, phooey. Only in name.' Child's voice once more, sulky, wheedling. 'See if I can't turn you on. Promise I won't tell.'

'Pa'd do –' Loaf was up from the bale, free from her, head high in the darkness, running, breaking through the green square of sky, feeling the familiar catch of the back door under his fingers . . . The stairs, then, two at a time – the noise, never mind the noise . . .

He threw himself on the bed. His heart battered at his ribs, his trousers strained round the crotch, his whole body was clammy. He closed his eyes : darkness replaced by a million scarlet chips, spinning, spinning. *You'll pay for this, Gracie, with your airs and graces . . .* The words a banner in his head. He groaned out loud.

Loaf lay quite still for some time. He had no energy to get up, undress, put on the light, get into bed. Only a different kind of energy within him, disturbing, wakeful, prowling his blood, weakening him.

His door opened gently. He reached up and switched on his bedside light. He knew it was Gracie. *You'll pay for this Gracie* . . . The interval without her had given him time to muster a little of his reasoning.

She stood there, defiant, beautiful, in a blue dressing gown. Make-up still on, but stick legs bare now. Bare feet, too. She closed the door behind her.

'Sorry,' she said. Loaf swung his legs on to the floor.

'You must go back to bed, Gracie,' he said. The words were difficult. 'You must. You must, Gracie . . .' Looking away from her, he knew his head had lolled to one side.

'I know I must.' She giggled. 'It's just – I didn't want to go with you so mad at me. And I was feeling so – you know. I couldn't help it. I should've gone home with Derek.'

'Go, now,' said Loaf.

'Yeah, all right.' She opened her dressing gown. 'Just thought you'd like a look at all of it before I do.'

Loaf jerked up his head. The scarlet chips, blasting his eyes again, crowded the slice of her body that the dressing gown exposed. They gathered, crazed, round her breasts and stomach, darkening as his eyes lowered. Then she ran towards him.

'I'm not revolting, am I?' she screamed. 'Why won't you touch me?' She threw herself upon him so that for a moment he felt her soft warm flesh against his face, his hands. He pushed her from him, lifting her up as he did so. She weighed no more than a large box of apples. When her feet reached the floor again he supported her crumpled body, watching her sway. Then he hit her, heavily, on the side of her face.

'You little . . .' No word came. He watched her fall. She screamed. The noise was a profound exacerbation in his soul, causing his skin to contract, to go cold. He looked at her, lying on the rug, face down, dressing gown covering the bony little back. Breasts too heavy for those bones perhaps . . . She began to cry. Perhaps that's why she was crying. A child's noise. Loaf had forgotten she was a child. Forgotten why he hit her.

He looked up to see the door had opened. Mother and Pa stood there, Pa first, in old woolly night things. Faces askew.

'What happened?' Pa was at once kneeling beside Gracie. Loaf whimpered. Tomorrow, they'd send him away. Maybe tonight.

'What happened, child?'

'I don't know. Loaf . . .' Gracie was sobbing badly. Mother looked down at her, severe, drawn beige mouth.

'Best carry her to her room, Pa,' she said.

Pa picked the child up, averting his eyes as he wrapped the dressing gown over her nakedness. He carried her out of the room.

Loaf hung his head, listening to her diminishing cries. He could feel his mother's eyes searching him, silent. He could see her hands kneading the clotted wool of her night-gown. She had brought a powdery, angry smell into the room.

'I didn't . . .' he said. 'I'll go in the morning. Pack my bags.'

'Look at me, Loaf.' Loaf raised his head. Mother's eyes, always small, were shrunk with tears that gave them an extra skin, but the tears stayed poised where they were, no signs of over-flowing. He'd never seen her like that before.

'She'll have to be the one to go,' Mother was saying. 'We've had this trouble before, Loaf, so many times. Didn't you under-stand? Had you no idea?'

'I'll go,' Loaf persisted. 'I'll be the one. Gracie's your real daughter.' The words all rushed.

'I said : don't you understand, Loaf? Others . . . many others in the village. Complaints at school. Why do you think I asked you to go with her to the dance, to take special care of her? She's fourteen.'

Loaf found his mother's quiet words beating themselves into a pattern in his head. A shape he was beginning to understand, though not believe.

'What's the matter with her?' he asked.

Mother hesitated. Chose her words carefully. 'She's very precocious. But we thought at least with you, her brother – '

'But I'm not really her brother, am I?' New confusion : the chips gathering again in his eyes.

'I'm not, really . . . you know I'm not.'

He remembered quite clearly Gracie saying that in the barn,

lying back, lying back. He'd always known.

Mother turned, eyes dried out and larger, neck pulled high. 'It's how we think of you, Loaf,' she said, and left the room.

They sent Gracie to a special school, far away, and Loaf continued his work on the farm. But since the dance an increasing listlessness came over him. He found it hard to concentrate on the simplest job. Pa snapped at him, doubly confusing him, and Mother seemed to notice him less than was her custom. From time to time he begged them to let Gracie come back. It was his fault, he said, and he didn't like to see her punished. But they wouldn't listen, said they didn't want to talk about her. She was ill, was all they would say: better get her cured while she was young.

Loaf spent more time than he used to in the hills. There, he was alone with his picture of Gracie lying back in the barn, the most beautiful thing he'd ever seen. She'd done something to him that night, Gracie had: just to think of her he trembled.

He trembled and bashed at the bushes with his stick. Restless, up in the hills, he'd bash till the butterflies flew out, pretty butterflies not half as pretty as Gracie, Gracie who'd done something to him that night damn her lovely mouth and breasts and eyes. Restless, bashing butterflies, he knew he'd not resist her when she returned. Mother and Pa'd do their nuts, send him away, next time. Still, he knew what he had to do. Restless, bashing butterflies . . . He'd wait.

Consequences

Professor Gerald Bravington met Leonora Thorne on the 8.15 from Pewsey to Paddington. He noted with pleasure that by some chance, for a Tuesday, the train was not crowded. The professor chose the compartment she alone occupied. He sat by the window, opposite her, back to the engine : his favourite seat, when he could get it. He observed that Miss Thorne, as he later discovered was her name, wore a red coat and was filling in the *Times* crossword with considerable speed.

It was a fine morning, but condensation on the window obscured the view. The professor wiped his hand across it, making a wide ribbon through which he peered at the familiar landscape. After a while Miss Thorne, who had been clicking her pencil against her teeth, said :

' "Our sincerest something with some pain is fraught". Do you know what ?'

The professor drew his eyes from the fields to her face. She had good teeth, white and even.

'Laughter,' he said.

'Thank you. That's it. I can never do the quotes.'

'They're all *I* can ever manage,' the professor answered, who was not a crossword puzzle man.

There were papers in his case that he should attend to : he had planned to read once more through his notes on Carlyle, in the hopes that he would not have to refer to them on the platform.

'If it wasn't so heavy I'd bring the *Oxford Book of Quotations* with me,' said Miss Thorne. 'If it wasn't for the quotes I'd get it done most days by Hungerford. My father, before he retired, always managed to do it between Newbury and Reading.'

She folded the paper and put it on the seat beside her. Her eyes were restless, grey. They turned down at the corners, matching the slant of her mouth. The professor put a hand on his briefcase, making to open it.

'Haven't I seen you somewhere recently?' she asked, frowning. 'On television or something?'

'Could have done,' said the professor. 'I show my face from time to time.' He disliked being recognised, and thought attempts at conversation too bold, so early in the morning. Women's Liberation had killed the art of the subtle approach.

'Thought so. Do you live down here?'

The professor considered not answering her question. It was no business of hers where he lived, and probably of no interest. Yes, he did live down here, in a seedy rented cottage on the banks of the Kennet and Avon canal. Damp all year round : no heating, unreliable light. Three thousand books and a broken sofa. A willow warbler outside the kitchen window, milk in bottles left to clot, used tea bags cluttering up the sink. It had all got on top of him, somehow, since Mrs Jenkins had given up her weekly bicycle ride across the fields to help him out. Yes, he lived there, if you could call it living : reading, writing, eating out of tins, swallowing pills to induce a few hours of fretful sleep.

'I do,' he said eventually, eyes back out of the window. He heard her cross her legs, the rasp of her tights.

'Sorry to have interrupted your concentration, but I knew you'd know your Shelley.'

Was that sarcasm in her voice? Or merely the impatience of a woman used to men reacting to her swiftly? In any case, her guess might easily have been wrong. She was taking a silly line.

'Ah,' he said. 'I'm little acquainted with Shelley, as a matter of fact. Not very fond of him. I learnt *The Skylark*, at school. It was drummed into us along with *Ode to the West Wind*.'

But Miss Thorne's head was bent over a book now. Huffy. She shrugged, but said no more. The professor had offended her, he supposed. In the old days, when he was more concerned about doing right by women, he was always offending them. He possessed no talents to charm them; that had always been his problem. He had felt uncommonly – quite disturbingly – inclined towards one or two of them in the past (the names Patricia and Teresa came briefly to mind), but the partial independence he had always insisted upon had not satisfied them. They required more than he had been prepared to give – his entire being, his every private reflection, a whole mass of promises concerning love and fidelity in the future. So far he had never felt all that was worth bargaining for, and so, some twenty years ago, the professor had abandoned the search for an ideal woman with whom to share his life. He decided that no such thing existed. Those who thought they had found perfection fooled themselves, as the years would show.

Out of the running, the professor was a happier man. Disillusion no longer disturbed him. The occasional woman who attempted to glut her own loneliness, desirousness, whatever, upon him, he could treat with impressive indifference : Madam, he would say, don't waste your time. I have no sympathy, no compassion. Go elsewhere. And at the ice in his voice they would give up, knowing he meant what he said. Now, the only women he depended upon were those he paid to ease the domestic side of his life. He missed Mrs Jenkins because without her the rubble of the cottage had become almost unbearable. When he could summon the energy he would have to try to lure some other woman from the village, by means of extravagant wages, to replace her. The professor sighed at the thought.

The train pulled into Paddington. He saw that the uncovered ends of the platforms were wet, and wondered at what moment of the journey the skies had changed without his noticing. Foreboding gripped him. He hated London rain.

'Taxi,' he said out loud, standing up.

'Taxi,' said Miss Thorne. 'I never take the tube, I'm afraid. I can't bear it.' She spoke vehemently, as if the tube was someone who had offended her in the past.

They walked together up the platform, stood side by side in the queue. A silent wait for ten minutes. It was always like this on rainy days. For practical reasons the professor asked Miss Thorne where she was going : to share a cab would at least halve the wait for one of them. Ludgate Circus was her destination.

'Well, how extraordinary,' remarked the professor, 'for I myself am bound for the City. Therefore it would seem sensible to share . . .' Miss Thorne nodded without interest.

In truth, the professor was going to Baker Street, the opposite direction. But there was plenty of time. If he had made his way directly to the lecture hall he would have had to spend a dull hour in the canteen. Half an hour in a traffic jam with this strange red lady seemed preferable. Nonetheless the professor felt himself blush at his own lie. A man much concerned with the truth, to hear himself lie with such easy spontaneity was disturbing. He turned away to concentrate hard on an advertisement for hair oil that blared across the murky walls of the station. Goethe was right: 'Man thinks he directs his life, leads himself: but his innermost being is irresistibly drawn in the direction of his destiny.' Destiny had decreed that he and Miss Thorne should share a taxi. Therefore the lie was forgivable – indeed, imperative.

At last it was their turn. They sat side by side on the beige leather seat, encompassed in the stuffy air that smelt of old cigars. The professor's briefcase lay between them. Miss Thorne's gloved fingers played scales on her navy leather bag. She wore shoes of matching blue decorated with gold chains. Good ankles.

'Wish I could remember where it was I saw you,' she said, turning to look at him. 'Some programme about education, could it have been?' Her eyes held such enquiry that the professor felt afraid.

'Ah,' he said. 'I'm asked from time to time for my opinion upon diverse subjects, and find myself accepting with little relish.' What he had meant to say was that he did a bit of television in order to pay the bills. But the red lady's musky scent, which the professor had not noticed in the train, had stifled the cigar fumes and rampaged through his senses in a curious fashion. He noticed that the buildings of London, this morning, seemed to be made of coarse grain, shifting as if in a wind. Through the rain-pearled windows familiar streets were quite distorted so that it was difficult to be sure, on this well-known route, precisely where they were. And it was necessary to hear more of the lady's voice.

'You do have a funny pompous way of talking, if you don't mind my saying so,' she said. 'Wonderfully old-fashioned.' She smiled kindly. Extremely kindly, white teeth a-dance among scarlet lips.

'Really? I wasn't aware . . .'

'I shall look out for you,' she said, 'on television.'

As far as the professor could tell, they were passing the Savoy. It was then he asked her name, and was told Leonora Thorne.

'Beautiful name, Leonora,' he said, wondering if that, too, sounded pompous.

'Probably helped me more than anything to become an executive secretary,' she said.

'Is that what you are?'

'That's it.'

'Very impressive.'

'Quite dull. But well paid. In a year's time I shall stop commuting and stay at home.'

'What will you do at home?'

'Help my father with his orchards. We sell apples and plums.'

'Ah.' The professor could not imagine her, red-coated, up a tree, basket over her arm. 'Crossword in the lunch hour, then?'

'I suppose so, or I'll become a complete cabbage, won't I?'

A cabbage among the apples. The professor smiled as the taxi pulled up at the door of a stern building. Miss Thorne opened her bag, fumbled for her purse. The professor touched her gloved hand : he would not hear of it, he said. It was on his way. Miss Thorne looked at him in belief. She got out of the taxi, tossed her hair in the rain. The professor leant out, shook her hand. She thanked him. He said perhaps they would run into each other again one day on the train. Perhaps, she said, and ran to the door. Rain splashed her shining blue shoes. Her red back disappeared quickly, impervious. As the taxi moved away the professor noticed the name on a small brass plate : Benson & Benson Ltd., Engineers. To whom in Benson & Benson was it the happy destiny to have acquired Miss Leonora Thorne, dreaming of her orchards, as executive secretary? Silly thought : but the professor would have given much to swap places with that person this morning.

As the taxi made its slow way towards Baker Street Professor Bravington found himself thinking about the exceptional white-

ness of her teeth. Over a cup of tea in the canteen, guest of
several students, he found the chains of her shoes glinting in his
mind. On the platform itself he managed to banish Leonora
while he concentrated upon Carlyle, and was rewarded by
keen applause. But on the train returning to Pewsey – empty
compartment very bare without her – she returned to him : the
lilt of her voice, the funny way she boasted about her ability to
do the crossword. The professor, repeating his earlier gesture,
wiped a clear space in the steamed-up window, and watched the
rain slant across fleeting trees. He thought about her father's
orchards : apples and plums, she had said.

Professor Bravington was set upon a course from which he knew
there could be no diversions. Exactly when the climax of that
course would come he did not know, or care to know. It was a
subject on which he would not question himself. He was content merely to let himself drift from day to day, without anticipation, until the right moment became recognisable.

When he arrived back that raining day from London, a feeling
of unusual melancholy hung over him. His bicycle dripped in
the station car park, its seat quite sodden. The rain battered
into his eyes as he rode, and walking across the field to his
cottage the mud seeped into his shoes. He was used to such
things. They did not bother him. His mind was normally on
bookish matters, too involved to be disturbed by the heaviest
rain. But today, detachment from physical discomfort was
suddenly not possible. There was no ignoring the wet, the chill,
the bleakness of the evening ahead.

And the cottage itself, he noticed, was particularly desolate.
The thatch was black with water. A thick curtain of raindrops
fell from the eaves. Inside, the sickly smell of damp. Water
dripped from a yellow patch in the kitchen ceiling and over-
flowed from a saucer the professor had laid on the floor in the
morning. The sink was full of dirty plates, gaudy smears of dried
egg yolk and baked beans – horrible colours in the gloom. The
professor, still in his gloves, lit the kettle. Its instant hissing made
a companionable noise, but the tin of tea bags was empty. With
some distaste he plucked a damp tea bag from the pile under

the plates in the sink, and put it in a mug. Through the window
he could see that the solitary white duck, which of late had fre-
quented this stretch of the canal, was huddled in the reeds on
the bank. Head under its wing, it lay quite motionless.

The professor put logs on to the ash in the grate and lit a
fire. The small flames had no power to slay the feeling of damp –
they barely warmed his feet. He kept his coat on and lay back
in the broken armchair, mug of revoltingly weak tea to warm
his hands. Later, he ate some dry cream crackers and drank
several glasses of whisky.

He watched himself steering his way down the narrow course
he had set, eyes strictly ahead, not glancing in any direction for
indications of help. There is no likelihood of rescue if signs
of desiring rescue are not given, and the professor was not one
for troubling others with his trivial depressions. The apparent
futility of his life, he believed, was something that concerned
him alone. He had always believed in the protection of one's
friends from oneself. And besides, these days, due to his own
apathy, his friends were scarce. They saw him from time to time
on television and wrote letters of congratulation on his dazzling
articulation and good sense. 'Saw you in excellent form as ever,'
one of them had written only last week, 'country life must suit
you.' The professor was grateful, but only required that these
few remaining friends should keep their distance. He never invited them to the cottage, and refused invitations so constantly
to their London dinner parties that they had long ago given up
asking him.

Professor Bravington played with a small pile of biscuit
crumbs on his thigh, dividing and sub-dividing them into patterns. It seemed to him that what had happened today had
caused the faintest – indeed an almost imperceptible – hesitation
in his journey. Leonora Thorne, her wonderful conventionality
shining brightly in train and taxi, had stood like a stranger on
the bank and waved a wave of recognition. The gesture was a
a little unnerving. The professor desired no recognition on his
solitary way. And yet . . . the smugness of her tailored coat,
her dreary bag, her matching shoes – they symbolised a gentle
pleasure he had ceased to imagine many years ago would exist

for him. Perhaps to pause with her for a while, a mild autumn picking fruit in her father's orchards, would cause no harm. Not an affair, of course. At the thought of the absurd process of shedding clothes only to cling to another body in the dear privacy of his single bed, the professor blew all the crumbs from his thigh on to the floor. Not an affair in that sense : just a rewarding union of minds. (Maybe she would be interested in Carlyle). The temporary cheer of companionship – a drink in the pub, scrambled eggs in here by the fire. (He could clean the place up, somehow). Walks down the towpath. She might like the smell of wild chives in spring, if their association lasted that long.

The professor would not let her come too close, of course. All she would see of him would be the public man, the humorous intellectual who smiled on television. He would not warn her of his destiny : that would be unfair. All he would ask was her response : smiles and laughter for a while, before he pursued his way.

For a drunken fantasy, as the professor realised the whole thing was as he stumbled to bed much later that night, the idea had taken a curious hold. It had not faded next morning, as soberly he regarded more rain. And a week later it was still vivid, providing him with a new energy. He preoccupied himself with trying to clean the place, though was soon diverted from this hopeless task by renewing acquaintance with old books. Each day he walked far along the towpath, watching swallows swoop to dip their breasts in their own shadows on the water's surface. He would walk until he was cold and wet and tired, and then have a lukewarm bath in his damp and peeling bathroom, which scarcely warmed him but afforded an illogical pleasure.

One afternoon, some three weeks after he had met Leonora Thorne, the professor, inspired by a silvery rainless day, decided to be practical. He would buy provisions at the post office, then make his way to the call box.

For once, he enjoyed the shopping : bought the entire stock of Ambrosia creamed rice, four dozen boxes of matches, firelighters, tinned pilchards, raspberry jam, sliced bread, sausages, margarine, Pears soap, and a packet of toffee, which he liked to suck on his walks along the towpath. He felt there were other things he should have remembered, but for the time being they escaped his memory. He tied the box of provisions on to the rack behind his bicycle seat, and pushed the heavy machine the few yards to the call box.

Inside, he gasped for air: vile smells of wet cement floor and stale cigarette smoke. He leant against one glass-paned wall, heart beating jumpily like it used to in the early days of appearances on television. Directory Enquiries gave him the number of Benson & Benson. He made a small pile of ten pence pieces, in case the call should be a long one.

'Benson & Benson, good afternoon.'

The chink of his coin.

'Miss Leonora Thorne, please.'

'Miss Thorne?'

Terrible silence, bringing back to the professor his first teen-age date acquired through a telephone call to some nubile girl in Windsor. He remembered the trapped isolation of a call box, only possible to escape from by the cowardly act of putting down the receiver. He remembered the alarm of silence. The fear brought about by his own determination to hang on.

'Mr Wheeler's office. Can I help you?'

'Leonora?' Surely it wasn't her voice.

'I'm sorry, Miss Thorne is in South Africa for a month on business. Can I take a message?'

'No. No, thank you. No message.'

The professor put down the telephone. Silly not to have rung before. But a month was not so very long, he thought. Why, it was almost a month since he had seen her. Thirty days. Give him another chance to clear up the cottage.

But stacking the tins of rice and pilchards into the kitchen cupboard – mice droppings on every shelf – it seemed longer. Tea! That was it. He had meant to get more tea. The professor swore out loud. Tea-less, thirty days was hopelessly long.

Then he began to laugh at himself, at the absurdity of the whole plan, at the weeks he'd waited brooding upon it when it was in fact irrelevant to his central strategy. He cursed the disease of hope, for the restlessness it caused, the silly flutterings of the heart. Damn Miss Leonora Thorne and her thoughtless waving : she had lost her chance. He would not recognise the signals. Like all the others, having offered some fragment of hope, she had failed. He was no longer interested, he no longer cared. There was tinned rice enough till spring. Tomorrow he would clean the shelves – for himself, not for the benefit of Miss Thorne. Tonight he would read Carlyle, and eat pilchards straight from the tin.

Much later it rained again. The professor tried to block his ears against its battering of the window, but the sound penetrated the sparse feathers of his pillow. Miss Leonora Thorne, as he sailed once more down his course, still waved from the bank, smugly, in her tailored scarlet, with the mocking smile of one whose existence is to remind. Damn her : she would fade. Trespassers upon solitude were easily cast out. They had no power to distress, and what most concerned the professor at present was the itching of his eyes.

For several days he had been afflicted by irritation of the eyelids. Each time he blinked they seemed to scrape his eyeballs with filaments of glass. As a result, the eyeballs were raw and tearful. He bathed them night and morning, but felt no improvement. Now, in the dark, heart pounding from half a bottle of whisky, and head bleary from sleeping pills, they fiercely hurt. The lids scratched the balls in a way that made sleep impossible. Reluctantly, the professor got up and went down to the kitchen.

There, the fire was dead and water dripped from the ceiling again. Black rain slashed against the windows and the wind keened with horrible self-pity. In his half-drunk state the professor felt a sense of shock : he was used to such depressing things, but not in the middle of the night. He poured himself the rest of the bottle of whisky and, not counting them, swallowed a clump of sleeping pills. Then he went to the sink and chose two damp tea bags from the pile on the draining board. He had heard they contained antiseptic and could soothe sore eyes.

He carried them upstairs and returned to bed. After turning out the light he lay down and arranged the tea bags on his closed eyelids. Almost immediately, he thought, he could feel some improvement. In celebration he drank the rest of the whisky – an awkward feat in his recumbent position : some of it ran down his chin and wet the neck of his pyjamas. Perhaps this is the right time, he thought : then, confused by the pills and alcohol, he remembered it was not so. Another thirty days. If Leonora Thorne had not faded in another thirty days . . . He might give her one last chance.

His eyes ceased to hurt and the wind faded. The sound of the rain dulled against the windows, no longer to be avoided, quite soothing in the dark.

They found him ten days later, decomposing in his narrow bed, tea bags dry but still in place upon his eyes. No one in the village could imagine his motive for suicide : he was a quiet man, the professor, they said – kept himself to himself, but always so charming to talk to. He seemed happy enough, full of smiles in the pub on the rare occasions they saw him – just as he was on television. Pity.

Leonora Thorne's trip to South Africa was cut short by three weeks due to an economic crisis in the firm in London. On the train, her first day back to work, irritated by the change in plans, she completed the *Times* crossword with particular speed. All but the quotation. Further irritated, she turned to the obituaries, which she always enjoyed. There she saw a picture of Professor Gerald Bravington, described as an eminent man of letters. She had not thought of him since the day he had given her a lift in the taxi. Now, she remembered, he had helped her with the Shelley quotation on a rainy morning such as this. He had struck her – in as far as she had thought of him at all – as being an eccentric old thing, nervous – not at all as he appeared on television – and pompous at the same time. Inquisitive, too. He had asked her questions about her life, she recalled, with an eagerness which had exceeded the bounds of mere politeness. Perhaps she should have been more friendly in return, but she was fed up with men pestering her, seeking her out for comfort and all the rest of it, but never offering permanence. Still, it was always a pity when someone of such ability died before his time.

Leonora Thorne turned back to the crossword. For some reason the news of the professor's death inspired in her a determination not to be defeated by today's quotation, at least. She read it again.

The whirligig of time brings in his —

The line was quite unknown to her, she had never been good on Shakespeare. But, with uncanny speed, the word was suddenly there, dazzling her mind.

Revenges, she wrote, and smiled to herself, knowing it was right.

Had there been time, she might have paused to reflect upon the strange coming of her inspiration. But the train was already drawing into Paddington. Leonora Thorne stood up, smoothed her scarlet coat with her navy glove, as was her daily habit, and thought of the fortune she was obliged to spend on taxis, these days, due to so much rain.

Thinnest Ice

Laura's cheek was cold.

Apart from that, it was a perfectly normal evening, a Tuesday. Philip stuffed his glass full of ice before filling it with gin and tonic, a trick he had learnt in America. He liked to show, through gestures rather than words, that he had been about a little in his time, although he had given up the travelling side of his business when he married. In spite of Laura begging him not to – she knew how much he had enjoyed his jet life – he had been insistent. Of course they could trust each other, but he had seen enough of what could happen to the most trusting married couples when one or the other of the partners was much absent. But his peripatetic bachelor days had left their mark. He still wore Indian cotton shirts and suits from Hong Kong, smoked Russian cigarettes and drank bourbon on the rocks.

Laura sat opposite him on the sofa, her evening face ready with concern. In two years, he had never come home to find her anything but full of love, welcome and interest. She had learnt, from her meticulous mother, that a man is entitled to be selfish at the end of a day. He needs to come home to a wife who casts aside – at any rate to begin with – the petty cares of her own day, and is all sympathy for his. On this score she never let him down. She was always there, ice in the bucket, dinner prepared, curtains drawn in winter, cushions on the garden chairs in summer. Philip had come to rely on these things, and would no longer trade for them a business trip to any part of the world.

He had, in fact, only the vaguest idea of how Laura spent her day. He imagined she shopped, and took care of domestic things in the morning; lunched with a friend, went to an exhibition in the afternoon – he was quite proud of her interest in the arts. One day a week, he knew for certain, she devoted to a group of disabled people in Kensington. But she rarely spoke of her activities at the Day Centre, perhaps for fear of boring him. Sometimes she mentioned taking a job – what job, exactly, was never discussed, and none of the plans had ever materialised. She seemed content enough with her quiet life. Soon they would have children and the peace and privacy would be changed. It was her right to enjoy the peace while it lasted. Philip approved.

In the dappled light of their sitting-room he studied her face. Such innocence, he thought. Such innocence, and a fist of pain screwed round in his chest. He had telephoned her at five, to check what time they were expected for dinner, and there had been no reply. There was never no reply at five o'clock. Laura was always there at that time, in her apron in the kitchen eating ginger biscuits (he liked it very much when he caught her on the telephone with her mouth full, barely able to speak) sifting through her cookery books choosing something for their dinner. He had rung at quarter past and half past. Still no answer, and he had left for home. There, of course – and the underground had never been so slow – she was waiting for him by the fire, holding up her peculiarly cold cheek for him to kiss. He had managed not to ask where she had been. Now, he studied the familiar patterns of room, aware that he was seeking something as he looked at the framed prints on the silky walls, plump cushions, fringes that hemmed the sofas and felt table-cloths – the autumn colours of the square conventional place, their sitting-room, that he loved so much. For a moment he found that each piece of furniture, each ornament, was back-lit by a strong light, making it strange. He struggled with the illusion, fighting it off like the end of a nightmare, pressing his fingers against his icy glass, and the room returned to normal. First signs of flu, he thought. Several people had it at the office. Or, as Laura had often said recently, he had been working too hard.

'So what've you been up to this afternoon?'

Laura looked surprised. She shrugged.

'Nothing much. The cleaners. Boring things.' There was a lilt in her voice, an unusual brightness. She paused. 'You don't have to change,' she said, 'but I shall. We're meant to be there at eight-thirty.'

'What are you going to wear?'

The gin had melted the odd pain in his heart, replacing it with warmth. Laura's smile, with its power to reassure, had become part of his existence. The spell of black fantasy, the signs of encroaching flu, were over.

'You'll see. Surprise.'

She surprised him in a flurry of smoky velvet that he had not seen before; jet beads at her neck, amber gloss on her cheeks. Philip frequently suggested she should buy new clothes, but, with a nice sense of economy when it came to other people's money, Laura rarely took advantage of his encouragement. When she did, Philip was always pleased. She had taste, the girl. Wonderful taste. In the narrowness of their hall he congratulated her.

'Christ,' he said, 'all those husbands will be after you.'

'Nonsense,' Laura laughed, spiralling about, making the velvet flutter with shadows. 'You carry on just like a newly married man.'

They drove through fog to Hampstead. At dinner Philip was aware of every movement his wife made at the other end of the table. Bored by conversation with the high-pitched women on either side of him, he fell to musing, as he often did, on his luck in having found Laura. He quite understood why other men envied him. She was not only beautiful, as now, in the candlelight, but she was spirited. Exuberance blew off her like gold dust, touching other people, so that in her presence they found themselves reflecting her brightness. Her head was bowed. She was listening carefully to the man on her left, who taught Russian at Oxford. Philip heard the word Chekhov several times, and saw Laura smile. Ah! She was intent on educating herself. Having been unenthusiastic about coming to this business dinner party, she was now revelling in the don's company. *Revelling. Smiling. Smiling almost constantly.*

With a sharp movement Philip pushed back his plate. The duck stuffed with brandied plums quite suddenly sickened him.

The old pain stabbed at him again. He closed his fists on the polished table.

Philip was a man of instincts : this he often claimed. Several years back, big game hunting in Kenya with experienced guides, he had suddenly sensed the dangerous proximity of an elephant. His companions had scoffed at him; they had seen it charge, enraged, in the opposite direction. It would never have returned so soon, they said. But such was Philip's conviction that they were persuaded to return to the Range Rover. No sooner had they done so than they saw the elephant a few yards from them, half hidden behind trees. It bellowed, prepared to charge; they escaped. Another time, alone in a bar in London airport waiting for a plane to Switzerland, Philip heard with uncanny clarity a voice telling him to switch flights. Without asking himself any questions at the time, he did so. A few hours later, he heard that his original flight had crashed in the Alps.

And now his instinct was at work again, gripping him in its horrible conviction. Laura, after only two years, was being unfaithful to him. What's more, she was being pretty blatant about it. The previously innocent, once embarked upon deceit, are often the most skilful. Here she was, not six feet from him, putting up an immaculate show. No one would ever guess she and the arrogant don had spent afternoons, days, months, for all he knew, in some form of contact. Not just talking about bloody Russian writers all the time, either. Christ, what a fool he was not to have seen it all before. Philip's mind jerked back to other occasions when they had met the don, Crispin – ridiculous name – with mutual friends in Oxford. Now he came to think of it, Laura had always made a point of paying him special attention, asking him questions and listening to his interminable answers with her big eyes. She said, he remembered, Crispin was shy – shy! But that when you got to know him, he was wonderfully entertaining.

Philip refused the cheese, the soufflé, the coffee. The heat of the room tightened about him; the candle flames, magnified by their own halos, pained his eyes. Only a lifetime's training in the art of politeness enabled him to contribute to a conversation about

43

duck-shooting with the woman on his left.

After dinner, regathered in a beige drawing-room, Philip saw a look pass between Crispin and Laura as they chose their places : Crispin sat by his wife on the sofa, Laura talked to her host. Unspoken calculation. A tedious hour passed until the goodbyes, when Laura and Crispin merely nodded to each other. Admirable restraint. Philip took Laura's stiff velvet arm. Then they were in the car again, pushing through the solid fog.

'Well, that wasn't so bad, after all, was it? I was lucky getting Crispin. You know what he was telling me? He was telling me that the problem at Oxford these days – '

Philip wiped the windscreen with the back of his hand. Laura watched his face.

'Are you all right, darling? You didn't eat a thing.'

'I'm all right. Get that rag and keep wiping.'

They concentrated on their journey.

The next morning the feeling of unease had died. On his way to work Philip convinced himself he was being ridiculous. It had all been in his imagination, due to overwork perhaps. He spent a contented two hours reading through a long report, able to give it his full attention. At eleven Laura rang. This was unusual. She did not like to bother Philip at the office. There was some minor problem about servicing the car. The conversation was brief. Laura ended :

'See you at the usual time this evening, then.'

'Of course.'

It was only when he had put down the receiver that Philip realised what Laura had done. By ringing him now, she was making fairly sure that he would not ring at five : there would be no need. Thus he would not discover her absence. She would have no need to lie.

Philip's afternoon passed in a turmoil of disbelief. How could she? Laura? What had he done to deserve . . .? Where had he gone wrong? At five, hand shaking, he rang her. No answer.

Laura's cheek was cold again. And again, apart from that, it was a perfectly normal evening. They watched a documentary on television and ate devilled chicken's legs in the kitchen.

Philip opened a bottle of her favourite Sancerre.

'Why such extravagance?' she asked.

'I don't know.' He wondered if she noticed the quaver in his voice. He wondered why, when one human being can see a beast that haunts him, revolting as some creation of the devil, another person can remain unconscious of the vile, almost tangible presence.

'I don't know,' he said again. 'I was thinking. Laura : I was thinking – if ever all this . . . If ever you decided all this wasn't what you wanted after all, you'd tell me, wouldn't you? I mean, you wouldn't put up with it, bravely, just for my sake, without telling me, would you?'

Laura looked at him in amazement.

'What a funny idea,' she said. 'What on earth's on your mind? You look quite pale.'

With a tremendous effort of will Philip forced himself to laugh.

'I expect I sound quite mad. It's just that – I don't know. Such innocence as yours, such continuing innocence, makes one quite suspicious sometimes.'

'Oh, you silly idiot !' Laura laughed and blushed. 'You should find yourself something *really* to worry about.'

She was so convincing that for a moment, in the warmth of their kitchen, Philip felt the chill of shame. In bed he made love to her with unusual violence : she responded with surprised pleasure. If she was tired from her don lover all afternoon, then she did not show it. If there were recollections of his touch in the recesses of her mind, they stood little chance of survival while Philip thrust himself, full of his own agony and love, upon her. In his frenzy he bruised her, hurt her, and she cried to him to stop. She slept quickly, as she always did, her body curved into his.

Philip lay on his back listening to her breathing, and watched the picture show of his wife's infidelity glitter on the ceiling. She and the brute don lay on an anonymous bed, location impossible to define. Where did they go? How often and for how long? What did he do to her? The academic hands, luminous in the darkness, stroked Laura's thighs, Laura's cheeks,

Laura's . . . Sickened by the vision, Philip took a sleeping pill, shut his eyes, tried to shut his mind. But sleep would not come. Both drained and alert, he watched the fogged dawn infuse itself into the room. When Laura eventually opened her eyes Philip buried his face in her hair, clinging to her, murmuring he had had a nightmare.

He drank only a cup of black coffee for breakfast, and left for the office feeling icy cold, flesh taut against his bones. He crossed the road and stopped to look back at the leaf-green façade of their house – a small, narrow house in a quiet street behind Notting Hill Gate. They had found it soon after they married. In summer, Laura filled its window boxes with pansies and geraniums; now, they were planted with small evergreens bright with orange berries. It was a nice, conventional house, with a welcoming look about its windows. One of them, the kitchen, was lighted. Philip could see Laura moving about, a grey silhouette, gathering up the breakfast things. He wondered how long it would be before the telephone rang and she and Crispin arranged today's meeting. As he wondered Laura bounced towards the telephone on the dresser. Philip saw her nod. He saw her smile. He felt his breath come very fast – for a moment he opened his mouth and gasped the air, letting out a small moan – then struggled for control. Laura put down the telephone and left the room. A light went on upstairs, in the bedroom. As Philip's eyes travelled towards it he noticed a web of cracks over the green paintwork of the façade. The paintwork is cracking, he thought to himself : it's time we had it done. I must tell Laura to organise repainting. He turned away, began to walk towards the underground. How strange, he thought, that green paint should last so little time. Must be pollution. Pollution destroys everything.

When he rang Laura from the office at five she answered the telephone. Relief confused him. He could think of nothing to say.

'It was just – I noticed cracks all over the front of the house this morning. The paint. It's worn so badly. We must get it done. Could you ring the builders before – '

'Cracks? What are you talking about?'

'Cracks, darling. All over the front of the house. Honestly.'

'But there isn't a crack to be seen.'

Philip could sense her puzzlement.

'Well, never mind. Maybe, in the fog – I must have imagined it.'

'You must have.'

'Be back in an hour.'

So today she and Crispin must have done it at lunchtime. Crispin must have had to get an early train back to Oxford. The weekend. Of course, the weekend. How would they communicate between tonight and Monday? Philip decided to make sure he would answer every telephone call. He could not bring himself to ask questions, but if he caught her out she would have to explain.

And there was nothing else for it. He would catch her out. Exhausted by the thought, he set off for home.

Philip unlocked the front door very quietly, a sense of horror at his own action. He could hear Laura talking on the telephone in the kitchen. Unusually low voice. A laugh. Noiselessly, Philip pulled the door shut behind him, crept a few paces further into the hall. Then he stood, quite rigid, and listened.

'That's funny,' he heard her say. 'That's terribly funny. I want to hear more when I see you.' Oh, they had their jokes, she and Crispin. Riotous jokes he knew nothing about, killingly funny jokes to make them squirm and giggle between kisses.

'So you'll be here tomorrow, then,' she was saying, 'about three. We might see if there's something good on locally.'

Tomorrow? Michael, her younger brother, was coming to visit them tomorrow. A great heat exploded in Philip's head. He swung round, opened the front door, banged it shut, pulled off his coat, ran up the stairs as the telephone clicked. Laura must not see him in this state.

He shut himself in the bathroom. Its familiar pinkness was unstable, as if he had cocooned himself in a shaking blancmange. Breathe deeply, Philip, he said to himself, leaning against the basin, and take a look at yourself.

He saw in the pink glass mirror the face of a man who had been spying on his wife : a man haunted by suspicion, convinced by instinct. Wild hair, huge eyes, fear.

'You're loathsome, you're despicable,' he said. 'How far will you go?'

Later, some measure of equilibrium restored, he poured himself an extra large gin and tonic and paced the small sitting-room. Laura sat in one corner of the sofa doing her tapestry, half-smiling, innocent as usual.

'You're restless,' she said.

'I am, rather.'

'Anything the matter?'

'No. Not sleeping very well, I suppose.'

Sated by her own life, Laura had no notion how troubled were his nights. He had often thought of waking her, asking her for the truth which would put an end to his own suffering.

'Come to think of it, you seem to be rather thin.' Laura's eyes travelled all over him. 'Perhaps you're getting something.'

'Perhaps.' Philip sat down at last, crossed his legs, spun one ankle. 'I often wonder,' he said, 'how you fill your days. Sometimes at the office, you know, I try to image what you're doing, and I've really no idea.'

Laura glanced at him. Quickly smiled.

'I think I'd better keep you in the dark. If I told you the truth you'd not only be bored, you'd be ashamed of me for not thinking up better ways to pass the hours. But I've decided quite seriously that after Christmas I'll get a job – in fact I've more or less found one. That art gallery in Notting Hill Gate – you know – they apparently want someone half-time. That would suit me very well. Be a good idea, don't you think?'

'I should think it would.' Philip plucked at his Hong Kong trousers. Of course a part-time job would suit her well. Regular hours would mean terrible complications, maybe even the necessity of deceit. *Oh Laura! So quiet, so tranquil, in the lamplight, how is it that you love someone else, that you count the hours till you see him, that you let him into the most private parts of you . . .?*

'Oh, Laura!' he cried out loud.

'Philip!' She ran to him, put a cool hand on his forehead. 'What is it? You're looking most . . . peculiar.'

'Don't touch me, please.' He removed her hand.

'What is it?'

'Leave me. I'm all right. I just . . . I'll ring Dr Bruce in the morning. Get some tranquillisers.' He rose and went to the tray of drinks. 'Worry about all this . . . redundancy. It's affecting us all.'

'Of course.' Laura's face expressed perfect concern. 'But you don't normally let office worries get on top of you like this. Perhaps you need a break. Perhaps after Christmas we should go away for a week.'

'Perhaps. But you wouldn't want to go away for a week, would you?'

'Of course I would!' Her indignation was genuine enough. 'What do you mean?'

'All right, then. I'll get tickets for one of those cheap tours to Venice.' *You lying little hypocrite, I'll take you at your word.*

'What a lovely idea!' *What's more, you bloody little actress, not for one moment will I let you out of my sight – no chance of your slipping off to the Poste Restante . . .*

Philip half filled his glass with gin.

As far as he could tell Laura and Crispin had no form of communication over the weekend, but the private canker within Philip spread. Tranquillisers did nothing to abate the torment of his suspicions. He could neither eat nor sleep. And yet, some basic habit of maintaining appearances kept him going, while within him a devil voice lashed constant abuse at Laura. Outwardly he was friendly, gentle : they continued to lead their quiet lives with little reference to Philip's disintegrating appearance. He could sense Laura's concern but, knowing he abhorred fuss, she refrained from questioning him, merely said all would be well in January.

Two weeks went by. During this time Philip rang Laura every day at five, and she was never at home. On his return each evening she flourished her cold shining cheeks, the sparkle in her eyes betraying her rewarding afternoon. Still Philip endured her condition in silence, though some evenings the physical pain in his chest was so bad he would shut himself in his study for half an hour, and bend double in the armchair to alleviate the ache.

Then, one morning after a particularly bad night, he came down early to make Laura breakfast. Having inwardly riled against her most of the night, he thought this was the least he could do for her, to make private amends. On his way to the kitchen he picked up the post from the mat, shuffled through the letters.

There was one with an Oxford postmark. Stiff white envelope, intelligent writing in black ink. Philip stared at it till the words blurred before his eyes, and a vile sweat pricked over his back.

He made two cups of coffee and took them upstairs on a tray with the letters. Laura was waking, stretching, smiling, pleased at the treat of breakfast in bed. For the first time for many mornings a pallid sun slanted into the room, cheering the timid blues of curtains and walls. Philip, conscious that the sweat that now covered his body smelt strongly, sat on the edge of the bed and watched his wife closely.

She was very clever. When it came to opening the thick white envelope she made no comment, simply slit it with a knife. She pulled out a white card, read it quickly, and passed it to Philip.

'Crispin and Moira want us to go to some lunch party on Sunday.' Voice quite level.

Philip held the card between finger and thumb as if it were edged with blades. This, of course, was all part of a well-constructed plan. Crispin and Laura apparently saw no treachery in organising social meetings as well as clandestine ones.

'Don't let's go to that,' he said.

'Why ever not? It should be rather fun.'

'Well, I'm not going. I don't like Moira and I like Crispin even less. Pretentious man, to say the least. And most of all I don't like donnish Oxford parties.'

'Oh, Philip.' Laura's mouth, rather thin, was not made for pouting. It curved downwards. 'That's silly of you. You can't generalise like that. You can't simply say you don't like *all* Oxford parties. Moira's and Crispin's might be quite different.'

Philip stood up.

'It might, but I'm not going. You can do what you like.' His dressing gown fell apart. Glancing down, he saw the gleam of sweat on his stomach, realised the ridiculous sight he must be to Laura. She smiled up at him.

'No need to sound so fierce. I don't really mind – '

'And don't lie to me, Laura!' The roar of Philip's voice shook the room. 'Go to the party without me if you want to – I don't care a damn how many parties you go to, but don't lie to me!' The sudden fear and miscomprehension in her eyes goaded him. 'Go on, go! D'you hear me? All the way to Oxford for another little lesson in Chekhov. God Almighty!' He flung off his dressing gown: the sour smell of his own sweat almost stifled him. He ran one hand down his stomach, wet flesh upon wet flesh: with the other he pulled back the bedclothes, watched the lilac slip of Laura's body cower into itself like a night flower at dawn. She screamed.

Philip was upon her. He was aware, from the way she turned her head from his mouth, that his breath was evil, and that his jowl scratched her cheeks, inflaming them with ugly red. He was aware of tin tacks in his flesh, of the dryness of Laura, of terrible moaning noises from them both.

When it was over he left her exposed and crying on the bed. He dressed quickly and went from the house without saying goodbye.

In Holland Park the sun was gentle among bare trees. Philip sat on a bench, head in hands. I am ill, he thought. I have a virus that turns reason to unreason, makes me savage my wife, abuse her, suspect her. Dear God, he thought, I am a man debased by a feeling I should be able to overcome. I understand it to be irrational. Understanding that, perhaps it will go from me. He looked slowly about as if searching the air for a cure. The bare branches were cruel against his eyes, flaws in the winter sky. His whole body ached with the kind of pain caused by flesh that is too thin to protect raw bone from the elements. He stood. He began to walk back down the path, heavily as a man breast-high in water who pushes against a strong current.

At the office, dully, no greeting to his secretary, he shut the door. Telephoned Laura.

'I'm sorry.'

'Oh . . . that's all right.' Pause. 'I mean, it's the first real row we've ever had, isn't it? It had to happen some time. Though I'm not sure what it was all about.'

'Nor am I.'

'Are you all right?'

'Yes.'

'Well . . . thank you for ringing.'

'And thank you for being so . . . I don't know what came over me.'

'No need to go on.'

Philip called for black coffee and a glass of brandy. The relief of his wife's forgiveness gave him strength to start the fight. He would rid himself of the disease through an act of supreme will. He was, after all, a strong man. First thing to do was to resist ringing Laura at five. He achieved this. But when, on reaching home, he kissed her cold bright happy cheek, the physical pain restruck with a force that overwhelmed all his good intentions. He realised, as he lay awake that night, mind seething with vile possibilities, that it was going to be a long battle.

A week later, swallowing tranquillisers with his coffee in the office – they merely misted the superficial pain, did nothing to banish the fundamental ache and racing mind – he decided to tell Laura what had happened. This would mean risking possible disaster. There was also a small chance it might save and cure. A chance worth taking. Tonight. The positive decision fanned a small flame of strength. Philip picked up a long report, began to read. The uneasy looks of his colleagues, of late, had not gone unobserved; their concern for him was plain. He would now concentrate on putting their minds at rest. Then his private telephone rang. Laura.

'Sorry to bother you – but do you think you could *possibly* take the afternoon off?' She sounded breathless, excited.

'Well, yes, I dare say. But why?'

'It's quite important.'

'What is it?'

'I don't want to tell you now. Just come home in time for lunch. Please.'

'All right. How very mysterious.' He tried to sound light hearted.

He put the report back in a drawer knowing that further work that morning would be impossible, and decided to walk home. It would take an hour and so exhaust him, in his weakened state, that, by the time she broke the bad news, he would have achieved a protective sense of stupor. He strolled along the City pavements, St James's Park, Hyde Park, afraid. When finally he reached the front door he felt faint and dizzy, as he had felt on occasions in church as a child.

For the first time Laura did not try to conceal her anxiety. He looked dreadful, she said, and insisted he should see the doctor again tomorrow. Philip, with little energy left to argue, let the warmth of the house seep into his cold flesh. Gratefully he drank a glass of red wine and managed to eat half a plate of soup.

'Now,' said Laura, 'I'd like you to come with me in the car.' She was authoritative, bossy, pretty. The warmth of her reached through Philip's fatigue. In the car, he wanted to touch her. But he remained quietly with hands in his lap, asking no questions. He assumed they were going to some mysterious rendezvous to meet Crispin and decide upon their future.

Laura drove to Queensway and parked in front of the skating rink.

'Here,' she said. 'We're here.' She paid their entrance money – Philip's reactions were too slow to reach for his wallet – and led the way downstairs. There was a heavy chill about the place that made Philip visibly shudder. It vaguely occurred to him that this was a strange place to meet with an Oxford don : too cold. Perhaps they would sit in the cafeteria behind the glass screen. It would be warmer there, round a small Formica table with a cup of tea.

'You wait here,' Laura was saying. 'I'll be back.'

Philip sat on a chair behind the barrier at the edge of the rink, no longer much in possession of his senses. Before him several dozen skaters, mostly women and children, skittered about the ice. A few of them were fast and competent, masters of their movements, spinning and zooming in tight-lipped silence, the keen wind of their own speed their only awareness. Others clutched, squeaked, fell, and rose again without the benefits of grace or balance. Nightmare people. None of them was Crispin.

A gong boomed. Philip jerked, afraid : felt a skein of sweat over his back. Clutching at his neck with a cold hand, he looked about for Laura. Where was she? And what was he doing here?

The skaters crowded to the exits in the barriers. Only the good ones remained on the ice. Music, suddenly : an organ blurred by bad acoustics playing a tune from a fifties musical. The skaters, in pairs now, began to dance.

Not far from Philip a familiar girl stepped on to the ice. Laura, it was. She wore a short pleated skirt, red tights and new-looking boots. She waved at him, smiled. Behind her came a thin figure all in black, except for a small badge on his breast. He had the impassive look of a skating instructor, his sharp face frozen into inanimation that comes from years of skimming over blank ice. He put an arm round Laura's waist.

The music changed to a slow waltz. Laura and her partner moved, cautiously. They were straight-backed, fluid. Gradually, they gathered speed, dipped and swerved in unison. They reached a corner : turning backwards, Laura quavered a little. The androgynous black arm tightened round her waist, supportive. Laura's face was pinched with concentration. She did not look towards Philip.

Philip's eyes never left the scarlet and black pair. They blurred and fuzzed, became dots, then fur, then for a moment hardened into sharp focus. All the while, beneath his raw skin, he felt the blood seep from his veins, taking with it the old pain in his breast-bone, and leaving an overwhelming feebleness. He lifted one arm on to the edge of the barrier, lowered his head on to the coldness of his sleeve. Beneath his feet the black rubber flooring, holed like crochet, gleamed with the water of melted ice. The dreadful organ thumped out a Beatles tune. Philip put his free hand to his face to prod the numbness. He felt a hot mess of tears on his cheek.

A hand ruffled his hair. He looked up. Laura was pink and laughing, leaning over the barrier. Her partner backed away, with little swerving movements, knees dipped.

'How about that? Are you all right?'

'Amazing. Cold.'

'Bet you never thought I could do anything like that?'

'No.'

'So you'll never again be able to say what do you *do* all day, will you?' Gently accusing. 'I was *determined* . . . I was determined to surprise you before Christmas.'

'You have.' Philip felt his icy lips draw back over his teeth into something which he hoped would resemble a smile.

'I didn't want to tell you. Though I nearly did because I began to think you thought . . .' She laughed. 'I'll just go round a couple more times, then we'll go home. You look frozen.'

She swirled away, too daring. Her partner darted forward, stretched out an arm, but she fell. Philip stood up, one hand on the barrier. Against the horrible slur of music, he heard himself laughing. Laura, scrambling up, regaining her poise, laughed with him.

Philip remained standing, hands in pockets, shoulders hunched, his breath regular globules ballooning over the rink. All those secret afternoons, he thought, and his instincts, a little late for once, flashed benevolently towards Crispin. Dear God, he thought, that such an innocent conspiracy should cause such thunder in a reasonable man : may she forgive me, should she ever guess.

But Laura came off the ice with no sign of ever guessing. Philip met her at the barrier, briefly aware of his own width compared to the svelte shape of her skating partner. He took her arm, kissed her cold cheek, and told her she was an amazing creature : yes, he could hardly believe it. Pleased, she strode off, unusually tall on her skates, to fetch her coat.

Philip enjoying waiting for her. Still weak from shock, he felt the strength seep gradually back along his blood, and refrained from smiling only for fear of looking foolish. His damned instincts had nearly destroyed him, but recovery was here. When Laura came back he would drive her home : he felt more able to drive, now. She would enjoy recounting the difficulties of carrying out her plot, words tumbling almost into incoherence, as they did when she was excited. When they reached their green and uncracked house, they would resume their normal lives.

Philip would listen quietly. Knowing the wisdom of occasional silence in marriage, he would admit only one thing: that in all truth he had not guessed she was learning to skate.

The Friend

Muriel was very happy surrounded by an organised mess of glue and scissors and photographs. Albums were spread about her wide-winged on the table, and she felt at peace. Janice would be here soon. It was a Thursday night and Janice came over every Thursday night. Tuesdays Muriel went to her house, which she never enjoyed quite as much as having Janice here. She couldn't be doing things with her hands in Janice's house while they talked. At home, when she had made the tea and fetched the plate of iced biscuits – she had perfected a shade of green icing which had forced Janice into reluctant praise – she could carry on with her albums, or darning, or whatever, and it didn't seem impolite.

There was a noise behind her. Muriel turned to see her neighbour, Gerald, edging his way through the door. He had never been a man to enter a room boldly.

'You're always leaving the door open like this,' he said. 'You'll have burglars one day.'

'Oh, Gerald, it's you.'

'I just popped in. Everything tidy, everything trim?'

'Fine, thanks. Fine.'

'What are you up to, so busy?'

Gerald moved to stand behind Muriel. She felt him looking over her shoulder.

'You can see. I'm catching up on my scrapbooks.'

Gerald peered more closely. Although she didn't bother to look, Muriel knew his nose would be wrinkled with concentration.

'That's you and Bob, isn't it?' he asked.

'In Ireland. Sneem. We found it years before General de Gaulle. There's a village near there with all the houses in the main street different colours, like children's bricks.'

'He didn't quite come up to your shoulder, did he?'

57

'Who?'

'Bob. Your husband Bob.'

'He wasn't a tall man,' said Muriel, after a while.

'He looks quite slight.'

'He wasn't tall. He wasn't a big build.'

'You can never tell in a photograph, though, can you? Don't tell me snaps are true to life. I take a very bad picture myself.' Gerald pulled up a chair and sat at the table beside Muriel. She didn't seem much interested.

'Do you?' she said. 'Don't get too close, there's a dear. You'll jog.'

Gerald pointed a finger to another picture.

'Where's that?'

'That? That's the first house we had. At least, not the whole house. The house we had a flat in.'

'Looks nice.'

'Wasn't bad. A bit on the noisy side. Bob never liked noise, what with being at sea so much.'

'Do you mind if I light up?' Gerald was taking out his pipe before Muriel could answer.

'Not much use if I do, is there? Go on, move over. I'll murder you if you jog.'

'You've got a nice way of putting pictures in,' Gerald observed, moving very slightly.

'I used to be quite artistic, actually. Bob always said I had a good eye. For colour, and that.'

'I should say you have. What's that party?'

'Tenth wedding anniversary. That was a lovely dress I had, a mushroom silk. Bob gave me a lovely present that year – a little silver boat brooch. I should have a picture of me wearing that, somewhere.' She shuffled through a pile of pictures.

'From what you say, it sounds as if he was a good husband.'

'You couldn't have found a better, though I say it myself. Every little thing, every little detail – he remembered. No, I can't lay my hands on the picture.'

'He's been gone, what, five years now?'

'Six. Six in May.'

'But you're – settled now, aren't you? Over the worst of it.'

Muriel sighed.

'I'm happy enough. I have my life.'

'You're a sensible woman, to my mind. Like you always say, there's no use crying over spilt milk. Get on with your life. There are other fish.'

'I never said that.'

'What?'

'The bit about the fish.'

'Well, there are, you know.' Gerald sniffed.

'It could never be the same with anyone else. I wouldn't like to try second best. I've plenty to remember to keep me going.' Muriel plumped her fist on to a close-up of Bob's face. Gerald let a spiral of evil-smelling smoke out of the corner of his mouth.

'I've never found the perfect woman myself,' he said.

'That was it. Bob was perfect.'

'I gave up looking some years ago, you might say. I thought : if she's going to come, she's going to come. No need to go out looking. Had a good face, in his naval cap and that, Bob. Did other women fancy him?'

Muriel felt her arms flush.

'He'd no more look at another woman than he'd go in the Air Force,' she said, quite snappy.

'You were lucky, then.'

'I was. That's just what I realise.'

'You were lucky all round.' Gerald paused. 'But it seems to me a pity, sometimes. A waste, your life now.'

'What do you mean? Here, pass me the glue.'

'A good looking woman like you, with all the talents, but no one to spread them on.'

'Get away with you.' Muriel couldn't quite contain a smile.

'I mean it. You've all the accomplishments a woman could want. You cook a lovely meal.'

Muriel knew when to be modest.

'Average,' she admitted.

'Sew, stick in pictures better than most, do a vase of flowers like the wedding people.'

'Nonsense !'

'You do.'

'No, but I used to sing a little in the choir. And Bob said I had a light hand making pastry.'

'There you are, you see. All the accomplishments.' Gerald was becoming quite warm, dispensing so much praise. He stood up. 'Well, I'd better be getting along. I was on my way down for a quick one. Can I tempt you?'

'No, thanks. It's Thursday. Janice comes Thursdays.'

'Who's Janice?'

'Janice Sullivan. My friend. She comes over Thursday evenings.'

'Never heard you mention her before. You're a dark horse.'

'She gets off early, Thursdays. From the beauty parlour. She's got a nice little business going there. But then anything she turns her hand to she does well. She's one of those.'

'A beauty parlour?' Awe in Gerald's question.

'Oh, she's quite glamorous. But a good sort for all that. She'd do anything for me – anything. When Bob died, you'd think it was her own husband gone. She was a tower of strength.'

'Is she married, this Janice?'

'No.'

'Ah ha.' Gerald gave a lusty laugh.

'She's not your type, I can tell you,' said Muriel.

'Maybe she's my dreamboat.'

'She's not your type.'

'Who knows? My dreamboat may not turn out to be my type. What's she like?'

Muriel thought for a moment, careful to choose the right word.

'Petite,' she said.

'Raven-haired?'

'Blonde.'

'Interested in the horses?'

'Not that I know.'

'Easy-going?'

'Beautiful laugh. You never forget her laugh once you've heard it.'

Gerald laughed again. He wondered whether his own hacking sound might possibly be called memorable, too.

'I must meet this Janice,' he said.

'Well, she's due any minute.'

'I might pop back later.'

'Don't go giving her any of your sauce, will you? Remember, she's my friend.'

'Would I let you down?' he asked, indignant, and went to the door. 'Might see you later.'

Muriel hoped he would return. She couldn't abide the smell of his pipe but he was a kind enough creature and it would be nice to bring him together with Janice. Show him off a bit. Mention he was a figure in the racing world. Janice had so much to boast about : there could be no harm in grabbing her own rare chance. Funny she hadn't thought of it before.

Moments after Gerald's departure Janice bustled through the door.

'Anyone at home?' she said, seeing Muriel at the table.

'Oh, Jan, hello.' Muriel turned away from her photographs.

'And who was the tall dark handsome stranger I just saw leaving your house? Or did my eyes deceive me?'

'That was Gerald.' Muriel felt an edge of triumph in her smile.

'And who, may I asked, is Gerald?'

'Oh, just a friend.'

'I've never heard you mention him before, have I? You are a dark horse.'

Odd how two people thought of her in the same way, thought Muriel. She had never thought of herself as a secretive person, but maybe they observed in her something she herself had not noticed.

'He stops by sometimes. Lives just down the road. Sit down and make yourself comfortable, Jan, won't you? I won't be long till I've finished.'

Janice stumped across the room to stand behind Muriel, just as Gerald had, and look over her shoulder.

'Proper old memory lanes, scrapbooks, aren't they? You do them very nicely, I must say. Very neat.' She slipped off her emerald coat with a mock beaver collar, and slung it over an armchair. 'Has he got his eye on you, then?'

'Who?'

'This Gerald.'

'Good heavens, no! It's not like that at all. He just wants someone to talk to.'

'You shouldn't have sent him away.' Janice dabbed at the blonde tentacles of her fringe.

'I told him you came Thursdays and we liked our private natter.'

'I wouldn't have minded, just for once.' Janice sat down and crossed her plump knees.

'Well, he's not a ball of fire.'

Janice sniffed. Then, to remedy the vulgar act with a more refined one, she dabbed her nose with a lace-edged handkerchief.

'I wouldn't be surprised if he fancies you,' she said.

Muriel's steady hand, pushing a snapshot into place, gave a small dart of surprise.

'What makes you think that?' she asked.

'Well, dropping in and out like that. Men don't just drop in and out like that unless they have their eye on something, mark my word.'

'Like a cup of tea?'

Janice stood up bristling, Muriel thought, with funny suspicion.

'I'll make it,' she said. 'I know my way around. Any of the green biscuits?'

'In the tin,' said Muriel.

While Janice was in the kitchen Muriel made some attempt at tidying the rubble on the table. Then she took a lipstick from her bag, went to the fireplace and contemplated her image in the speckled mirror. She reddened her mouth with particular care. Janice returned, more quickly than Muriel had anticipated, with a tray of tea and biscuits.

'What, dolling yourself up for a night out?'

With some guilt, Muriel returned the lipstick to her bag.

'As a matter of fact, Gerald said he might stop in on his way back,' she said.

The news made Janice swerve round the low coffee table, and

almost drop the tray.

'Ooh, and I haven't changed either. I came straight from work.'

'Don't worry about Gerald,' soothed Muriel. 'He won't be expecting something from the Folies Bergère.'

'No, but I don't want to create a bad impression, do I? Not being your friend.' She opened her bag, took out powder and lipstick and began to repair her face. Then she sprayed herself from a bottle shaped like the Eiffel Tower. 'Like a bit? Essence of Paris. Sample offer. I'm very lucky that way. I get all the samples.'

'No, thanks.' Muriel poured the tea. 'I'll stick to my lavender water. That's what Bob always liked best.'

'So he did,' said Janice.

'Business good this week?'

Satisfied with her face at last, Janice leant back on the sofa.

'Never better, though I say it myself. They're all coming in to get their skins back into condition now their suntans have worn off. You should see some of them. Crusty old necks, yellow between the wrinkles. They expect me to do miracles, no less, honestly. Well, I suppose I do do miracles, or they wouldn't keep coming back, would they?'

'That perfume's mighty strong,' replied Muriel, sniffing the air.

'Essence of Paris, as I said. You'd expect a French fragrance to have body, wouldn't you?' She laughed a little at her own joke.

'I went to *The Sound of Music* again last night,' said Muriel. 'Fourteenth time.'

'Did you really? Such stamina. My father's people, you know, came from Walton-on-Thames – same place as Julie Andrews.'

Muriel had heard this boast so many times before she had run out of comments of awe and amazement. Instead, she scratched at the folds of her neck, which reminded Janice.

'You know what?' She looked closely at Muriel's face.

'No? What?'

'I said I'd give you a free facial, any time. Christmas present.'

Muriel stopped scratching her neck.

'Do you really think I need one?'

'Well, to be honest, I'd say you do and you don't. Seeing as you're a friend, I'll tell you this, truthfully : your skin's not too bad. It's not too bad, but it's a tired skin. You can tell that a mile off. It needs a spring clean, same as a house. A bit of nourishment, it needs.'

'That's all?'

'Look, I'm telling you the truth. All I'm saying is, a common garden facial would do you a power. You'd come away feeling a different person. Don't bother with an appointment. Just come in, say who you are, and I'll fit you in.'

'That's very kind, Jan.'

'And I'm telling you – don't take it amiss – your Gerald will notice.'

'He's not my Gerald.'

'If he's anything of a man, he'll notice.' Janice lifted her cup towards Muriel as if silently drinking her health. 'Went to a fête yesterday,' she went on, 'Winstaple. Lovely afternoon. You meet a nice type of person working for charity, you know. The Honourable Mrs Jolliffe opened it. She knows me quite well, as a matter of fact. To be honest, at one point she came right up to me and addressed me — a little business matter – and then she complimented me on my blue spotted two-piece. And she's someone who knows the difference between plain *smart*, and *flair*. She can tell.'

'Oh.'

'How was Julie Andrews?'

Muriel sucked the beautiful green icing off one of her biscuits. Her mind tore itself from the dazzle of Janice's honourable acquaintance to the pleasure of her own film-going. She had always meant to try to explain to Janice the precise quality of that pleasure.

'It's always the same, I find,' she said, 'coming out of the cinema. When the lights come on you stand up and feel even smaller than when you come in. You realise that life size is very small. But then walking out into the street I always feel that if only someone would come along with a camera, just at that moment, why, I could perform for them just as well as all the people I'd seen on the screen. You know – dance for them, sing for them, do a beautiful tragic scene, cry, anything. I feel quite elated, thinking what I could do.'

'Bob used to talk like that,' said Janice.

'Only of course nobody ever comes along with a camera, and you wither back into being small again.' She paused. 'What do you mean, Bob used to talk like that?'

'Not about films, about the sea.'

'About the sea?'

'He used to say that standing on deck, out on the ocean, looking at the sunset on the waves – that it took him out of himself, he used to say.'

Muriel's cup hesitated towards her mouth. She tried to remember.

'So he did,' she said.

'Once, that time you were ill, you remember, gastric flu I think it was, you had gastric flu – Bob and I took a stroll along the cliffs, and he said just what you said he said about sunsets at sea.'

'Did he? Asian flu, it was.'

'Asian. That was it. Well, human nature couldn't do without its uplifts, sunsets or whatever.'

'I didn't know you and Bob had gone along the cliffs.'

Janice helped herself to another biscuit.

'Only for half an hour or so after we'd picked up your medicine. We didn't leave you long, did we?'

'I don't remember,' said Muriel. She stirred her tea, a small frown between her eyes. 'Gerald, now,' she said, 'with him it's the horses. He knows racing people up and down the country. He says watching a race is a shot in the arm, the excitement.'

'You said he might drop by later?'

'He might.'

'I'd like to meet a racing man. Did you tell him anything about me?'

'That you're my friend.'

'What else?'

'You come over Thursdays.'

'Nothing else?'

'That you're quite a glamour puss, I think I said.'

'Go on! He'll be expecting Marlene Dietrich. Wish I'd known, I'd have got myself up a bit more.'

'You look all right, Jan. Don't worry. Anyhow, he's not the world's greatest noticer.'

'All the same, I like to create a good impression.'

'You do create a good impression,' said Muriel, warmly, and patted her friend's knee.

Gerald arrived an hour later, slinking through the door again, so that he was halfway across the room before they noticed him.

'Hello, hello,' he said. 'Looks as if I've barged into a regular hen-party. Excuse me.'

'We were expecting you,' said Muriel. 'This is my friend, Janice Sullivan.'

Janice stood up. A blush curdled her matte foundation. She and Gerald shook hands.

'Glad to know you,' said Gerald, his earlier pertness a little subdued. 'Never seen it so crowded down at the Bell. Fridays, you expect the crowds. But Thursdays, no.'

'You don't really, do you?' said Janice.

Muriel stood up.

'I'll brighten the pot for Gerald,' she said to Janice, and went out to the kitchen. Gerald cleared his throat.

'Mind if I sit down?'

'Make yourself at home.'

Gerald sat beside her on the sofa.

'Mind if I light up?'

'I like a man who smokes a pipe, actually, better than cigarettes.' Janice smiled.

'You must be a woman in a thousand! Muriel, now, she doesn't care for my pipe. She never complains, mind. But I can tell.'

'There's no accounting for tastes, is there?'

Gerald looked at Janice carefully, and puffed at the stem of his pipe. Then he said:

'Do you mind if I make so bold as to make a personal remark?'

'Fire ahead.'

'The colours of your dress. They remind me of something. Soon as I saw them something clicked in my mind . . . Archie Fellows. That's it. Ever heard of Archie Fellows?'

'Can't say I have. A racing man?'

'Archie Fellows from up Wetherby way. Born and bred there. String of horses from here to kingdom come. Maroon and pink – I've seen those colours flashing past more winning posts than I'd care to mention.'

Janice, taking this as a compliment, smiled again.

'What a coincidence,' she said.

'Coincidence! I came through this door not five minutes ago. I looked at you, and something rang a bell.'

'I must admit, I know little of the racing world myself.'

'Ah! It's a grand life. If I hadn't gone into business I would have trained, myself.'

'To be a jockey? You have the build.'

'Trainer. That's where the creation comes in. And here comes the light of my life with a new pot of tea! Your friend, Muriel, it turns out, is wearing old Archie Fellows's colours.'

'Is she, now?' asked Muriel, pouring him a cup. Gerald took it from her, and turned back to Janice. 'Must be a very meticulous business, beauty,' he said.

'It's meticulous, all right. Skilful. Nothing amateur about it. As a matter of fact – has she told you? – Muriel's going to come to me for a facial.'

'What's the matter with her face? What's all this, Muriel?'

'On the house, of course,' said Janice.

Gerald wrinkled his nose towards Muriel.

'You let me catch you coming back with the skin all hitched up over your ears, Chinese eyes, and there'll be hell to pay.'

'Nothing like that,' said Janice quickly. 'Not a *lift*. Just a little refreshment.'

'Just to tone me up. I'll be in safe hands with Jan,' added Muriel.

'Rainwater: that's the best treatment I know,' said Gerald. 'Well, I expect you ladies know what you're doing, but she looks all right to me as she is. Till Bob died she never looked a day over forty, did you, Muriel? Haven't I said that before?'

'Thirty-eight, you said.'

'Well, thirty-eight, forty.'

'Were you a friend of Bob's, too?' asked Janice.

'Never met him. Never had the pleasure. But if I ran into him in the street, I've heard that much about him I'd feel I'd known him all my life.'

'He was a wonderful man,' said Janice.

'So I understand from Muriel.'

'Wonderful.' Janice paused, glanced at Muriel in the silence. Then she went on: 'Of course, there weren't many who knew him well, were there, Muriel? I mean, there were those who thought him aloof. It was his quiet manner. You had to get under his skin to know him, didn't you, Muriel? There weren't many who managed that.'

'Some men are darker horses than women, I've always thought,' said Gerald.

Janice shifted her look from Muriel to Gerald. She spoke quietly.

'Once, you know, he told me something I've never forgotten. He said, Janice, he said – he never called me Jan like everyone else – there are some things a man must never reveal. That makes you think, doesn't it? There are some things a man must never reveal. I went cold all down my spine, I remember, when he said that. He said it so mysteriously.'

'When *did* he say that?' asked Muriel.

'Oh, I don't know. One day. In the Badger, if I remember rightly.'

'We hardly ever went to the Badger.'

'It must have been on one of the rare occasions, then, mustn't it?'

'But he never said anything to me like that. About not revealing things. Bob told me everything.'

Janice gave her a smile.

'That's what every wife likes to think, dear. That's where men are so clever.'

Gerald, sensing it would be beneficial to divert the line of conversation, scratched his ear. He was not inspired, but did his best.

The Friend

'The three of you were, what, lifelong friends, were you?' he asked.

'Oh no, not at all,' said Janice, quickly. 'We only met in the war. Muriel and I worked side by side in a rubber factory.'

'Bob and I had already been married years,' Muriel added.

'Muriel and I hit it off straight away, didn't we?'

'Jan came back to our house one evening for supper and from then on, somehow, she became part of the family.'

'I remember that evening.' Janice lit a cigarette. She smiled nostalgically through the smoke. 'Bob came home so late I was beginning to think Muriel had been kidding me, and hadn't got a husband after all. He came in in his uniform, very smart. Always made a good impression. We had Spam fritters for supper and Bob opened a bottle of sherry.'

'So he did! Your memory, Jan. You don't forget a thing.'

Gerald turned to Janice and gave her a wink that Muriel was also meant to appreciate.

'But how come such an attractive lady as yourself, if you don't mind me saying so, didn't get a husband for herself?'

Janice settled herself more comfortably, her bosom swelling with the truth she was about to reveal.

'Well, to be honest, it wasn't for the lack of offers, was it Muriel? I turned down more honest offers than I can remember. None of them suitable. None of them worth half of Bob, for instance. It's all a question of standards, you see. If you can't get what you want, rather do without than drop your standards. That's always been my motto.'

'They were round Jan like flies,' Muriel said to Gerald after a small silence.

'Well, a little exaggeration, but I have to admit they were.' Janice lowered her eyelids, revealing immodest blue lids. 'But I spent all my spare time with Bob and Muriel, didn't I? Sometimes when I was working different shifts from Muriel, I'd come here and do Bob's supper for him so he wouldn't come home to an empty house. He was a fiend for stew and cabbage – very easy to feed, even on rations. Sometimes, he'd come to my place and have a black-market omelette. Well – ' (she gave Muriel a quick look) – 'on a couple of occasions. Muriel and I always thought we should put the man first, give him the delicacies we managed to scrounge . . . didn't we?'

'That's the right attitude,' said Gerald.

'He never told me about the omelettes. When did you give him omelettes?' asked Muriel.

Janice shrugged.

'Oh, I don't remember exact *dates*, dear, do I? Even my memory doesn't stretch that far. It may have been only once. In fact I think it probably was only once. But you know what an impression a real egg omelette made on anyone in those days.'

'I gave him every egg I could lay my hands on,' said Muriel. She brushed some crumbs from her knee, hand shaking very slightly.

'Of course you did.'

'But he never mentioned you gave him an omelette. Never once.'

'Of course he didn't.' Janice sounded quite scornful. 'Really, men had better things to talk about in the war than their stomachs. He didn't tell *me* about the boiled egg *you* gave him for breakfast. He didn't tell *you* about the omelette *I* gave him for his supper. To him, they were just eggs, served up by his two loyal women.'

'But I was his wife!' Muriel's protest came out like a small moan. It was followed by a moment's silence. Then Janice smiled. Calm. She turned to her friend.

'So : you were his wife. I was his wife's friend, remember? And therefore his friend. That was all.' She paused. 'Though I daresay if you'd been blown up by a bomb I would have considered looking after him for you. I daresay I would have done that.'

'Come along, now, come along,' said Gerald. 'The conversation's getting morbid. Why don't we all go down to the Bell for a drink?'

'I don't feel like a drink, thank you,' said Muriel. 'But don't let me stop you two.'

Gerald waved his fist in mock despair. He turned to Janice. 'There you are ! What do you do? I try to take her out of

herself, try to give her a bit of the old romance – and what do
I get? No : I don't feel like a drink. No : don't feel like going
to the races. It's enough to make a man give up, isn't it?' He
turned from Janice to Muriel, feeling himself now to be in com-
mand of the situation. 'You can't live with a memory for ever,
you know, love. Bob's dead. Remembering him won't bring
him back to life. You must help yourself a bit. Let others help
you . . . If you didn't give me quite so much of the cold shoulder, I'd be quite willing to come to any terms . . .'

'Well, she's never been much of a social butterfly, have you,
Muriel? Even when Bob was alive they never went out much.
Often I'd come over and find the two of them crouched by the
fire just listening to the wireless.'

'Bob liked being at home,' said Muriel.

'Of course he did.' Janice was patient. 'What man doesn't?
But I can tell you this : he once told me he'd give his eye teeth
for a night on the tiles – '

'He never said that !' Muriel was shouting.

'I'm telling you, he did.'

'I don't believe you.'

'I'm telling you the truth. He sat in that very chair and told
me he liked a bit of a night out,' Janice stood up and went to
the fireplace, ran a finger round the oval frame of a picture of
Bob.

'Where was I ?' asked Muriel.

'Late shift, I suppose.' Janice held up a finger, slightly grey
with dust.

'I don't believe you.' Muriel snapped her knees together, indignant. Angry. 'Bob liked quiet evenings here. That's what he
liked.'

Gerald, his nose wrinkling with the strain, made an effort.

'I like a night out myself, personally,' he said. 'But on the
other hand I understand those who don't.' Neither woman seemed
to hear him.

'When did Bob say he'd like a night out?' asked Muriel.

'Oh, off and on. From time to time.' Janice returned to the
sofa and sat down.

'*When?*' Muriel was firm.

'Well, if you really want me to be so precise, that time you were with your mother for the night – her ulcers. One of those nights was my birthday.'

Muriel frowned, trying to remember.

'I sent you a card from my mother's,' she said.

'So you did.'

'What did he say?'

'Now, let me get this right or I'll be up to my neck in hot water.' Janice winked at Gerald then turned back to Muriel. 'He said : Janice he said, seeing as it's your birthday, perhaps we ought to have a little celebration. There's a dance on tonight at the Town Hall and I got a couple of tickets – '

' – a couple of tickets?' Muriel's voice was faint.

' – like, as a birthday surprise for me. Well, what could I say? He'd thought it all out, hadn't he, to surprise me? I couldn't let him down. So, anyway, we went.' Janice paused, eyes carefully on Muriel's face. 'He was a lovely dancer, actually. Waltz, tango, Gay Gordons, the lot . . .'

'But he never danced with me in twenty years !'

'Keep your hair on ! He said you didn't like it.'

'No : he said *he* didn't like it. I don't believe you.'

'Well, it's true. We had a very nice night out. If you don't believe me I can show you – he made mention of it in one of his letters – '

' – *one of his letters?*' Muriel had sprung to the edge of the sofa, appalled, cheeks quivering.

'You weren't the only one who got epistles from sea, you know,' said Janice. 'He sometimes managed to drop me the odd line.'

'But, Jan, I read you out bits of his letters ! The times I read you bits of news and you never let on *you'd* heard from him.' There was a sob behind her voice, but she managed to contain it.

'Oh, for heaven's sake.' Janice was brusque. 'A person likes to get her own letters.'

'Now, you two, no quarrelling,' ventured Gerald, but they paid him no attention.

'And why didn't you tell me you'd been out dancing?' went on Muriel, kneading her hands. 'If only you'd told me . . . Why didn't you tell me?'

'There are some things, as Bob said to me, that a man – or a woman, for that matter – should never reveal. That was the wisest thing he ever said. But don't blame *me*. I said to him, I said, Bob, we must tell Muriel about this and perhaps she'll come with us next time . . .' Janice trailed off.

'With you? I like that!' Muriel was more deeply flushed with indignation.

'But *he* said, better keep it quiet, not because we've got anything to hide, but because Muriel might feel a bit hard done by, sitting there looking after her tiresome old mother while we were out on the tiles.'

'He loved my mother! He never said that. Don't go on, Jan. I don't want to hear any more. I don't believe . . . it's all lies. Lies, lies, lies you're telling me. Anyone would think Bob was *your* husband, the way you're talking. But he was married to me, remember? Twenty-six happy years. He loved me. He loved me more than anyone else in the whole world, didn't he, Gerald?'

'I, er – don't bring me into this,' said Gerald.

'Well, he did,' went on Muriel. 'He told me. Every day he told me, or if he didn't tell me, he showed it. He was kind to you because you were my friend. No other reason. He wouldn't have laid a finger on you, or any other woman, for anything in the world.'

'I'm not saying he did, am I? Glory be, the suspicion in some people's minds. It's an illness, you know that? Suspicion like yours is an illness. All I'm saying is that Bob became my friend – a man can have friends besides his wife, can't he? Sometimes they say it even *helps* a marriage. It's healthy to have a friend outside – '

' – our marriage didn't need any help, thanks very much.'

'In that case, there was nothing to fear from me, then, was there?' Janice stood up. 'I was no threat. I was just a friend. A friend to you both, I thought.'

Gerald stood up. He picked up Janice's coat and helped her on with it. He tried to be cheerful.

'Now come along, you two. How about that drink?'

'Thank you, Gerald. I'll accept, for one,' said Janice, fumbling down the long line of fancy buttons, little finger crooked as if for a refined tea party. 'I mean, the atmosphere in here's getting a bit over-heated, isn't it?'

'Lovely colour, your coat,' said Gerald. 'Froggie Moore's racing colours . . . a similar green.'

'There's one more thing I'd like to know,' said Muriel. She too was standing. She took Bob's photograph from the mantelpiece, held it to her breast.

'Oh yes? Oh, I see.' Janice began to laugh. 'I know what you're getting at, love. I know how your mind's working, don't I? Well, blow me. What a scene after all these years. We've never had a cross word. Can you imagine?' She linked her arm through Gerald's. His mouth sagged unhappily. 'Come on, Muriel – where's your smile? Where's your humour? What's the matter? You're put out because I'm off for a drink with your beau, now, are you? First your husband, then your boyfriend? That it? Really, Muriel. You ought to know me better than that. We're old friends, aren't we? Can't you trust a friend?' She paused. Silence. 'So, you've nothing to say. Well then, Gerald and I might as well be on our way. Illicit drink. Come along, Gerald.' She tugged at his sleeve.

'Sure you won't come, Muriel?' he asked. She shook her head. 'Well, whatever you like. I'll pop in again some time soon, anyhow. Drop by, you know. Next week, perhaps.'

Janice tugged at him again.

'Honestly, all this unpleasant atmosphere just because I mentioned an omelette and a couple of tangos,' she said. 'You wouldn't credit it.'

Muriel put her hand to the mantelpiece, held on to it.

'That would be nice,' she said to Gerald. 'Please do.'

'Any evening suit?'

Muriel regarded him, smaller than Janice, kind eyes, thin frame weighted down one side by Janice's arm. Janice herself held her head high, cigarette stuck in her plum mouth. Smoke blurred the triumph in her eyes. Muriel wondered. She sighed.

'Not Tuesdays or Thursdays,' she said quietly, to Gerald. 'You see Thursdays Jan – Janice Sullivan, my friend – Thursdays she comes here. Tuesdays I go to her house. Twice a week, every week, since the war, since Bob died.' She saw Gerald nod and let himself be led away by Janice. 'Twice a week . . . just quiet evenings, we have, talking over old times.' She paused. 'So Tuesday it'll be my turn to go over to Jan, you see . . .'

But by then Gerald and Janice were out of hearing, gone. Muriel realised her explanation was left only for Bob, in his oval frame. She replaced the photograph carefully on the mantelpiece, and looked at it, and wondered again. It took her quite some moments to realise how silly she was being – to scoff at her doubts, and to brace herself to the task of her albums again, where she could be alone with Bob and remember, as she looked at the hundreds of photographs to prove it, the happiness of their marriage.

Monday Lunch in Fairyland

She met him at a party somewhere. Noticed the decayed state
of his leather jacket before his face. Neither heard the other's
name in the mumbling that goes for an English introduction.
But they danced. When the music came to an end he said he
was K. Beauford. The K stood for Kestrel. He liked it, but
everyone else thought it so pretentious that he had long ago
given up using it. Except his mother. And her name? Anna.
O-oh, he said, giving the word two syllables. She thought,
from his smile, it would have been nice to talk to him. But the
music smashed into the room again, and he disappeared.

'Saw you having quite a dance with K. Beauford,' said Mark,
driving home. They both sat upright in their lumpy marital
car. 'Met him once, years ago, fishing. He kept us supplied with
the best white wine I've ever drunk. Called something like
Annaberg. Never met it since. Cooled it in rock pools. Bloody
marvellous.' He smiled. Fishing memoirs always made him
smile. Smiling made his moustache hunch up to brush the keel
of his nose. Sometimes this would tickle, and he would push
it down with a thick finger.

'O-oh,' said Anna.

Breakfast in their London kitchen. Perhaps three weeks later.
Feeling, as always, of an indoor storm. Flurry of cornflakes.
Thunder of fists on the table. Rain of splattered milk on chairs
and floor. Years ago, as lovers, Mark and Anna had calm break-
fasts. Years ago they would speak, and gaze, and pour coffee
absent mindedly. Now, a child clutched a postcard in a sticky
hand. Anna snatched it. For her. Picture of Buckingham Palace.
Strange writing. *Nineteen days to track you down, am no detec-
tive. Love K. Beauford.* Oh, yes. Leather jacket. Pale as milk at
the elbows. Fishing with Mark. Mark quite hidden behind *The*

Times. Anna propped the postcard between two mugs on the dresser. If he hadn't been so deeply into Bernard Levin she might have said something about it.

'Get your *coats* on,' she shouted to the children.

Next card three days later. Buckingham Palace from the air, this time. *Would you consider lunch as my reward? Love K. Beauford.* Hooting outside of the school-run car. Lost satchels. Running noses. Smudgy kisses. Mark's baggy morning eyes dull with the promise of a hard day. All gone, suddenly. Alone with the silence of 8.45 a.m. This mess to be cleared before she could begin her own day. No immediate impetus, though. She sat. Dabbed at toast crumbs on the table, letting them prick her finger. Would she consider lunch? Yes, she would consider mere lunch. So innocent an event could not affect the order of her life. She had no wish for anything, ever, to affect the quiet order of her life. Its domestic tides, its familiar routines. Books for intellectual stimulus, flowers for pleasure. Small clinging arms for love, Mark's good-humoured laugh for companionship. Yearly holidays for adventure, Christmas for excitement. Smug, perhaps, but orderly. Compared with so many, after fifteen years, happy. Untempted by the shoddy delights of extra-marital associations. Those who had vaguely supposed had been severely snubbed. But lunch, just lunch. The smallest of treats. Preceded, if necessary, by a lecture on the lack of future. And of course not a secret. I'm having lunch with K. Beauford, she would say to Mark. If she remembered.

The quiet of the house, daytime, rose up : bulbous, engulfing, warm. Only to be shattered at four. That clatter of footsteps just as silence could be borne no longer, its peace grown chill. Squealing bell. Rush for television and instant tea. The noise. The telephone.

'I must have caught you at a bad time.'

'Rather. Only by five minutes. Who is it?'

'K. Beauford.'

'Oh, yes.'

'How about Monday? That lunch.'

'Yes. Why not?'

'La Cuisine, at one.'

'Sorry, I can hardly hear. La Cuisine?'

'At one.'

'Lovely.'

'Bye.'

She had let the toast burn, felt no concern at the lack of peanut butter. 'You're so bloody *spoilt,* you lot. It's Marmite or nothing.' Unfamiliar puzzlement in their eyes. The whole weekend ahead – the smallest one in tears. Oh God, make up for it with an extra long story . . .

. . . Increase of the size of the Round Pond that Saturday. Mark's kite entangled maddeningly in the trees. Hours till it was brought down. All absurd, such impatience. Just for lunch. Mark's hands efficient on her body after his favourite braised celery and *coq au vin* for Sunday dinner. Things she hadn't cooked him, come to think of it, for a long time.

Monday, noon, she thought she looked quite old. Brushed her hair to cover a lot of her face. Wore clothes she hoped might seem like ordinary Monday clothes. Paid for the taxi out of the housekeeping money, disloyalty shaking her hand.

K. Beauford sat in a distant corner of the restaurant. Its kitchen air. Strings of onions and garlic hanging from the ceiling, like unfinished chandeliers. He stood. Same leather jacket. Deep lines round his smile.

'Hello, hello.'

'Hello.' Anna sat.

'I thought I'd always send you pictures of Buckingham Palace.'

'I wondered at their significance.'

'No significance. I recommend the watercress mousse.'

'I don't know what I'm doing here, really. I'm not used to lunch. I never go out to lunch. You're almost a blind date, aren't you? At my age.'

'Oh, do stop twittering,' he said.

Very pale green, the mousse. White wine that tasted of grapes. Trout. Fennel salad. He said he lived far away, by the sea. Hardly ever came to London. Had a wife, mostly absent, to whom he would always remain a husband. So no need for the lecture. Relief. Such relief Anna's hands sent her hair scattering backwards, revealing all her face.

'At last I can see you,' he said. 'Scrutinise.'

Confused, she told him something of her orderly life. Very brightly. Made it sound desirable. Which it was. The children would be having mince at school now. Mince on Monday, so fish fingers for tea. Never imagining their mother . . . Mark at the Savoy with a chairman. Making an important decision. Never imagining his wife . . .

In the end she had not told him. Would later. Tonight. K. Beauford was pressing her to pear flan. She was not resisting, liking his laugh. A furry quality. He was telling of his evenings. Alone with his dog. Not a reader, but a maker of complicated model cars for his sons. No, he felt no need to see people. So long as lunch appeared at one, and dinner at eight. Orderly, too, you see. That was the way to keep going. Invent one's own discipline to prevent floundering. Protect oneself from intrusion. Plant trees. Visit people's lives. Resist indulging in explicitness. Catch the train you first intended to catch. Which was in half an hour.

No word of ever meeting again.

Orderly life quite intact.

Goodbye, goodbye.

Nothing to fear. The children wanting tea. Full of relentless instinct. Mama, why are you wearing *that* dress? She knew quite well his part of the coast. Yes, darling, now I'll help you with your Geography. And after Geography, listen to news of Mark's lunch. Glad you've come to that decision as last, darling . . . . No time to reflect. Seas very savage in winter down there. Dinner at eight alone with the dog. Postcard writer. Visitor.

Eleven days without a signal. Then third picture of Buckingham Palace by the second post. This one from an engraving, 1914. *Have discovered the Whitlaws nearby are mutual friends. Possibility of plans? Love K. Beauford.*

Possibility of what plans? The telephone, startling.

'Hello, hello. Are you coming to the Whitlaws?'

'What? I've only just got your card. I don't know what you mean.' Outside, movement of the one bare tree. In summer its shadows blurred the geometric shadow of the wrought iron gate. Any minute now the car would be drawing up, bearing children.

'When are you coming?'

'When?'

'Couldn't you make next weekend?'

'Mark will be in Brussels . . .'

'Someone can look after the children. Surely.'

The children. There they were. Scrambling out of the car. One school beret falling into the gutter. Anna waved, smiling, through the window.

'What? Next weekend. I must go, I'm afraid. The bell.'

'I'll be expecting you.'

Apologies for keeping them waiting at the door. Exclamations at a cut knee. The *arrogance* of the man! The ridiculous nature of the summons. Of course, it was out of the question. Quite impossible. Where would the children go? She buttered their crumpets, full of love.

Mark, with the enthusiasm of the innocent, thought her idea a very good one. Nice to see the Whitlaws again and he loathed it down there. The children so pleased about going to their aunt. Plans falling into place with horrifying ease. For what?

On the long train journey she wondered. Just another lunch, perhaps. A long way to go for just another lunch. But no use speculating. In effort to remain calm, heart strangely beating.

The Whitlaws made no mention of K. Beauford for twenty-four hours. They were pleased to see her, pressed on her more food and wine than she cared for. The children rang her. She rang the children. Snow on the moors, forsythia in the courtyard. Mark rang from Brussels. Marvellous sun there, he said. But progress slow. Not back till Tuesday. Why had she come all this way to be without her children? Then it was announced : K. Beauford was coming to lunch on Sunday. Hadn't they met somewhere? He could give her a lift to the train.

Monday Lunch in Fairyland

Sunday was dour. Unbroken cloud. Anna pulled her belt into its tightest notch. She felt thin.

K. Beauford was punctual. Talkative. A bit wicked.

'Having discovered we all knew you, the next thing I hear is you're *down* here. It's an awfully long way to come for a weekend. Isn't it?'

'She'd come any distance to stay with us,' said the Whitlaws.

They left after tea. Late sun through a flurry of snow. Drove over the moors. In silence. Then K. Beauford said,

'There are all sorts of fairyland, you know.'

His car skidded through the thick gravel of his drive. In the snowy dusk, giant clusters of weeping copper beech trees. Indeterminate parklands.

He led her through outer and inner halls. Dark pictures. A room whose crimson silk walls twitched with firelight. She sank on to a broken sofa. Its stuff scratched the back of her knees. He pulled the curtains against huge panes of black snowflakes. Muffling a church bell.

'We can have dinner and I'll put you on the sleeper,' he said.

They explored the cellars. Gloomy stone passages veining the foundations of the house. Hundreds of bottles of orderly wine, dust obscuring the labels. Strong rooms of polished silver chalices. Crates of yellowing books, first editions waiting to be sorted. Kitchen tall as a barn. Old-fashioned black range. Mixing bowl and pile of chopped onion on the huge wooden table only signs of culinary activity.

Dinner at eight. The gong as the hall clock struck. Two places at the far end of a long white-clothed table. A silvery butler who poured Mark's remembered wine : Annaberg.

'I don't know what I'm doing here,' Anna said.

'Three postcards then a visit. That seems to me the proper order of things.'

'Do you eat like this, every night, by yourself?'

'Of course.'

'The table laid like this? The candles?'

'How else?'

'It seems so odd, these days.'

'Have to keep things going. There's not much of it left.'

'Kestrel Beauford,' she said. As if trying out the name for the first time.

'Silly whim of my mother's, really.'

'K. Beauford. I don't know what I'm doing here.'

'You keep saying that. I suppose you ought to be at home with your husband and children.'

'Yes.'

'Well, I'm glad you're not.'

They drank port by the fire. Wine red against fire red against red of silk walls. All reds confused. Billy Paul singing.

Me and Mrs Jones
Have a thing going on . . .

One hour, she was thinking, till the train.

'Alternatively,' said K. Beauford, 'you could go back in the morning. Or the afternoon. Or tomorrow evening.'

'Quite impossible.'

But there she was making telephone calls. Very calmly. To Brussels. Quite right, you stay on, said Mark. To the aunt. Oh, very well, she said. No, it won't be much of a bother. The children are quite happy. Elaborate stories. Everyone believing her. Guilt dulled by wine. Wine making the stories of her life quite funny, so that K. Beauford was laughing in his endearing fashion. Hand stretched out towards her. But at rest on the crumpled sofa. As if frozen on its journey.

Very late he showed her to a cold room. Switched on the one-bar fire. Double bed with icy sheets.

'Only three postcards and here I am. What am I doing here?' she said.

'Do stop asking that question,' he said. 'You can go tomorrow on the five-thirty. I promise.'

'You promise?' she said.

'I absolutely promise, my love,' he said.

Five-thirty. On the train in the stuffy carriage. She quivered. Next to her, cartons of farm eggs, pots of Devonshire cream. He had given them to her. Saying : for the children's breakfast. She would explain they were from the Whitlaws. The train jerked, moved forward. Dark bare platform where moments ago

Monday Lunch in Fairyland

K. Beauford had been kissing her goodbye. I shan't wait and wave, he said. And had not mentioned when, or if, they would meet again.

Oh my love that wet and shining winter beach the sandpipers pecking at the frills of sea you said they were sandpipers I didn't know and you said quietly now if we go quietly we won't disturb them and we came so close before they flew away a small bush of wings in the grey sky urged higher by their own cries of alarm and me with my arm through yours absurdly bulbous in a puffed anorak of dreadful tangerine so out of place I said on this empty shore shouting against the wind so you could hear and laugh and feeling you shorten your step to coincide with mine . . .

All well at home. All pleased with eggs and cream. Stories of the aunt. Stories of Brussels. Scarcely a thought for her weekend. Thank God. For it hung, indelible, a double image upon her daily life. Which had resumed its normality so fast. Only, within, the orderliness had flown.

Impatiently she waited. Afternoons were worst. Then, in the silent house, the churning mind that nothing could divert. Fear of going out for fear of missing the telephone. The pacing, the trying of all the old familiar chairs. Mind a visible thing in the mind's eye : a yellowing ivory ball as carved by the Chinese. Intertwined rats of miniscule teeth and savage eyes. Twisting, turning, never still, gnawing at the memories. You're very thin darling, Mark said. Never usually noticed such things. And you're restless at night. Can't sleep? What's the matter? Concerned eyes. Oh don't be so silly, she said, hating his hands. And in the morning shouting at the children.

Because you are far away by the sea in the private ocean of your park knowing that lunch is at one and dinner at eight and your dog will sleep by your bedroom fire and you plan the planting of more melancholy trees and spray silver paint on to plastic motorbikes and maybe sometimes think of me though you didn't say you would you said in fairyland the figure is there all the time unconsciously conscious if you like you said K. Beauford why don't you ring me?

Complications of infidelity unimaginable to those who have not experienced them. He rang too late one evening: Mark's car drawing up outside. So she sounded terse, bright. Yes, tomorrow, three o'clock. No, not here. Not possible. She would meet him somewhere. Put off the dentist and the meeting with the headmaster. Mark asking for ice. Nothing, nothing of the days that had passed. I'm coming, Mark, with ice: her voice almost a scream.

And terrible hours, fighting for calm. Till she met him in a dark wine bar in the Kings Road. His jacket black with rain. They watched its streamers liquidise the windows. Stabbed out cigarettes in a plastic ashtray. Arms touching, and their thighs.

'When are you coming again?' he said.

'I can't really come again, can I?'

'I hope you can and you will,' he said.

'It would be so difficult, another time. The plans. The lies. I'm not very good at the lies.'

'Divided worlds,' he said. 'We should all have our divided worlds. They shouldn't conflict, or be hard to separate.'

She laughed.

'Do you find that easy?' she asked.

'Well, yes, I do.'

'You're lucky,' said Anna.

'I mean, visits to fairyland are nothing to do with anything else. If you plan them right they can go on for ever and ever. Just things to look forward to, and to look back on. With tremendous excitement. And pleasure. Aren't they?'

'Oh, yes.' She had to agree. Couldn't explain.

'Well, it's up to you,' he said.

'I've seen it happen so often. When people start this kind of thing,' she said. Trying. 'It's the stuff of divorce.'

'It needn't be,' he said. So easily. 'It's only difficult if fundamental, impossible changes are visualised. Best only to think of the good, possible times. Within their limitations.'

Monday Lunch in Fairyland

'The strength of you,' she said.

He drove her home on the back of his motorbike. Nose in his wet hair. Arms round his shoulders. He kissed her without heed by the front gate. Said she smelt wonderful in the rain. Some kind of flowers. And he'd be in touch. Exhilarated by such parting news, tea with the children was a lovely time. Mama, you look so happy today, one of them said. But such wet hair.

Well you see that's because K. Beauford insisted I should ride on his rusty old motorbike in all this rain dodging the buses I thought death every time smelling the earthy smell of his hair shouting into it be careful for God's sake I'm the mother of three children and now my love my love not many days will pass before we'll speak again . . .

Next postcard of Buckingham Palace behind the Victoria Memorial. From somewhere in Wales. *Am writing this in a bus shelter. Two days later – sorry I forgot to post it. Will ring Tuesday morning, much love K. Beauford. Much,* Anna noted. Before it had been just love. Much love, and by now the destructive forces of infidelity crowded in all about her. Her family all strangers. Resentful of them. Resentful of their needing her presence. Their demands so irritating. Their puzzled eyes sniping her guilt at her own unfriendliness. Nothing was but what was not. Lady Macbeth's undoing. The house itself was an insubstantial thing. Tiny flaws in the fabric of daily life. The clear picture, familiar for so long, shattered. A private mosaic. It couldn't go on. She couldn't survive it : Mark's appalling tolerance. The children's constant forgiveness. The sleepless nights. Where had all the orderliness gone? Quiet content? Precious habit of unexciting love? All she had thought she wanted. Could never return, now. Not in the same way.

In the silence of a dun-coloured afternoon Anna stood by the tall windows of her house, fingers hunched up like spiders on the cold glass of the panes. Blasted, her life. Inadvertently, she had let it happen. Linen cupboard disorganised. Deep freeze empty. Husband and children squeezed by the rats of her mind to a faraway place. No longer of prime importance.

85

Rain. It began to rain on the leafless trees. Falling silent on the square of plantless London earth she liked to call her garden.

Oh I'm not as strong as you K. Beauford at dividing worlds perhaps because I love you and that's where it's all gone wrong though you must never know but in the spring I'll visit you again and we'll send postcards of Buckingham Palace for years and years until we grow old and calm and the visits between our separated worlds can't unground us any more. But oh, my love, can that ever be?

Dirty Old Man

After Lily died, Tom fell very quiet. There was no lack of people – his old friend Jack Grass, for instance, and a couple of neighbours – who were prepared to listen, had he wanted to talk to them. But the fact was that nowadays the small things that used to flow into his mind, the trivial observations of everyday life that invariably made Lily laugh, no longer came to him. He felt quite dead himself.

After Lily died, Tom forced himself to pack up her dressmaking things. He covered the old sewing machine that had stood for twenty-five years in the corner of the front room with a polythene sheet, and sent a bundle of old materials to a jumble sale. These scrap ends of fabric made his hands tremble for a while, as he gathered them up awkwardly, pricking his fingers on pins that only Lily would have known were there, and tied them with a ribbon from the neat sewing box. A triangle of shiny green satin brought back to him the trouble Lily had had with Vera Finch, fat old spinster, self-important member of the council who, convinced she would be mayor years before she actually was, got Lily to make up a whole trousseau. A more unlikely set of clothes for a stumpy mayor-to-be Lily and Tom had never seen: décolleté evening dresses to show off the spongy flesh of Miss Finch's appalling breasts; frills round every hem to call attention to her thick ankles; huge sashes that spread over her wide bottom. Lily had done her best to persuade Miss Finch into something a little plainer, but Miss Finch remained adamant. She had stamped her solid foot in the front room crying, 'Flair! I know how to dress with flair, Lily Greville, and you would do well to learn a thing or two from me.' Lily good-humoured as ever, gave up the battle and laughed about it with Tom later.

A small piece of cream calico dropped to the floor. As Tom bent to pick it up he recalled the skirt it had come from – a

voluminous thing with an elastic waist that was meant to hide
poor Lovelace Brown's condition. Lily and Tom had been the
only ones to know her secret for a while, until the skirt, for all
its cunning folds, swelled to obvious proportions. Lovelace had
never managed to pay for it and Lily had told her to forget it.
She was a good dressmaker, Lily. Good in many ways.

Tom locked the door of the front room and never went in
it again. Otherwise, he resumed his normal life. At eight-thirty
every morning, having cooked his breakfast and washed it up,
he walked a mile to the small brown room behind a shop that
sold antique pictures, and settled himself to the restoration of
frames. He had spent his entire working life in this room, start-
ing as apprentice at sixteen. Now, forty years later, he was the
most skilled and conscientious frame restorer the firm had been
fortunate enough ever to employ. He in his turn had no assistants to teach. Times were hard, prices rising : people had better
things to spend their money on than repairing frames. The
firm was struggling for its life, and although nothing was ever
said, Tom and Mr Lewis, the kindly owner, silently acknowledged that the struggle would soon be over.

While he worked, no such melancholy thoughts were able
to trouble Tom. He concentrated wholly on his tiny world of
scarred wood and chipped gold paint, filling the cracks with a
fine paste of his own invention and, when each crack was
smooth and dry, covering it with the blob of gold that swelled
his paintbrush – each stroke delicate and light to avoid the gold
leaf clotting.

To concentrate wholly on his craft, Tom worked in near
silence. The radiators choked, sometimes, and he himself hissed
a little, mid-winter, when his asthma was bad. But to Tom,
to whom these noises had become part of his being, the silence
was pure and satisfactory. Often, at twelve-thirty, he would
forget to stop work to eat his pork pie and half a pint of brown
ale lunch, and be surprised to find that when Mrs Lewis came
in with a cup of tea, at three, he was quite hungry. When he
did stop for lunch he took off the minimum amount of time, sat
happily among the waiting frames, looking forward to the afternoon.

Dirty Old Man

It had always been his habit, when Lily was alive, to join Jack Grass at the Fighting Cock on Friday nights, on the way home, for a couple of pints. He did not look forward to this Friday night date with any particular enjoyment, as he had no great partiality for beer, crowds, or noise. But he felt it was a friendly thing to do, and Jack Grass was his friend. When Lily died, Jack had sent a wreath of pink carnations in the shape of a racehorse and jockey. Lily had known or cared nothing for horses, but Jack was a great betting man and the idea had obviously been an inspiration to him. Tom appreciated this and when, the Tuesday of the funeral, Jack had suggested Tom should join him at the Cock for something stronger than beer, Tom, who had nothing else planned, hardly liked to refuse. Since then, two nights a week at the pub had become the custom. That was the only major change in Tom's life since Lily died.

And she had been dead nearly three years now. The small terraced house, so full of her for thirty years, functioned still, but without life. Increasingly, Tom was aware that without her he was a dying thing himself, a mechanical being devoid of spirit. Time did not heal, time did not numb. Jack, with his theories about time taking care of all things, was talking nonsense.

Once, guiltily aware of the indulgence, Tom tried to express the ashy feeling within him in his weekly letter to his daughter, Betty. In the old days he and Lily had written a joint letter, two sides, every Wednesday evening. Betty lived in Bristol, married to a man who had made something of a name for himself in sherry, and had no time for his working class parents-in-law. Betty never replied to the letters : a card at Christmas, and one when each of the grandchildren was born, was all they ever heard from her. She didn't manage to come to the funeral, and the brief letter of condolence and apology to her father had been without thought or feeling. But for all her rejection, Lily and Tom would have no word said against her, and however little it meant to her, to them the weekly letter was a point of honour.

Now, Tom found the whole responsibility of writing two sides once a week a struggle : Lily had always written the greater part of the letter. She had been the one with the news. He had no news : he found himself stretching his hopes for his grandchildren's well-being in to a whole paragraph, and report- ing on the state of the weather for the last six days. He bought writing paper without lines, which meant that he could make bigger spaces : still the letter took him an hour or so of careful thought. The week that he decided to confess his feelings of increasing despair to Betty meant a particular battle. After many attempts, all of which he deplored and rejected because of their self-pity, he ended up with a single sentence : 'It is rather lonely here without your mother.'

Three weeks later Betty replied on a postcard : 'Cheer up, life's not so bad', and Tom, trying to control an imminent sob, brought on a fit of asthma. That evening, at the pub, he decided to tell Jack Grass.

'Jack,' he said, 'my hands, they feel like paper.'

'Do they now?' said Jack.

'And my body,' Tom went on, 'feels all dried up. It feels as if there's no blood in my veins. No life in me.'

'Ah,' said Jack, 'now you're talking.' He thought for a while, the concentration pulling his forehead into a pattern of deep jagged lines. Then he said : 'You know what you want, Tom me old fellow, you want the odd thrill.'

'I'd like to feel full of fire again, full of life,' replied Tom, not understanding. Jack wiped his mouth, which always seemed wet whether he was drinking or not, with his sleeve.

'Tell you what,' he said, 'leave it with me. I'll fix you up so you never had a better time.' He looked at his friend and, for the first time that Tom could recall, winked.

'How?'

'My sideline. I've always had a sideline, matter of fact. Reason I haven't brought it up with you before is, I thought you wouldn't be interested. You can usually tell. But try any- thing once, that's what I say. Friday, after our drink, we'll go back to your place for a natter.'

This prospect filled Tom with some apprehension. No one had been to the house since Lily died, and he did not know how he would feel about voices in the kitchen again, albeit his own and Jack's. But he was eager to know what his friend was plotting for him.

It rained hard on Friday night. Jack and Tom walked back from the pub hunched up against it. They had drunk more than usual during the evening and clutched each other, stumbling a little, as they crossed roads.

In Tom and Lily's cold and cheerless kitchen – cheerless now it was no longer filled with Lily's flowers and warm cooking smells – they huddled round the small fist of fiery coals in the grate, and hung their dripping coats over chairs to dry. Tom brought out half a bottle of whisky, which he'd been keeping for years for some unspecified occasion, and they drank from the bottle in turn.

After a while Jack tapped at the inside pocket of his jacket.

'Well,' he said, 'I've brought the goods.'

He took from the pocket a bulging unclean envelope from which he extracted a bundle of photographs in an elastic band. He handed them over to Tom.

'Take a look at these, mate. Just for starters.'

Curiously, Tom looked at the first picture, postcard size, underdeveloped, cracked till its surface was soft. He saw a middle-aged woman lying on a bed, legs wide apart, no clothes on apart from a cardigan which covered one breast only. She had very made-up lips and was smiling a horrible smile.

'What's this?' he asked.

'Pictures to keep you happy,' said Jack. 'Porn.' He gave a smile.

'I've never seen anything like this before in all my born days.'

Fascinated but shocked, Tom continued to study the picture. There was quiet for a while, except for the dripping of rain from the coats on to the floor.

'Flip through them,' said Jack, at last. 'There's a good assortment.'

'I don't know whether I should like to, Jack.' What with the beer and the whisky, Tom was feeling a little out of control.

Only one thing was firm in his mind : these weren't the sort of things that should be in Lily's kitchen.

'Go on,' urged Jack, 'they're lovely. Full of imagination.'

With some reluctance Tom went through the pictures. It turned out the cardiganed lady was mere *hors d'oeuvre* : compared with some of the photographed activities performed by Negroes, muscle men and tarty girls with vast breasts, she was pure innocence. Tom could think of nothing to say.

'Do something to you, don't they? Make the old blood run faster? You're never alone with a bit of porn, Tom, take it from me.' Jack laughed.

Tom blinked. He handed the package back to Jack who shuffled through it, chuckling.

'I don't like them very much,' Tom said at last.

'Well, it's something takes some people a little time to get round to,' replied Jack. 'You may not feel full benefits right away. Tell you what, keep them a few days. Take them to bed with you. Look at them under the sheets, if you know what I mean. And if you're not a happier man in the morning, I'll be surprised.' He got up, in a sudden hurry to go, picked up his coat and shook it. Tom stared with distress at the muddy marks their shoes had made on the kitchen floor. 'If they do the trick, I can supply a lot more – films, stories, books, anything you like. It'll cost you a bit, mind, but it's worth it, I reckon.' He left the envelope on the kitchen table.

When he had gone Tom threw it in the fire, watched two small hands of flame leap up and devour it, then fade. He felt quite sickened, and set about cleaning the floor.

But having found a possibly new ally in his old friend, Jack Grass was not one to give up easily. Over the next few months he persuaded Tom to persevere, and gave him every encouragement. Tom, dizzied by the pressure Jack was putting upon him, found himself leading a new and furtive life : two to three nights a week he would go with Jack to Soho and pay large sums to see erotic films. On other occasions they would loiter in the back regions of sleazy bookshops flipping through pictures of people performing revolting acts with animals or children :

the kinkier the more expensive. Once, they watched a live orgy through a peephole. Screwing up one eye for an hour gave Tom a headache for days. Whatever they did, whatever literature he took home to read, sickened him; and yet believing that among all this filth he would find something to cheer him one day, he continued to follow Jack and do as he advised.

On one occasion, after several months of relentless porn pursuing, Tom tried to extract himself from his new life. He and Jack sat opposite one another on a late train home. Tom was very tired. He knew his work next morning would suffer. He looked forward to it, though, with greater fervour than ever before. Only in his world of gold leaf paint could he put away the horrible images that now constantly plied his mind.

'It's not that I'm not grateful for all you're doing for me, Jack,' he began. 'It's just that, well, the thing is it's not exactly *sex* that I'm looking for. Who'd want that, after Lily? What I'm looking for is something, you know, more to live for.'

'Ah,' replied Jack, 'sex is the remedy. Sex mends all things.' He chuckled to himself. Tom despised him for the evident pleasure Jack found in their pursuits : but in despising his friend he felt he was being disloyal. He said nothing and reprimanded himself. 'Had a bloody marvellous night with the Girls of Corsica book,' Jack added, and Tom felt very weary.

He had been a good sleeper all his life and now his undisturbed nights had gone. He would toss and turn in the bed, straying into Lily's side (a thing he meant after her death never to do), head aching, throat dry, his body wracked with asthma, his mind tortured by pictures of people doing things to each other that he and Lily could never have dreamt of in their wildest moments. Would these pictures be with him for the rest of his life? Was he ill, that they didn't excite him? Was he mad that he should be sickened by them?

Then he began to worry about money. At Jack's request he was spending far more than he could afford on their film shows, books and pictures. Once he was late with the rates, a thing that had never happened before, and he began to save by cutting down on food. His appearance changed, and Mrs Lewis, who brought his tea every afternoon at work, noticed it.

'Anything wrong, Tom?' she asked, when he jumped at her entrance. 'You do look poorly. All pinched and thin. Anything I can do?'

'Nothing, nothing thank you,' said Tom, alarmed. It worried him that he should look ill: everything worried him.

The next morning, an unusual event took place. Mr Lewis, whom normally he only saw about once a month, entered the room without knocking. Tom's hand jolted, spilling gold paint on to his trousers. Quickly, he stood.

'Good morning, sir,' he said.

'Good morning, Tom.' Mr Lewis patted a book under his arm. Tom, seeing its title, was incredulous. It was the new volume of colour plates he had received yesterday morning – £10 it had cost him. He had imprudently brought it to work to look at in his lunch hour so that he could report on it to Jack that night. But a few pages had depressed him, brought on his asthma. He had hidden it behind some frames, meaning to take it home, and had returned to work on a particularly valuable frame. Mr Lewis tapped the book again.

'Sir,' said Tom. Fire burned under the flesh of his face and his eyeballs scorched. Mr Lewis looked very sad.

'Not here, Tom,' he said. 'Please, not here.'

He put the book on the table and was gone.

Tom stood quite still for a few moments, not knowing what to do. Seared with shame he had never experienced or imagined before, a trembling that began in his knees spread over the rest of his body. Blindly, he reached for a scrap of paper, scribbled an almost illegible note of resignation, put on his coat and slipped out of the shop the back way. He left all his tools, paints and brushes behind. The Lewises, whom he had respected for many years, would never see him again and, at his age, there would be no other jobs.

At home, stupefied, he lit the kitchen fire and proceeded to burn every one of the loathesome books and pictures that he had collected. By evening they were all ashes. He hurried to the Cock to meet Jack.

'What's up, mate?' asked Jack, seeing his friend unusually bright of eye, and with two red spots on his cheeks. 'Hit you at last, has it?'

'Jack,' cried Tom. 'Jack, what have you done to me?' He fell against the bar. Jack supported his arm, saying there, there, everything's all right, mate.

But Tom pulled himself away from Jack, turned, and shouted : 'No, it's not all right, Jack Grass. It's not. I never imagined, in all my days, I'd sink to this . . .'

He heard his own voice, distant and hollow. He ran to the door, stumbling against people, aware that he was causing a scene, that people turned their heads and stared. He ran most of the way home, realising that would be the last he would see of Jack, as well as the Lewises. Coughing from the exertion of it all, he struggled for breath and felt a cold, clammy sweat coursing down his limbs.

Tom went to bed late that night. He was much weakened by the attack of asthma : weakened and appalled. He let his eyes wander round the cracked old room, stripped of Lily's things now, murky by the light of the dim lamp on the bedside table. Then he took the photograph of Lily from under his mattress, where he had hidden it the night she died. There she was, smiling still, hair blowing in the wind by the front gate, hands screwed up in her apron pocket. He touched her face with his finger and put out the light.

In the dark the image of her continued to shine, a tangible thing. He lay the photograph under the jacket of his pyjamas, its cool glass on his heart, and pulled the hard sheets up round his chin.

Quite suddenly, he heard himself cry out loud for Lily's forgiveness. At once a warmth flowed back into his body. Then he smiled to himself, as he used to last thing at night when Lily was alive, knowing he would sleep.

Maternity

He'd brought no present, nothing. The prefabricated stall outside the hospital reminded Romilly of his forgetfulness. He
chose a small bunch of expensive freesias. She would know, of
course. She would know by the scrap of brown paper they
were wrapped in they had come from the hospital steps. She
would remember he was like that.

On the long journey to her room the muted smells of disinfectant, ether and polished linoleum gathered in squalls about
him and made him feel sick. He wondered if he should look
for a lavatory. But there was nobody about to ask. Dizzily, he
spun a complete circle on his heels, a trick he had learnt as a
child, a trick that had driven his mother to high-pitched screams
of annoyance. The floor of the corridor felt mushy. He knew his
heels must have made dents. Luckily, nobody had seen. He
pressed the button of the lift, dreading its arrival. He might
well have chosen the wrong lift, the one that took trolleys of
corpses down to the mortuary.

It was empty of corpses, just the slightest smell of death, and
took him to her floor. Private, of course. Plenty of nurses starch-
ing about in their small black shoes, there, thermometers like
wicked fingers sticking out of their breast pockets. One of them
stopped and asked Romilly if she could help. Her white hand
fluttered round her cap. He wondered how many purple bloody
heads she had pulled from how many gaping wombs with those
hands. She asked him again. He gave the name. Ah, she said,
you must be the lucky father. He followed her, silently, to the
room.

Jane sat in the high bed propped up by a mound of white
pillows. Staring, blaring white they were. The whitest pillows
he had ever seen. A bed in a greenhouse. For all around her were
flowers, a hundred pounds' worth of flowers, bright expensive
colours, their heads bowed down by their own heavy scents. Pot

plants whose earth had been disguised by moss: miniature rock gardens with dwarf trees. Bows round vases. Messages tied to bows. Bows tied to messages trailing from veinous leaves. Romilly's feeling of nausea returned – the travel-sickness of one whose eyes lurch through a jungle.

'Hello, Romilly,' Jane said, and her eyes fell to the brown paper bunch in his hand.

He heard the door close behind him. He sniffed the tide of terrible flowers. He took two paces to the end of her bed, and held on to the white iron rail.

She was unnaturally propped up. Perhaps she needed to be. Perhaps having children – or at any rate your first child – did something to your back. Made it weak. Made it so that you needed pillows to keep you upright. Yes, she must be very weak. Etiolated face, white as the pillows, ashy under the eyes. Something had happened to her breasts. They seemed to have been propped up, too. Bolstered, padded, or something. Their upper curves were also tinged with the prevailing whiteness. Blue-veined. Vast blue veins, an aerial map of trunk roads. She never used to have blue veins or this white skin. He often told her she was the colour of a free-range egg. Speckled. Lovely speckled breasts that weren't caught up in slings like this. And brown arms, all year round, and capable hands. Even they were pale now, lying on the sheet stiff and helpless. She had scraped her hair back, a thing she had never done even in the rain. It was tied with red ribbon. The ends of the ribbon lay against the pillow, streaks of blood.

'Well, do I look so terrible?'

'Course not.'

'I'd like a kiss, then.' She patted the sheet with her useless hand. Romilly went to her, bent over, kissed her on the temple. He could smell warm milk. She used to smell of salt winds and grass after rain.

'Sit down, go on. Don't look so awkward.' He sat on the upright chair beside her bed. Put the flowers on the floor. 'It's lovely, your coming,' she said, 'but you've been a long time.'

'I'm sorry.'

'You were the second person I rang.'

'Thank you.' He smiled a little, listened to the silence between them. 'I can't remember . . . what you said it was.'

'Romilly! Really. You are a dopey old thing. I told you quite clearly. A boy. Orlando.'

'Oh yes. I knew it was some funny name. Is he all right?'

'Of course he's all right. He's absolutely marvellous. Beautiful, in fact. No, really. Everybody says he looks exactly like . . . Sorry, Rom,' she added.

Romilly looked through the density of flowers to the grey sticks of high-rise flats beyond the window.

'Was it quite easy? Not too agonising?' Once, he'd imagined she'd give birth to his child under a haystack. Lying on tarpaulin. A warm day, the smell of harvest, no pain, very easy. He would have been calm and helpful.

"Course it was easy, a cinch. What do you think I am? He started in the middle of the night. Quite bearable pains, so we waited till after breakfast till coming in here.'

Romilly listened to her voice as she told of the birth. (Geoffrey, as he might have guessed, hadn't been there.) Her voice was the same. Maybe that was one thing birth didn't change, voices. It chopped up and down, changing pace in its funny way, just as it used to on the boat, a small murmur against the waves so he would have to ask her to shout. She was quite capable of shouting. Braced squarely against the wind, brown hand resting on the boom, she could shout against the waves all right.

'And you – what have you been doing?' As usual, when she'd exhausted stories about herself, she remembered to ask about him.

'Nothing's changed. Quite a heavy lambing season.'

'Still got the boat?'

'Still got the boat.'

'I miss the boat. We don't sail.'

'No.' He paused, thinking of things to tell her that would please. 'Oh yes. One bit of news, I suppose you could call it. I'm putting in an Aga.'

'Taking my advice at last,' she laughed.

She had said so many times they should have an Aga. It was the only thing she had asked for in three years. It would make all the difference to the stone kitchen, she had pointed out. Take the slate-chill off the shelves and floor. She had been right, of course, but Romilly had always been reluctant to make swift changes. He liked their evenings poking at the surly fire, encouraging the logs to flare through the smoke. He liked the long ceremony of the lighting, the eggs and bacon fried in the iron pan over the eventual flames. It occurred to him, too late, he should have made his decision sooner.

'I suppose you have all mod cons, now,' he said.

'Yes. We do rather have that sort of house.' She was honest, as always, but apologetic. 'Did you come up from Cardiff by train?' Romilly nodded. 'That was awfully extravagant of you, Rom, coming all that way just to – '

'What's happened to your breasts?' he asked.

Jane looked down at the swelling lace frills beneath her chin. Slight colour came to her cheeks.

'They get like that when you have a baby.'

'They didn't used to be like that, I remember.'

He remembered her moon flesh under night skies, cold on the mountains. They never slept in the tent. No – he would open her to the cold, clamp his mouth over each part of her. Slow, nudging movements of his tongue that made her writhe, and made the earth beneath her move like the sea. Now that she'd had a child . . . would she want all that? He remembered the dew, mornings, on her sleeping face and hair; the promises they'd made each other in midday bracken, that this simple life would never change. Neither had wanted change, then. They had no need of other things.

Her hand hovered above a bell.

'Would you like to see him?'

'Who?'

'Orlando.' She said the name as if already she was used to it. 'I don't mind.'

'Perhaps I won't show him to you. You'd just say he was like all babies, which he isn't.'

'All right.' He had intended for her sake to say yes, he would like to see it. Instead he touched her hand and asked the question he had been determined not to ask.

'If I'd given up the life we had, and offered you all this, would you have said yes?'

'Oh, Rom.' She laughed lightly, protected as she was from him by her new state of motherhood. 'You were the most lovable adventure I've ever had. Ever, ever. Honestly. But you never made any suggestions about permanency. That was part of the adventure. Permanency might have spoiled it.'

Romilly nodded, reflecting upon himself as an adventure. To him, it had been ordinary, perfect life.

'Nor I did. It might have, yes. You're right. Is marriage to Geoffrey a good adventure?' He managed to keep his voice quite flat.

Jane smiled, pausing while she thought up a comparison he would understand.

'A life-long cruise on an ocean liner,' she said, 'rather than one of our jaunts in a precarious little sailing boat.'

Romilly appreciated her care.

'Well,' he said, 'there's no one else. So far.'

'But there will be. A beautiful Welsh wife who will sing over the new Aga.' The gaiety of her voice hurled him away from her. She should give up trying to make it easy. 'Next time you come up, won't you come and see us? Could you bear to? I mean, I don't think you'd hate Geoffrey, exactly.'

'I don't come up very often.'

'No. I suppose you're too busy. The farm and everything.' Her voice faltered. Romilly scraped his chair back from the bed, sensing danger. He watched as she untied her hair for him. It fell darkly about her shoulders. It made her face so familiar that a physical pain burnt through him.

'Why did you do that?'

She shrugged. He smiled – weak, desirous. 'Can I see your breasts, too?'

She paused.

'No. I'd like you to remember them as they were. Besides someone might come in.'

Romilly took his hand from hers.

'Do you ever think of those days in the mountains? At sea? I can never remember our being in rooms, except the kitchen when it snowed. Some people might say you were a bloody fool, leaving.'

'Oh, shut up, Rom. You promised you wouldn't mention any of that.'

'Sorry.'

Jane glanced at the clock at her bedside, a battered brass thing with bells each side of its face like earphones. The only present he had ever given her, bought in the local market. It had never failed to wake them. They would wake just long enough to register the pleasure of returning to sleep in a new, entwined position.

'Time for me to go?' he asked.

She smiled uneasily.

'Visiting hours are any time in this sort of place,' she said, apologetic again. 'Geoffrey comes in every evening on his way back from the office.'

'I'd better go, then.'

'They'll be bringing Orlando in for his evening feed any minute.'

'I've got to catch the seven-ten, anyway.'

'That means you'll be back dreadfully late.'

'I can't imagine you in a lot of well-ordered rooms,' Romilly said, standing. 'In a real house with carpets.'

'I like it. We all change. We grow up.'

'We don't all change. And we can't all give up things to fit in with other people's growing up, however much we may love them.'

Jane frowned, careless.

'Don't let's get into one of those conversations, please don't let's.'

'No.' Those sort of reflections, now, were unnecessary to her. He could understand. He bent down, kissed her on the temple again. She shifted, a sudden movement she would make when some new idea sprung her with enthusiasm.

'Listen, would you like to be a godfather? I'm sure Geoffrey –'

'No – for Christ's sake.' He went to the door.

'I only meant to show you that I . . . Oh, don't go away looking so furious, Rom. You didn't used to take things the wrong way, did you?'

'Be a good mother,' he said. 'I'm sure you will.'

'Romilly!'

He left quickly.

On the train back to Wales he leaned against the black window. He remembered he had left the bunch of flowers on the floor, but didn't care. It had been a bad idea, the visit. Hadn't worked out as he had planned. Things rarely did. In future, he wouldn't make plans. He sniffed at the rough sleeve of his jersey. It smelt of warm milk, the milk with which she was to feed someone else's child. Suddenly, he could not remember why it was not his. Nor, in the following weeks, as spring came to the Welsh hills, could he precisely re-envisage Jane's present whiteness, the bulging softness that had come to her with maternity. He recalled only that she had changed, and was glad that his child – their child – had not been the cause of that change. Against all facts she remained in his mind the girl he had loved, the girl he had lost through his inability to see what she required beyond the life she had seen as adventure. He didn't blame her: his own way of seeing the enemy within was not much understood. He tried to convince himself that she was happy with her kind of permanency. For his part, farming his land, sailing their boat for the first time without her, he occasionally allowed himself to think of the years they had had, and found himself reasonably content with his.

Mind of her Own

'Think the big one'll win, Jack?'

'Chancey.'

'Small one looks as if he could do with a square meal.'

'Wiry, though. Muscle through and through.' Jack Lee tapped his thigh through his office trousers. 'Here, budge up, will you? You're cramping my style.'

Alice had slumped a little towards her husband's end of the sofa. She remembered the old days. 'Here, snuggle up a bit, Al. Keeps the chill out,' he used to say then. But that was twenty-eight years ago. Then, she would give him her hand. He would squeeze it, a passionless pressure that would cause no look of alarm in the eyes of his parents, who chaperoned Jack and Alice for five years while they waited, in their uncertainty, to marry. Now, she shifted her position obediently so that there should be a few more inches between them.

Co-operation was pale yellow in Alice Lee's mind. A primrose yellow, to be precise, sometimes almost metallic : a colour that started in her head, flowed down through her body filling it with warmth and making her limbs waxy, deliquescent, so that her movements, to onlookers, would sometimes appear clumsy. Most days Alice experienced these yellow sensations in some measure. The fact that she was used to them in no way diminished their rewards. They represented an inexplicable happiness that was her only secret, her only area of absolute privacy.

Alice Lee was born a good woman. As her friends said, there was no trace of malice in her. When all around her bitched and snarled, she remained full of charity. As far as she could tell – as she often laughingly said – the Lord had forgotten to plant in her any form of neurosis. In appreciation of this blessing she was a willing listener and adviser to many friends and neighbours. And as a wife and mother, Alice was conscientious and sympathetic. She put her family's interests always before her own, and thus never had the time to doubt that this was the best thing for herself. But for all her virtues, Alice ran no risk of being saintly. Sometimes, evenings like this, when Jack sat in front of the television thinking out loud about his day in the insurance office (he didn't require any response), Alice would find her concentration wandering far away from her husband's problems. Staring at the wrestling match before her eyes, she would see instead the woods of her childhood where she and her brother Sam would gather birds' nests and blow the pale eggs. Next best, she would let herself become enveloped in what she called her Brontë cloud : magically, she would turn into Jane Eyre at that climactic moment when Mr Rochester sees her through his veils of blindness. Not that she ever wanted Jack to be blind, of course. Alice would rouse herself guiltily, glancing at her muttering husband, important things on his mind. He was a fine, healthy man, for all his years of desk work. But in some strange way he'd never given her the thrill – not even in their earliest days, picnicking Sundays on Box Hill – that in her view Mr Rochester had given Jane Eyre.

'Where are Denise and Robbie ?' asked Jack. He felt easier now that Alice had moved. He asked the same question most nights. Always prepared to be surprised by the answer, he was always a little disappointed to find it much the same.

'Denise is washing her hair. Robbie's in his room.'

Denise washed her hair six nights a week. Robbie's habit was to go to his room as soon as supper was over to fiddle with his home-made radio set. Robbie was a mathematician, training to be a teacher. Denise, presently working as a receptionist in a travel agency, hoped one day to own a beauty parlour. Saving towards this end, she followed carefully the rules of dedicated parsimony, and grumbled at the self-inflicted hardship it caused. In his heart, Jack would have been delighted if his children had been a little more gregarious. But they didn't seem to have many friends. Certainly, none of them ever came to the house. However : he was not one to be ungrateful for his mercies. What he *did* have, and it was a pretty rare thing these days, looking round – was a close-knit family unit. As a family, they liked each other. They enjoyed doing things together. And nobody should under-rate *that,* thought Jack. With a small twist of his head he went on to reckon, as one wrestler flicked the other satisfyingly to the ground, that he and Alice had been married coming up to twenty-five years now. What's more, never a cross word. Alice had always had the good sense to agree with him, so there had never been any cause for dispute.

Denise came in, towel over her head, shaking her wet frizz of hair. Jack couldn't ever remember having seen a shine on Denise's hair, not even when she was a youngster. It was something she strove for, but, Jack imagined, considering its natural hazy texture, it was something she would never achieve. But he wasn't one to discourage anybody, let alone his own flesh and blood. So night after night, when Denise came in shaking herself like a dog after rain, Jack made an effort to restrain the criticism that welled up within him. It wouldn't do to criticise Denise on so vulnerable a matter as her hair.

A drop of water flicked Alice on the mouth. Even so small a drop smelt of expensive conditioner – Denise's only extravagance. A frail, flower smell. Alice brushed it away with her hand. She looked at her daughter. Looking directly at a real person like that, Mr Rochester vanished. Denise had a largish nose and large hands, like Jack. Her eyes were on the small side – though the blessing was she wasn't short-sighted. (Quite a wonder, considering Alice's mother, from Chippenham, had been nearly blind.) They were shut, as she towelled away at her wrinkled hair – cropped eyelashes barely reaching her flushed cheeks. In books Alice read the heroine's eyelashes always cast shadows upon her cheeks. Denise's didn't. Still, not everyone could give birth to a beauty, and Alice recognised the fact that Denise had a pleasant expression. What she'd call an open face.

'Cup of tea, Denise?'

'Thanks, Mum.'

Jack would be wanting his hot milk in half an hour, and no doubt Robbie would be down soon, that funny distant look in his eyes that always appeared when he'd been listening in to police messages – and he'd want something or other. Alice could never guess what. For a mathematician, Robbie was curiously irregular about his nightcap habits. To be on the safe side, Alice kept a good supply of everything so that she could never be caught off-guard. Sometimes, usually midweek, he liked a bedtime sandwich, too. You could never tell with Robbie.

Alice went to the kitchen. Denise took her place on the sofa, shaking her head, eyes smarting. Bloody wrestling. She could never persuade Dad to turn over to BBC2. That was the channel she liked : plenty of programmes about dwarfs and illegits and the educationally sub-normal – the sort of thing that reduced her to the warmth of compassion, and sent her to bed smug at her own good fortune. But she could only watch those sort of programmes when Dad was working late and she was here with Mum alone. Mum was easy. She'd agree to anything, and spoil her at the same time. Biscuits, little sandwiches made with salmon fishpaste and cress cut from the plastic dish on the window sill. Mum spent her whole life looking after them a treat. Sometimes Denise felt bad about it – but then it gave Mum such obvious pleasure. You only had to look at her to see that. She was quite radiant, sometimes, faced with a pile of washing that would have caused Denise herself tears of frustration. Well, some people were born housewives : that's all there was to it. They had no ambition to be anything else, no matter what Women's Lib might say. Denise wasn't like that. *She* had her ambition – her talent – and she wasn't going to give that up for any husband on earth. It would be plain stupid. In fact it would be foolish even to think about marriage at the moment. Besides, it would be hard to give up the comforts of home life before she had to.

Upstairs in his bedroom, Robbie, who had had a good evening listening in to trouble in a pub over Uxbridge way, felt the desire for a plate of ham and chips come upon him. The strength of the feeling wrung his mouth with a fresh supply of saliva, and he hurried downstairs to the kitchen. Mum had better be quick. He couldn't wait much longer. His stomach was a burning pit, empty, lusting for the food that had come to his mind in so tantalising a way.

Alice was making tea for Denise. Arranging a tray while a kettle boiled. She always did a tray, even for one cup of tea.

'Plate of ham and chips, Mum, please,' Robbie said. 'I'm

starving.' Alice looked surprised.

'But you've had your tea. A good meal.'

'Can't be helped. I'm famished.'

'Very well. Just a minute, till I've taken the others their drinks. Shall I put it on a tray for you?'

'I'll have it in here.'

Robbie liked to eat by himself. He liked his food after the others had finished, alone at the kitchen table, staring at the calendar of English cathedrals on the wall, his mind on other things. But what he couldn't abide was that the room should be empty. So his mother – wonderfully obligingly, really – stayed with him. The music of her washing-up was of such comfort that people would laugh if he told them how much it meant to him. Sometimes, Mum would say something. He would answer her, politely of course, but not with the warmth that encouraged further observations. He required silence with his meals as other men need wine. On holiday, that was the one thing that bugged him, communal meals on the boat.

'Days getting longer,' said Alice. She passed him a tube of mustard. Robbie liked English mustard with his ham, French with his beef.

'Yes,' said Robbie.

'Enough ham?'

'Thanks.'

'Shall I do you a slice of bread?'

'Thanks.'

'And a lager?'

Robbie nodded. When there was nothing more she could do for any member of her family, Alice felt flat. They were the moments she most dreaded. The yellow of co-operation thinned in her blood, leaving her physically lighter, feeling she might take off like an autumn leaf in a west wind. Tasks were her anchor.

Empty, she returned to the sitting-room. Her husband and daughter were eating slices of the jam sponge she had baked that afternoon. There was nothing she could do for them so, second best actions though they were, she plumped up the cushions and drew the blinds. She hoped they might all sit round for a while, now, and talk. She liked the sound of their voices. The drone of the telly, on most nights till closing down, was never the same joy.

But tonight she was to be rewarded. The news over, Jack switched it off. Robbie came in.

'You've turned it off.' His forehead was sweaty. It often glowed, like that, at any unusual change. Change of events confused him.

'Yes,' said Jack.

'You've turned it off earlier, though.' Robbie lowered himself into an upright armchair with aged caution. Five minutes and he'd go back to the set. See how Patrol 2 was getting on up in Uxbridge.

'Yes, I have,' said Jack, 'for a very good reason. Days getting longer – '

'That's just what I was saying to Robbie,' interrupted Alice.

'Days getting longer, and it's time to discuss our annual holiday. Not, I imagine, that there's very much to discuss. Need I ask where it's to be?'

'Broads, of course,' said Robbie.

Fifteen years they'd been going to the Broads, same boat, and Robbie liked it. He liked it best when it rained, sitting out on the deck, mack over his head, watching his mother peel potatoes at a sink no bigger than a pudding bowl. He liked watching the rain falling into the green weed on the water. He liked a drink in the local pub, evenings, talking to the local policeman in policeman's language, telling him some of the better stories he'd heard on the transmitter. Of course, the policeman had never been to Uxbridge but, as he said, he could credit the stories : the kind of thing the Force had to deal with these days. Robbie liked him. He liked everything in Norfolk but the communal meals, and more and more Mum was giving him sandwiches which he could take off and eat on his own.

'Broads, natch, silly,' said Denise. The thing that got her most about the place was the early mornings. You could hear birds and that if you woke early. Her sleeping bag, on the narrow bunk, was cosy. She could read her beauty magazines by the small light over the porthole, waiting till Mum got up to fry eggs and bacon for breakfast. *That* was a smell, on a boat. Not the same thing, in a house kitchen. Then, on the boat, Mum would offer her snacks all day long and she couldn't refuse.

'The *Lugger,* as usual?' Jack knew as he asked the question that it was rhetorical. There were many advantages to the *Lugger.* For a start, as the years went by and it grew more dilapidated, its rent decreased. To be honest, the Lees were the only family left who were still attracted to the boat : the only hirers. And in return for giving it a good spring clean on arrival – Alice was a wonder, the way she managed to clean a year's dirt and damp in an afternoon – they hired it for peanuts. That, in these days of economic crisis, was something to be considered. Moreover, it was *fun* the *Lugger.* A good time was had upon her by all, come rain come shine. Been the same for years. They knew their way around. They felt easy on board. They respected their captain – Jack : they took his word. If he said the engine was snarled up and there would be no cruise that day, they'd all potter off, quite happy, believing him. And the engine often *was* snarled up. Increasingly, over the years. But, in truth, it was no hardship to Jack to put it to rights again. In his heart, the task was a positive enjoyment. There was something about kneeling on the boards of the deck, feeling the muscles pulling in your back, greasy black fingers coaxing the tired parts . . . After eleven months in an office shuffling through clean white papers, Jack loved tinkering with an oily engine. So much so that, sometimes, he even prolonged the job, anticipating the cheer that would go up when he straightened his back and declared the fault mended. He knew the feel of the key in the ignition, familiar as his own front door. There weren't many greater pleasures than turning it, face against the wind and hearing, distinctly, the putter of the gallant little engine as the *Lugger*'s nose pushed once more through the reeds and into the open grey waters . . .

He'd write the usual letter. Tonight.

"Course, the *Lugger,*' said Robbie. 'You're very quiet, Mum.' He turned to her.

In the barren heath of Alice Lees's mind the yellow of co-operation failed to flower. She waited, stranded, helpless. But no warmth surged through her veins, as it usually did at this annual family conference. For years, she'd been just as delighted as the others at the thought of a summer holiday on the *Lugger*. Where was that most familiar of feelings, now? As she waited for it to infuse her limbs, in the silence of the front room, the eyes of the family upon her, Alice saw a kaleidoscope of all their years in Norfolk.

Potato peelings. She remembered them best. Miles and miles of brown spotted peelings uncurling from several tons of potatoes and overflowing the minute, discoloured sink. 'Here, be a love and get rid of these for me, will you?' she would say to no one in particular. But no one ever cared to hear her occasional cries for help. So – quicker to do a thing yourself, really – she'd push the peelings into a slippery plastic bag, feeling them curl like cold brown ribbons round her wrists, and squeeze the bag into the bin full of empty tins and egg shells and apple cores and lumps of cotton wool smeary with Denise's eyeshadow. Oh! The smell in the galley – Jack insisted they called it the galley. Funny the others didn't notice it. Tea leaves and baked beans, fried fish and pulpy fruit squashed under the superficial fumes of disinfectant. To Alice the smell was an obscenity, a tangible, creeping thing that crawled over her skin, into her hair, lapped in her nostrils at night while she tried to sleep. Not that she ever slept much. That awful plash, plash, thud, thud, a watery rapping hand against the boat. Then the lurching rock and the scrape of weeds when another boat passed, leaving behind its sickening wake. 'Jack!' she'd cry, queasy, head rolling about on the hard pillow. But Jack would be snoring, hands lumpy on the blankets, the oil washed to skeleton branches of black in the creases of his skin. Denise, too, slept peacefully beneath her face-pack, and Robbie was curled dreamingly under his mack on the deck. The moon, Alice knew, would be looking at itself in the black water. She didn't like the idea of two moons. They made her flesh prick. Also, she didn't like the idea of moorhens and water rats scuttling through the reeds on their night errands bumping, as they sometimes did, against the boat. The horrors of the night about her, Alice longed for morning. Stirring a tired fork among the bacon, at least there was light of a kind in the galley. The shopping to think of, the sleeping bags to be aired. Robbie's socks to wash : Denise's hair to set before she dried it, netted, in the sun or wind. Sometimes, on board the *Lugger,* every muscle in Alice Lee's body would protest, while the yellow of co-operation racing in her blood would urge her to go on. And go on she did. It was only conditions on board, being so different from home, made her so tired. Silly, really. The change itself probably did her good, and adversities were part of the fun, weren't they? Fun! Evenings, she'd let them all go off to The Jolly for a drink, and when they'd gone she'd sit out on deck, on the small plastic chair, alone, scuffing at the midges. Dreading the night. Counting the hours to go home. But not wanting to dwell on her *silliness* : for that's what it was. A five minute sit-down, a glance at the sunset clouds that dyed the water (she'd never been much of a one for sunsets herself, preferred grey skies that needed no comment) then back to the galley to peel more potatoes. They'd come back ravenous, wanting a big fry-up supper at once. Oh God ! The bin would be full again, plate scrapings from lunch. Lumps of meat Jack hadn't been able to chew. They'd arrive to find her started on the frying, smiling.

'Well?' said Robbie.

'I'm not going,' said Alice.

'Not what, dear?' Jack, a careless listener, could rarely believe what he heard.

'Not this year.' As she saw her own words spin into an incredulous void, Alice felt the gradual induration of her body. She leaned back in her chair, but her spine remained stiff.

'Mum says she's not going. Hark at that. She wouldn't miss it for anything.' Denise, filing her nails, was full of sarcasm. Robbie rubbed at the sweat that had accumulated on his forehead.

'Not going?'

'Am I to believe my two ears are deceiving me?' asked Jack, looking his wife directly in the eye.

'No, Jack.'

'Then what's all this about? I want to get the letter off tonight.'

'You can do that. You can get the letter off, go on your holiday. It's just that I'm not coming too.'

A film of blackness, like a year's dust, had gathered over the room. Alice felt faint. She held on to the arms of her chair.

'Mum's gone mad,' said Robbie, 'haven't you, Mum?'

'She's having one of her turns,' said Denise.

'She hasn't had one of her turns for twenty years, since she was pregnant with you. Or was it Robbie?'

'Could someone get me a glass of water?' Alice asked quietly.

Jack went to the sideboard, momentarily alarmed. He poured a glass of brandy from a dull bottle which he kept for victims of possible car crashes in their street.

'I said water, please.' Alice hated spirits.

'Go on. You need some of the hard stuff.'

Obediently, Alice drank. Jack watched her, uneasy at her paleness. Best to get her to bed as soon as possible, he thought. Then he could write the letter and post it in the morning. By then, she would have come to her senses. This turn was something to do with her time of life, more than likely.

When she had washed up the cups and plates and her own brandy glass, Alice went willingly to her room. In the morning she, too, knew she would feel better.

It was raining when she woke. Alice was immediately glad. She liked grey days better than bright ones. Her own internal yellow illumined the hours more satisfactorily when there was no real sun outside to compete with. Besides, there was more to do on rainy days. The lulling pleasure of sweeping and re-sweeping the kitchen floor, and the hall carpet where they all forgot to wipe their shoes. She sprang out of bed, looking forward to the day. Gently pulled back the curtains so as not to wake Jack for another ten minutes.

'I've written the letter,' he said. 'I trust you've come to your senses, so I'll be posting it this morning.'

Alice stood still by the window, a bunch of curtain hitched up in her hand, staring at the rain. She wriggled her toes in the warm burrows of her slippers.

'You can post the letter,' she said, 'but I've not changed my mind. I'm not going.'

Jack sighed. He threw back the bedclothes, sat up, slinging his legs on the floor, knees left wide to support his arms. His hands cradled his head.

'You're barmy,' he said. 'What's your objection?'

Alice was going to say the lavatory, the spilling bin, the potato peelings, the water rats – but it was none of those things, individually, or even together. What *was* her objection, she asked herself?

'Nothing in particular I could explain,' she said. Any more than she could explain how her body felt when it was drained of yellow. They'd think she was mad.

'You're barmy,' Jack said again. 'What you need is a tonic, too. A change. You don't look after yourself all that much.'

'Oh, I'm fine,' said Alice. 'I'll be getting the breakfast.'

And the strange thing was, getting the breakfast, she felt just as usual : the same subdued pleasure, a lovely saffron colour at this time of day, soon to flower later into the inevitable chrome. It was only when she let her mind alight on the holiday that the warmth of the colour in her veins ebbed from her. So she tried not to think. That wasn't easy, considering how the others kept on with their remarks. Then Jack gave her a strange look as he left.

'I'll be posting the letter,' he said.

For three evenings they tried to persuade her to change her mind. She resisted, simply, strongly. Nothing they could say would alter what she felt : she didn't want to go. Then what did she want to do, Denise, near to tearful exasperation, demanded?

'Go to the Lakes, perhaps.'

Alice had a vague idea in her mind of looking up Wordsworth's birthplace. Daffodils up there – she loved the poem. Though of course it would be the wrong time of year. Still, she could imagine them, a host of golden . . .

'What, alone?' Denise's voice, so hard.

'Yes. Why not?'

'Huh.' Robbie, gleaming again, his forehead.

'Don't be daft.' Jack kept saying don't be daft. Don't be daft, he said; don't be barmy; don't be mad. 'And who would look after us?' he added, this evening.

'You'd manage very nicely.' They wouldn't in fact. They all knew that. Denise would never get things going in the galley: she could scarcely fry an egg. No one would air the sleeping bags and check the bread bin for damp. Without her, it would be a disaster, not a nice holiday at all. But what could Alice do? Her mind would not change. Set on its own course, first time for years, it was quite adamant. No yellow to the rescue. A terrible black of stubbornness. And yet the red, somewhere, a strong and crazy flag, of knowing she was right.

Within a week a letter came from Norfolk. Jack read it and passed it to Alice with a silent smile. It confirmed, unsurprisingly, that the *Lugger* was available to them again this year. Alice smiled back.

'Well, you'll have to take a lot of cleaning things to get it into shape,' she said. 'I'll collect them up for you. I expect Denise'll manage.'

'You're off your rocker, Mum,' said Denise.

Off your rocker. It was a phrase which had begun to flaunt the household. They all said it. They said it straight out to her, over and over again, no attempt at hiding what they thought. Their questions *why?* flagged in the face of her taciturnity. She could not answer them. She remained silently knowing she was right, and as her silence increased so did their taunts that she was barmy, stubborn, selfish, foolish . . . The adjectives sprayed out, each painful new dart a further incentive to her resistance.

The day the letter came Jack left the house for work with a grim expression.

'You in all day?' he asked. He never asked such things: he knew she was in all day. The small mystery alerted Alice. When the front door bell rang, mid-morning, she was unsurprised. It was Dr Cairn, concern twisting his face.

He had been requested to do a difficult job by his old friend, Jack, and he did his best. He was gentle with Alice, quiet and patient. They drank tea in the kitchen, and he suggested she wasn't sleeping well. He could prescribe her something mild. Oh, but she was, said Alice. She was sleeping beautifully. Then she had something on her mind? Alice smiled. Only the usual domestic things, the horrifying price of . . . No, no. He didn't mean that. He wasn't making himself clear. Oh, but he was. Alice felt unusually bright this morning. In her brightness everything was particularly clear.

'What you're trying to say, like the rest of them, is because, for once, I've a mind of my own, I'm sticking to my decision, there's something *wrong* with my mind. A nervous disorder, perhaps? My time of life?' She was quite enjoying herself.

Dr Cairn crumbled a biscuit between his fingers. He had been convinced, by Jack's description on the telephone, that Alice was suffering from some kind of temporary aberration that a small bottle of tranquillisers would put right in no time. Now, facing her, he wasn't quite so sure. The problem seemed more complex. If there was a problem. Perhaps it was simply a matter of a spiritless woman – he had always thought her a wan old thing – showing a little temperament. But Jack had been so positive she was suffering. The way she had been going on – her silences. You could tell, he had said.

'Well, I don't know.' The doctor met Alice's eyes. 'But you can say anything you want to me, you know. Get it off your chest. Professional discretion.' He smiled a little. 'I wouldn't tell Jack.'

There was no clarifying response.

'I've nothing to tell you except that I don't want to go with them on the boat this year. No particular reason. I just don't want to go, that's all.'

From what he had heard of the Broads, Dr Cairn thought that mighty reasonable. It was Alice's calm and unshakeable determination not to change her mind that he found baffling. He left in some confusion, knowing he would have to think quickly. Jack wanted some kind of answer that afternoon. What should he recommend? All part of a GP's practice, mental disorders were not his forte. Best thing to do, obviously, was to pass Alice on.

Jack conveyed the message when he came home. Privately, in the kitchen. Gently. Worried eyes. Dr Cairn had said there was only one thing for it – and he was sorry, incidentally, that he had sent the doctor round without saying anything, like that, but he knew Alice would never have gone to the surgery. Dr Cairn advised she should see someone up at the hopsital. Some kind of specialist in psychiatry.

Oh, the easiness of such a request! The yellow flowers leapt. Alice clapped her hands, startling her husband. Of course! Why not? She didn't mind going to see anyone at the hospital if it would please him. She'd do anything to please. Except go on the boat.

The interview with the specialist, a few days later, took place in a small cubicle of frosted glass. The gas fire, a red-blue honeycomb on the fragile wall, filled the silences with its roaring, and the sun, through the ribbed window, made a halo of thorns above the specialist's head. He took off his spectacles and looked at her.

'They think I'm mad,' said Alice quickly, giving him no time to make up his own mind, 'because I don't want to go on holiday with them this year. Well, we've been going for fifteen years. It seems to me quite reasonable to want a change, but they're convinced I'm mad. Have you ever heard anything so ridiculous?' He didn't answer, but allowed his mouth a slight widening. His coat was blazing white. It would be good to iron, Alice thought. The idea exhilarated her. She liked the feeling of being enclosed with a man who was at the top of his profession. The blue of confidence swelled about her. At least he would understand, would dismiss the concept as nonsense . . .

'It isn't quite as simple as that, I think,' he said, and wrote something on his piece of paper.

'Surely it is.' Alice had imagined her voice would come soaring out. Instead she heard with surprise its minor tone.

The specialist tipped his head back to look at the ceiling. He made his fingers into a spire, their tips just touching, so that if prayer was made of incense, and he was praying, it would float through the stubby mesh quite easily. Nearer to God with unclenched fists. Alice hadn't prayed for years, not since she had asked Him to send her a Mr Rochester, and He had failed.

'Tell me all about it,' said the specialist, 'from the beginning.'

Although there was nothing to tell, nothing at all, really, the yellow of co-operation was flowing fast within Alice, and she tried. She spoke for a long time, twenty minutes, perhaps, saying how nice it had always been on the *Lugger*, how they'd always had such a good time – not mentioning the bin, or the two moons or the smells. There was no need to go into all that. But she ended, boldly, by saying the Lakes had taken her fancy. Wordsworth, the daffodils fluttering and dancing. They had a few in their own garden and, in the March winds, that's just what they did. Fluttered and danced. Didn't he think? For the first time in her soliloquy, the specialist revealed a touch of impatience in the arc of his fingers. He demolished the structure, which had weathered the whole of Alice's explanation, to take up his pen. He thanked her, told her not to worry, and she left.

In the next few days, Alice noticed, the jibes at home died down a little. There seemed to be a conspiracy of reticence which for the most part was kept to, although when discussing the holiday Denise, the most incensed by Alice's betrayal, continued to use the word daft. Robbie took a more tactful line.

'Poor old Mum,' he said, many times, 'think what she'll be missing.' Pity, it seemed, was now strongly within them. Strong as resentment.

On the night Dr Cairn arrived Alice was feeling particularly happy. The whole family had enjoyed her apple crumble for supper, and there was a good long play on television with three commercial breaks in which to fetch everyone their special drinks. But with Dr Cairn's entrance, the play was switched off. Denise, at some private sign from her father, fetched a tray of small glasses, and the brandy. Everyone seemed to know what was going to happen. Alice waited.

Dr Cairn explained it had come to this: all Alice needed, according to the specialist, who had diagnosed in a moment what was wrong – was a short spell in a home. A very nice home, all comforts, not too far away, no restriction on visits. There, they would look after her. Wouldn't fill her with pills – oh, no, nothing like that. Just, well, look after her in the way that she needed – in a way that her family or any unskilled person could never hope to accomplish – and after a while she'd be quite herself. How long, he couldn't exactly say. It would be partly up to her, depending on how she responded to the treatment. On how she co-operated.

Alice looked round her tidy sitting-room at the grave figures of her family. She felt a warmth of love for them, that they should care for her so. She felt guilty at their concern. And then their faces, very precise in their anxiety at Dr Cairn's words, wavered into marvellous oblivion behind the bands of surging yellow that rose before her eyes. The brilliance of the colour pounding in her veins made her very sure, very strong, with the pleasure of instant co-operation. Dr Cairn, had he known, would have been proud of her.

Jack was unsurprised at his wife's calm. He would not expect her to flap in a crisis. She wasn't like that. She had always been able to cope. They would miss her. But it wouldn't do to be selfish in a case like this. She would come back her old self : it was, after all, for her own sake she was going. They were doing the best thing for her. Denise sniffed a bit, rubbed at her eyes and shook her damp head. Robbie studied the carpet, thinking he would go and see his mother twice a week. A firm resolution, that. It would be an effort, the long bus ride. But he would keep to it. She deserved that from him.

And so, with no murmur of reproof, Alice packed her things and made arrangements for the perpetual delivery of milk and bread, and stuck reminders on the kitchen wall about the laundry and how to work the spin-dryer. They all went with her to the home, and saw her settled comfortably into her pastel room, with its linoleum floor and bright narrow bed. There was a nice garden outside, with a cedar tree and a bench made of knotted branches. The corridors made footsteps quiet, there was television in the lounge, only a few cries in the wakeful hours of the night. The staff were all so kind, always asking her if she would like tea, and the specialist who built prayers with his fingers came only once a week to ask her questions to which she had no answer.

They gave her a glass of pink stuff to drink every morning, saying how wonderful she was not to complain, how co-operative she was. She didn't worry much about life at home – Jack assured her, when he came on Saturday afternoons with a packet of chocolate wafers, that Denise had come out of herself surprisingly. She was being a good little housewife, doing very well. They all came quite often, as they said they would, interrupting her thoughts about Mr Rochester sometimes, but she didn't really mind. Then, in the summer, there was a break in their visits. Their holiday on the *Lugger,* of course. Alice quite understood, simply asked them to send her a postcard if they had time. A picture of the reeds at sunset arrived, with messages from all three of them. Having a lovely time, they said they were, but they wished she was there. Alice thought of their time, as she sat in her pastel room, and remembered the smells, the water, the potato peelings, the bin, and she saw the petals of the yellow flower in her mind were wilting, dying, falling all about her. She stretched out her hand to touch the petals, to feel again their warmth. But she knew, as she thought of them all in the boat, the yellow of co-operation would not come to her, and she was glad.

Loving Gourmets

We met again in Elizabeth Street, George and I. There he was, carrying a blue nylon shopping bag with immeasurable dignity. Flowering broccoli sprouted from its holes, brushing his legs as he walked, very upright, ignoring the purple heads that flirted with his twill knees. He stopped at once when he saw me, clicking his heels together : he'd never been able to shake off his military style.

'Why, good heavens, Diana,' he said.

'*George*,' I replied.

He had changed very little : same blunt face, a little baggier perhaps, startling green eyes. Red veins splintered his cheeks now (they were once solid red) and his paunch, safe as ever in its tweed waistcoat, had expanded by many pounds. I felt him looking me over, taking in equivalent changes, down to the waist. He once told me he never looked further, on an attractive woman, as this prevented him from being disillusioned by bad legs. I wondered if he noticed I had quite a show of bosom now (the menopause had brought that on) solid under my beige cashmere : I wondered if he recognised the same dull pearls with their magnificent ruby clasp that he'd played with sometimes between his finger and thumb.

'It must be twenty years,' he said. 'I live round the corner now.' It came back to me : I'd read in some gossip column he was married to his second – or was it his third? – wife. They had a penthouse in Eaton Square. The wife wouldn't speak to one of his hippy grandchildren, something like that. George had always had a penchant for difficult women. He swung the shopping bag a little.

'I enjoy doing the shopping – well, *you* know.' He smiled, darker teeth. 'Bloody Spanish servants always fiddle the bills.'

'After all this time,' I heard myself saying.

'Indeed, indeed : my dear Diana,' he was mumbling, and

from the look on his face I realised he was having some difficulty in recollecting, too.

We met at a cocktail party in the days when it was considered normal rather than daftly grand to send printed invitations to such functions. Him : blue pinstripe suit, red carnation in his buttonhole. Me : insignificant black dress, wavy hair. An immovable waiter held a silver dish of particularly ostentatious *canapés* between us, and we talked about mock caviare. We had to shout against the noise. He seemed to have a nice, resonant, shouting voice.

A week later he asked me to lunch at the Savoy – the restaurant, by the window, being summer. There was champagne waiting by the table, real caviar – my first, poached salmon with *sauce verte,* and a salad of translucently thin cucumber. Finally, *fraises du bois* flown from somewhere with, of course (*of course,* I quickly agreed) kirsch instead of cream. I remember coming away feeling, for the first time in my life, excited about food. Except for the caviar I had eaten all the things before, and was even acquainted with the Traminer and the vintage Moët et Chandon. But George, with his enthusiasm and knowledge, had a way of making them a new experience. I think we only talked of food : funny stories about some woman in Beirut who had forced him to eat rose-petal jam.

The lunch must have been a success because he then asked me out to dinner at the Caprice – iced sorrel soup and roast baby kid : marvellous. But we deplored the general standard of restaurant food in England – this was, of course, a few years before the birth of even the first trattoria. It was then that George admitted, diffidently, that he was shortly off on his annual gourmet holiday round France. Would I like to come?

This, it seemed, was a compliment. In previous years he had always been alone. In me, apparently, he confessed, he had found a soulmate. I had little knowledge but instinctive appreciation. It would please him so if I would come.

I looked at George. The red of his cheeks was a little deeper after two bottles of wine : his smooth, army hair was greased immaculately back, the thick silk of his tie an unblemished blue.

I felt a sudden stirring of anticipation. The wine had made the crimson room dance like tendrils in a wind. I imagined us eating like this – better – every night. Then making love in small *auberges* in the Dordogne, Normandy, Brittany, the South. I'd never contemplated any such escapade before – indeed, never before had I been offered the chance. I had been to bed (as it was referred to in those days) with only one gentleman to date, in conditions of utmost secrecy and discomfort. Today's permissive society was unborn : among my friends a week away alone with a man was rarely achieved and even more rarely acknowledged.

I accepted.

Along with his red Sunbeam Talbot, we boarded the ferry from Dover. In his holiday clothes George was perhaps somewhat less spectacular than in London, but very polished and neat in tweeds that merged into each other in a Scottish fashion. I noticed several middle-aged women turn their heads in admiration at the bar. After we'd drunk several pink gins we found two deck chairs on the deck. We sat enjoying the sun through the sea breeze, and looking in easy silence at the green-grey rocking waves. I thought perhaps he might hold my hand, not that he had ever done so before. In fact, he took a packet of *pâté* sandwiches and a bottle of hock from his briefcase. In my delight at his forethought (all around us people were eating packets of crisps) I made some extravagant remark about the receding cliffs of Dover. But George, concentrating on opening the wine, didn't seem to hear.

'It came to me in the night, about the sandwiches,' he said. 'I got up and made them then and there, in case there should be a rush in the morning.' I think it was at that moment I wondered how I should ever get through to George, apart from food. Maybe the nights would do it.

We landed at Calais, and with great modesty George fell into perfect French, only when necessary. No inessential observations to the porters to show how good he was. I was grateful for that. Leaning back in the comfortable seat of the Sunbeam Talbot I knew for certain that should we cross the border into any

European country, George would be just as at home, just as fluent in the language. Oh! he was wonderfully in charge. I shivered at the pleasure. He noticed, and covered my hand, which had strayed close to the gears, with one of his – gloved. Just for a moment.

'*Maintenant, mon chou,*' he said.

We sped away into northern France, dusk falling, the silence between us agreeable. Some hours later we drew up at an *auberge* set back a little from the main road. The Auberge Bon Femme, I seem to remember it was. A warm and cheerful place, a wood fire in the hall – the *auberge* of my fantasies. They seemed to know George there. The *patron* greeted him with many a jest, and kissed my hand, and called me *madame* with the seriousness of one who is always willing to partake of an English joke. We were shown to a room under the eaves, most of which was taken up by a vast double bed with brass ends. George began to unpack with great energy, almost filling the cupboard with his uncreased suits, leaving only two hangers for me. He seemed awfully happy. His walk, from cupboard to bed, bed to cupboard, was an anticipatory bounce. He hummed to himself, French tunes. Then suggested I should have a bath and change while he went downstairs to have a *verre* with the *patron.* We would dine at eight-thirty.

At eight twenty-five I made my entrance into the bar. I was wearing a modest little dress, sort of rhubarb colour which, I had noticed, glancing into the speckled mirror before coming down, enhanced the almost silly look of rapture on my face. The effect did not go unnoticed by George. He slid from his seat, welcoming.

'*Mon chou, mon ange,*' he said. 'You're beautiful. What will you have to drink?' He put an arm around my shoulder, his exuberance perhaps encouraged by the two or even three *verres* he had had with the *patron.*

We had the best table, by another fire. And a most exquisite dinner. *Pâté,* first, the *spécialité de la maison.* Slices of dappled, skewbald stuff that lay glinting on clouds of lettuce. As we ate it, with great reverence and much sighing, George recalled so many *pâtés* in his past: those smooth, bland concoctions of whipped goose liver spotted with fragments of truffle; the rougher, country *pâtés* full of zest and brandy. He had had such experience of *pâtés*, George. I was amazed. He liked to amaze me, I could see. He ordered wine without looking at the list, and when it came he sniffed it with just the right amount of disdain before acknowledging it perfect.

We ate *rougets*, next : such *rougets*, simply grilled. And finally a cheese *soufflé* that was a buttercup puff of foam – a *poem* of a *soufflé* as George said. By this time my head was cloudy bright from the beautiful wine. George's memories of past meals diminished a little with the *petits fours*, and he was quite silent by the time we went to bed.

The wine had made me careless. I undressed in a disorderly fashion, leaving my clothes in heaps on the ground. George was more meticulous. Under the camouflage of his dressing gown he slipped into silk pyjamas. There was some confusion about which side of the bed each one of us should have.

'You wanted . . . ?'

'No, no. I don't mind. You go there.'

'Which side of a double bed do you normally sleep?'

I blushed, I know.

'I don't normally sleep in double beds.'

'Very well, if you really don't mind.' He chose the side with the bedside table and the small lamp that glowed brownly under its antique shade. In bed, he took a tortoiseshell comb from the pocket of his dressing gown and resmoothed his already flattened hair with two quick, decisive movements. Then he lowered himself in the bed, and politely lifted the sheets for me to get in.

'Tomorrow,' he said, 'we shall go somewhere that has the best burgundy you've ever tasted.'

'That was a marvellous dinner,' I said. We lay a yard apart. My skin stretched too tightly over my surging veins.

'That was only a beginning,' he said softly. Lovingly, I thought. I let the words seep into my flesh. Then peered up at him.

'Do you always sleep in your dressing gown?'

His eyes were shut, his hands folded on his well-filled stomach. The position reminded me of those stone saints who lie on their graves, worn out by their good life, now happy in their good death. He snored a little. I reached across to put out the light. Well, I thought: I'm glad. It wouldn't have done, tonight. Not with him being so tired. It might have been an anti-climax. It's much better that he should get a good night's sleep. For one so young, I was something of a cynic.

George slept very well. He hardly moved all night. In the morning he woke vigorously, ringing at once for *deux cafés complets*. I realised, then, how I had misjudged him. He was not, after all, a predictable man – a perfect dinner, a heady bottle of wine, make love. Such a conventional pattern of things, thank goodness, would not appeal to him. No: his method was more interestingly spontaneous. He would ask for love when he felt the desire come upon him, no matter what time of day. And judging by this, his eager early face, it could well be morning. I trembled.

How delighted he was by that first breakfast! The warm *croissants* flaked away in our fingers even as we touched them. The rich black coffee flared through my wakeful body filling it with longing. I felt my legs squirm under the bedclothes – careful not to touch George, just to let him know of the movement. Outside the open window a blackbird sang, the sky was cloudless. It was going to be a good day, but I didn't want to enter it just yet.

'George!'

He turned to me, specks of *croissant* on his mouth and dressing gown. Took my hand, shifted himself a bit.

'Now. We're going to leap out of bed and get to the market while it's still early. It's always best, early. There I shall choose for you the most perfect peaches and cheese for our lunch, which we shall eat under a poplar tree that Manet might have painted.' His eyes strolled far away to this *déjeuner sur l'herbe*. 'Does that suit you?'

An infinitesmal silence. Then new hope: a checked table cloth, the car rug spread in the long grass – why else would he have brought the car rug? A few more hours, that's all.

'Oh, yes,' I said.

He was wonderful in the market. His fingers skimmed up and down fruits and vegetables, he muttered 'Bah!' sounds if he touched upon too ripe a flesh. Eventually he chose : two frail, dewy peaces and a wedge of Camembert that trembled on the brink of runniness. He bought butter and a knife and long *flutes* of fresh bread, and we roared off down empty roads between fields of smudgy lavender. He stopped at a place beside a small river for lunch : it seemed familiar to him. We spread the rug and sat in a cage of long grass, butterflies our only visitors. George took the corkscrew from his briefcase and uncorked a bottle of red wine, *château* something.

'This is the life,' he said.

In the sun, his brown shoes shone very brightly. There was something vulnerable about those shoes. I felt a surge of love for him : affection, regard, respect, desire. While he poured the wine I undid the top button of my shirt. After lunch, drowsy, we would sleep, perhaps. It would all happen, so drowsily, so drowsily. George's mind seemed to be following my own. He lay propped on one arm and lifted a gentle hand to my cheek, his eyes melting.

'There's a little place not far from here,' he said, 'that sells the most irresistible truffles. We'll go there directly after lunch, which will leave us plenty of time to get to the Bellevue by tonight.' And he broke the long, sweet-smelling loaf.

We accomplished it all, of course : stacked a dozen tins of truffles into the boot, and arrived at the Bellevue in time for dinner. There we had a room crowded with Louis XIV type chairs, and extravagant satin curtains. There we drank a sharp little muscadet on the leafy terrace before dinner, and between the *quenelles* and the *profiteroles* he fiddled with the ruby clasp of my pearls.

'You haven't enough bosom to show off such pearls,' he said, 'but you're becoming a delicious little gourmet.' In the confusion in my head I sifted the compliment from the criticism and hugged it to myself, and quickly drank another glass of wine to ameliorate the sadness of my inadequate bosom.

Then, to my shame, in the dreadfully hard historical bed, I

was the one to fall asleep first. Thoughtfully, George did not disturb me.

By the third day of our tour I learned that to join George in spirit, if not in body, was the only way. And so it was with greater, more desperate relish I came to appreciate the food. The days spun by, a galaxy of four-star interludes. I remember a hotel on a mountain top that overlooked half of France – the most delicate of boiled chickens under whose skin the *patron* himself had slipped fine slices of secret *pâté*. I remember the lightest of omelettes singing with fresh herbs (some of George's phrases rubbed off on me); I remember pale fish whose sea-taste glowed through the creamy sauce. And then the puddings – my particular weakness: the irresistible trolleys of cream cheeses spun with white of egg into airy blobs, and floating through primrose coloured sauces. I remember *sorbets,* and exotic pastry things oozing with cream and *fraises du bois,* and whipped *marrons* hazy in chocolate sauce. Less clearly I remember swaying up many a staircase to a sagging French bedroom whose once grand wallpaper was now quite faded. There, in a dozen different beds, exhausted by our gourmet day, overblown with food and wine, George and I slept at once. At least – did we? I could never be quite sure. Wasn't there the odd night when our bodies churned together, essaying some feat of love quite beyond us? I only positively know that we would wake each morning with our appetites for food renewed.

Somewhere in the Loire country I became aware of feeling a comfortable fatness. It slowed my movements: it happily dissipated all desire except for further food. George, I noticed, was at one with me in this feeling. The warmth of compatibility was upon us, and the days went fast.

We spent our last night in Paris. Began with champagne and those incomparable crisps at the Ritz Bar. Went on to a place whose menu, even to our experienced eyes, was dazzling. We took our time, weighing up the pros and cons of each dish, and indulged in a bit of connoisseur talk.

'How about the *pâté maison*?'

'But it couldn't be as good as the *Bonne Femme*.'

'Nor it could. But dare we try the *agneau*, after Mère Bise?'

In bed that night – a soaring cathedral of a bed, four posts and a domed ceiling of silk pleats, George remembered it was almost over. Sleepily, he held my hand.

'I don't know what you expected of this little *vacance*,' he said. 'I hope it hasn't been a disappointment.'

'Oh George! How could you? What an idea. I've never eaten such food in my life.'

With some effort he focused his eyes upon me.

'I wondered, from time to time, if you *really* loved food. If it could ever become a way of life to you, like it has to me. I thought, tonight – your face – that perhaps I've accomplished one thing: I've made you a gourmet for life. Haven't I?'

'Ooh, you have.' A slight, desirous stirring somewhere. But his eyes were half closed.

'I'm so pleased about that. Diana?' His stumbling hand felt for the clasp of my pearls. 'I'm really so pleased about that.'

On deck next day, on the way back to Dover, I tried my best to thank him. Without my knowing, he had slipped out early that morning and filled his briefcase with charming things for our lunch. We huddled to eat it, once again, in deck chairs in the shadow of a life boat.

'Thank you, tremendously, George.'

'Glad you enjoyed it.'

'Oh, I did. *Tremendously*.' This time, the rocking of the boat made me feel a little uneasy. 'But I think I was probably a disappointment to you, in some way.'

'Whatever do you mean?' His army hair glittered in the bright sun, his flushed cheeks bulged with surprise.

'I don't know, really.'

'Utter nonsense. We came to France to eat, didn't we? That was the idea, wasn't it? Thought we had some damn good times, myself. I'll never forget those meals. I shall remember them for ever and ever.'

'So shall I,' I said. 'Definitely. For ever and ever.'

Back in London he kissed me goodbye on the forehead, and gave me a couple of tins of truffles.

'Just to remind,' he said. And that was the last I saw of him till we met again in Elizabeth Street.

His face was beginning to clear.
'We had some good times in France, that, eh – wasn't it? That time. Lots of good grub.'
'Those *rougets*,' I said. 'Those puddings and *pâtés*.'
He paused. 'There's a new little French place somewhere near here. Not up to much, but the *escargots* aren't bad. I was wondering, would you like a spot of lunch?'
I looked at my watch.
'I can't really, George,' I said. 'Not today.' The shepherd's pie was already in the oven. I had to do the sprouts.
'Oh, well. It was just a thought.' He swung his bag of flowering broccoli so that it banged against his leg. He glanced at my mature bosom, gave an almost imperceptible sigh. 'Still, you might just come to Justin's with me and choose a decent bit of *quiche.* I can never decide between the spinach and the mushroom. What d'you think?'
In memory of our gourmet heydays I went with him. His pleasure among the shelves of delicious foods was as inspiring as ever. For a moment I caught my plump, middle-aged breath; remembered some distant thrill. Should I change my mind about the *escargots* after all? Would this not be my chance to find out the answer to that silly question, which had been puzzling me all these years? Would George remember?
But suddenly he was on his way, three boxes under his arm. How nice it was running into each other like that, after all this time, he was saying. We must . . . some time. But he turned as he spoke, so I was unable to hear what we must do some time. But knowing George – dear George! – I supposed it might be to experience once again the absolute happiness of a gourmet lunch.

The Fall

Mrs Grace Willoughby, seventy-three years old and reduced by circumstances to a diminished way of life, endured the present while she lived with the past.

She understood, philosophically, that there were good times and bad times, and when good times came to an end they were inevitably replaced by less good ones. That was the rhythm of things – it had to be accepted. Not unwillingly, therefore, she accepted it. Nourished by the better past, she concerned herself with making tolerable the present.

But it was a struggle. For all her efforts, she could never quite accustom herself to this high living. Her two-roomed flat was on the top floor of a tall block. Outside, when Mrs Willoughby dared look, were the summits of three other identical blocks; thin, soulless buildings with no form of life at their windows. Mrs Willoughby had looked *down* only once, on the occasion she had first been shown the flat by the estate agent and her married daughter, Rose. The small patch of green 'recreation ground', the ant people and toy cars had looked so terrifyingly far away that Mrs Willoughby had never repeated the experience. Rose, however, thought the view was 'lovely'. But then Rose was one of those people who, exhilarated by any journey up, only had to look down to find any view a delight. She was indiscriminate, like that, Mrs Willoughby thought privately. The estate agent, too, expressed an enthusiasm not only for the view but for the sparse qualities of the two rooms. He advised her to snatch at her lucky chance. Between them, they convinced Mrs Willoughby. Reluctantly, she snatched.

The idea of moving to London, after Edgar had died and the chemist's shop was sold, was to be near Rose. What had not come into the calculations was that while Rose lived in north London, Mrs Willoughby's new flat was south, and miles of difficulties lay between them. To begin with they tried to keep

some form of routine. Every other Sunday Mrs Willoughby
would set off early, negotiate a complicated route of trains and
undergrounds, and arrive at her daughter's in time for lunch.
Once there, she never felt wholly welcome. It wasn't that Rose
was unfriendly, just busy. She had her own worries : five children and a tight income. Her engineer husband, Jack, surly at the
best of times, spent their every spare penny on flying lessons. He
fancied himself as a swashbuckling pilot. Rose half approved
the fantasy and meanwhile had to do without a washing machine.
Mrs Willoughby, for some reason cynical about others' marriages
despite the experience of her own happy one, once suggested to
Rose that Jack might fly away for ever one day. Rose had just
laughed.

The first winter in London put an end to Mrs Willoughby's
visits to her daughter. A November fog gave her bronchitis,
and when she recovered she no longer had the energy, or, to be
truthful, the desire, to re-establish the old routine. Instead, on
one occasion, Rose came in the Mini to south London. But it
wasn't a success. There was no room in the flat for five children,
nothing to do. Rose was in a dither about getting the car back
to Jack in time to get to the airfield : she and her mother had
little to talk about. No mutual interest helped them, not even
the past. Rose had left home at fifteen. Her parents, puzzled
and hurt by this, agreed at the time their caring for their daughter would never be quite the same again. And things hadn't
changed.

Mrs Willoughby hadn't seen Rose and her grandchildren for
three years now. They were simply coloured snapshots on
the fireplace of shiny tiles above the electric fire. They sent each
other cards, Christmas and birthdays, but ceased to have any real
concept of the other's life. Rose would never have guessed that
her mother, so energetic, independent and gay, now spent three-
quarters of her time communicating with no one more rewarding
than the budgerigar.

In her three years alone, Mrs Willoughby's struggle to accept
her present life had become easier. In fact, it had almost come
to the point where she had no energy, or even wish, to change
it. She had long since ceased to hope for any companionship from

her neighbours. They were a reticent, dour lot who went up and down in the draughty lift with secret and uninteresting faces. Mrs Willoughby once invited the harassed young mother who lived next door for coffee one morning. But the woman said she hadn't time, thank you, and no reverse visit was suggested. It seemed that the policy of the building was to keep yourself to yourself. After several rebuffs ar the beginning, Mrs Willoughby fell in with this pattern.

All she had ever required in her life was to love someone in an atmosphere of peace. With Edgar, she had happily managed that for thirty-nine years. Now, she still had peace, but empty peace was a different matter. And as she could think of nothing to enliven the present – abhorring as she did any attempts to join old people's clubs – her days became a prolonged reverie of old times.

That was not to say she let things slide. A strict upbringing had had its impact for life : wash the dishes straight after the meal – no leaving them till later. Hair to be brushed fifty times night and morning, though all the brushing would not bring back its shine now – the shine that Edgar had so admired. Keep to a sensible diet – proteins, a little meat once a week, one slice of wholemeal bread and butter for tea. Lights out at nine-thirty after the news. These determined adherences to her own rule gave Mrs Willoughby an inexplicable satisfaction, and as a reward for keeping them she treated herself to a few minor luxuries : a box of milk chocolates once a fortnight, African violets the year round, an occasional expensive magazine.

She left her flat – each time dreading the precarious journey in the lift – only once a week, to do her shopping. She had no friends in the shops : after three years still none of the assistants seemed to recognise her, and the trips were not a pleasure. One summer she had gone to Kent for a holiday to stay with the doctor and his wife, old neighbouring friends. But she hadn't liked the experience, going up the stairs that for thirty years neither she nor Edgar had ever gone up, to their chilly spare room. Besides, she had been unable to resist taking a look at the chemist's shop. It was unrecognisable, brash with neon lights and selling shoddy clothes. After that, she decided holidays were of no use to her. She still wrote once a month to the doctor's wife, but stayed at home, reading, knitting, watching the news, and reflecting.

One October morning Mrs Willoughby's alarm clock failed her. It had been a wedding present from her mother-in-law and for over forty years had awakened her with its shrill old-fashioned voice at seven-thirty. The morning it died Mrs Willoughby slept till eight o'clock. When she did wake up she was surprised to find herself put out by the uncalled-for change in her custom. After all, there was nowhere she had to be at any time .It was her shopping morning, but there was still plenty of time to do the chores before setting out at eleven, which was the time she always left. Quite angrily, she rattled the clock. Its lack of response, for some reason, brought a ridiculous tear to her eyes. Silly to get so upset about a clock. She dressed quickly and went to boil the kettle.

In the kitchen Tina, the balding budgerigar, was chirping to herself in her usual monotonous fashion. Mrs Willoughby had hung her cage in the window to break the view of gaunt sky and neighbouring block of flats and she managed, when pressing her face to the wires of the cage, to distort her vision so that cheerless sight beyond the cage became out of focus.

Now, as always, Mrs Willoughby talked to Tina at breakfast.

'Morning, my lovely one : my lovely one. Slept well, did you? I'll tell you something, my clock didn't go off this morning. That's why I'm late. That's why I've kept you waiting for your breakfast. I'll have to get it mended somewhere. I can't be sure where. Now just a moment and you shall have your clean water . . .'

Mrs Willoughby fed the bird and herself. Even without looking directly out of the window she couldn't help noticing it was a fine day. Blue sky, sun. Wind down there, though, she wouldn't be surprised. She made a mental note to wear a hat-pin.

She washed up and wiped down the small Formica-topped table. Then, passing Tina's cage, she let her fingers slip along the wire sides gently as a harpsichordist feeling for her strings.

'We're all right, Tina, you and me,' she said. 'There's no doubt about it, we're very fortunate, all things considering.'

On mornings like this, she remembered, Edgar would be very alert at breakfast. She had never known anyone like him for responding to weather. There only had to be a glimmer of sun for Edgar to be out in the garden, checking that its life-giving rays were injecting themselves into the palm tree. That palm tree, that poor old palm tree! Mrs Willoughby smiled at the thought of it, battling for life like no plant she had ever known. She and Edgar had spent their honeymoon on the island of Tresco in the Scillies. There, Edgar had become so entranced by the tropical gardens that he had tried to recreate them, on a smaller scale, of course, in their patch behind the shop in Kent. But the climate in Kent is less temperate than in Tresco, the soil less sympathetic to highly strung plants. Exotic blooms withered before their prime. Only the palm tree, fed on strange potions from the chemist's shop that Edgar concocted over the years, clung tenaciously to life. This morning Mrs Willoughby remembered that, in her last letter, the doctor's wife had told her she'd heard the old tree had finally died, and the people at the boutique planned to chop it up for Guy Fawkes' night. Once again she wiped away a tear, despising herself for having to make the gesture as she did so.

Mrs Willoughby went to her bedroom and opened the small cupboard beneath her dressing table. There, in neat army rows, stood twenty-nine small bottles of old-fashioned lavender water. The sight cheered her immediately. The store meant much to her. When Edgar had died and the shop and all its contents had been sold, Mrs Willoughby had forced herself to go back to check the place finally. She had opened each mahogany drawer, each cupboard, all unfamiliar now they were empty, and on the shelf beneath Edgar's mixing sink she found the bottles. Somehow they'd been overlooked. Without a second thought Mrs Willoughby had taken them for herself. She knew quite well Edgar wouldn't have minded.

In her widowhood Mrs Willoughby had preserved the lavender water carefully. She wanted it to last till she died. She sprinkled a few drops on her handkerchief every morning, and every morning the smell brought back to her the polished wood of the shop, the sun making a streak of lightning in the scarlet liquid that filled the huge pharmicist's bottle, the anticipation that never dulled as to who would be the first customer, the reassuring early cough (never a worry till the end) as Edgar mixed the contents of his old brown jars.

Today it was time for a new bottle. With some reluctance Mrs Willoughby unscrewed the cap.

It was, as she had predicted, windy outside. She bent herself in the direction of the all-purpose shop, where she bought herself a small selection of tasteless packaged things, thinking all the while that she'd give her soul for warm crusty bread like their next-door baker used to bake, a bit of fish still smelling of the sea, muddy eggs instead of these anaemic things. Outside the shop again, buffeted by the wind whose direction changed every moment, and made it more disconcerting, Mrs Willoughby wondered where to take her clock. Opposite, through tears the wind made in her eyes, she could see a jewellery shop. Maybe they could help. Rattling her shopping bag, suddenly concerned for the future of her clock, she stepped off the pavement.

Mrs Willoughby was aware of a sharp pain in her leg, a screech of brakes, a shout, and a small patter of glass on the road. Then blackness. When she came to, a crowd of faces bobbed like yo-yos up and down at her. She was unable to feel her leg, but through a strange rug that covered it, seeped a widening stain of dark red blood. A folded mackintosh had been put under her head, but the pavement was hard beneath her spine.

She couldn't make out what they were saying at all. A confusion of voices, like a foreign language. She tried to ask them if they had seen her clock, but thought they wouldn't understand.

'Don't you worry about anything, dear,' a kind voice said, then, in a language she understood, and she heard the wail of a siren. At that moment the black spots cleared before her eyes and she gave herself up to the marvellous attentions of the ambulance men.

In a life of consistent good health, Mrs Willoughby's only suffering had always been from an incurable fear of anticipated illness and accidents. It was therefore with some surprise she found herself almost enjoying the trip in the ambulance, and still she felt no pain. They'd bandaged her leg and wrapped her up in a scarlet blanket to match the blood, and there was a nice fresh smell of disinfectant.

'What happened?' she asked. Her voice sounded shaky, she thought, but the ambulance man didn't seem to notice.

'Seems you had a fall, dear, and a car just missed you.'

'Oh. Anyone else hurt?'

'Not a bit of it, not a bit of it. Now you just keep still.'

'It doesn't hurt,' said Mrs Willoughby.

'You just wait,' grinned the man, cheerfully, but his warning didn't frighten her.

In the hospital they were swift and kind. She was wheeled to a cubicle, a doctor looked at her leg, a nurse cleaned it and dressed it and said they'd like to keep her in for a couple of days. When Mrs Willoughby protested, they insisted: it wasn't the wound, they said, but the shock. Shock had to be looked after carefully.

'Especially at my age,' conceded Mrs Willoughby, and two pretty young nurses smiled at her, even though they were so busy. One of them asked her about her nearest relative: they'd like to get in touch. Mrs Willoughby gave them Rose's number but asked that she shouldn't be troubled. The nurse made no reply, no smile this time, and wheeled her to a ward.

Mrs Willoughby was given a pain-killing injection and something to make her sleep. When she woke up the two old ladies either side of her, neither of whom looked very ill, were drinking tea. Drowsily, Mrs Willoughby began to heave herself up into a sitting position: she was immediately helped by a nurse who plumped up her pillows and went off to fetch her something to eat. There was a dull pain in her leg now, but it wasn't too bad. Quite bearable.

Glancing round the ward, Mrs Willoughby wished she had her own pink nightdress and wool dressing-jacket instead of this stiff hospital thing: still, it didn't really matter. She was warm and comfortable and they were all so nice and concerned.

Suddenly, through the swing doors at the end of the ward, she saw a familiar figure. Rose came stomping towards her, in a scarlet coat (so much scarlet today), bag swinging from her shoulder, a look of slight concern on her face which had, Mrs Willoughby thought, grown heavier.

'Oh, mother, there you are. You gave us all an awful fright.'

Rose looked down at her mother. As soon as it was apparent that she was in no actual danger, or even in any great pain, Rose's thin mouth drooped.

'I managed to get here,' she said, sullenly.

'That was good of you, Rose,' said Mrs Willoughby.

'It was a devil of a job finding someone to baby-sit at that short notice,' Rose went on, 'and then the traffic.'

'You shouldn't have bothered,' said Mrs Willoughby. 'I'm all right.' They kissed.

'Glad to see you are,' said Rose. 'They sounded fairly adamant that I should come. I've brought you these.'

She put a paper bag on Mrs Willoughby's bedside table. It contained half a pound of small white grapes. Mrs Willoughby, who had never liked grapes, thanked her daughter with convincing appreciation. There was silence between them for a few moments. Then :

'Your clock's stopped,' said Rose.

Mrs Willoughby turned to her bedside table again. This time she noticed the clock. In an instant she realised that someone must have rescued it, taken care of it, and seen it delivered safely to her. The thought of such care on the part of a stranger caused a constriction in her throat.

'I was going to get it mended,' she managed to say eventually, 'when I had the fall.'

'Poor old Mum,' said Rose, looking at her watch.

She left five minutes later and Mrs Willoughby drank her tea. The old lady on her left turned to her.

'That was a smart young woman,' she said.

'My daughter,' said Mrs Willoughby, surprised at her own pride.

'Lucky to have a daughter like that. I've only got a sharpjack of a husband. What's more, when he comes, he only talks to other people. You'll see.'

Mrs Willoughby smiled.

There was boiled fish and rice pudding for supper, and very good it was too. Then the visiting hour : the old lady's husband arrived, very smart, as she had warned, in beautiful big-checked tweeds and a stiff collar. He made several cheering remarks to his wife but she, who had apparently looked forward to his arrival, now wouldn't answer. He offered her a chocolate but she pushed the box away. So he offered one to Mrs Willoughby instead, who accepted with delight. They fell into conversation. He was a Mr Potterville and used to be in market gardening. His wife had insisted on their moving to London when they retired, but he was not enjoying the life. He missed his greenhouses. Mrs Willoughby understood. Then suddenly, without meaning to, she found herself telling Mr Potterville all about the struggle she and Edgar had had to keep the palm tree alive.

That night Mrs Willoughby's leg ached a little harder but the pain was still quite tolerable. Her last thought, before going to sleep, was that she was enjoying herself. Who would ever have thought it? Here she was in hospital after a nasty fall, with a wounded leg and the effects of shock, no doubt, to come, quite positively enjoying herself. Even the thought of Tina, alone in the flat, could not spoil the strange feeling of contentment. It coursed warmly through her body and she smiled in the dark.

Mrs Willoughby continued vigorously to enjoy herself in hospital for two days, then she was taken home by an ambulance man who escorted her to the lift. By coincidence, a middle-aged neighbour, face vaguely familiar, was also going up.

'We heard you had a fall, Mrs Willoughby,' she said.

Mrs Willoughby who had never, as far as she could remember, imparted her name to anyone, seemed surprised by the news. She stuck out her bandaged leg, tapping it with her stick.

'Oh, nothing to worry about,' she said.

'You can't be too careful,' replied the woman. 'I'll give you a hand to your door. Mrs Winner's the name.'

Mrs Winner ended by staying for a two-hour tea. She was remarkably interested in Mrs Willoughby's fall, and when the detailed story of it came to an end told three stories in return. They were about friends of hers who had had even worse falls, all with disastrous consequences. It seemed that the hospital, who had thought of everything, had arranged for Mrs Winner to look after Tina and the African violets. She was a friendly if somewhat tiring woman, and Mrs Willoughby asked her to come again. She quickly accepted.

When she had gone Mrs Willoughby felt quite tired, but pleased to be home, even if it all looked a little strange since her absence, and since the visit of Mrs Winner.

Next morning there was, surprisingly, an unexpected ring on the doorbell : Eileen – the young housewife next door, previously so cold, now full of offers to do the shopping. Mrs Willoughby made a short list, hands trembling with gratitude and excitement as she did so. From that time on it could be said that her flat was almost a-bustle. The news of her accident seemed to have spread round the building and, from whatever motive, strange neighbours came with offers of help and advice. They drank her tea and talked for hours, so that each night Mrs Willoughby fell into an exhausted and grateful sleep. Rose rang three times – the unexpectedness of the calls gave her mother three separate frights, but it was nice to be able to say to the companion of the moment, 'That was my daughter, you know, just checking up.'

On several occasions Mr Potterville, on his way back from the hospital, dropped by. Once he brought a bottle of sherry; another time Mrs Willoughby made him sardines on toast and they listened to a radio play.

'I positively enjoyed myself, Mrs Willoughby,' Mr Potterville said one night, as he left. 'The visit has quite bucked me up.'

'And so did I, Mr Potterville. I haven't **had** such a good time for several years. Please come again soon.'

'I will, I will. Never doubt that.'

But Mr Potterville failed to keep his word. As Mrs Willoughby had no address for him, and felt reluctant to go back to the hospital to see his wife, lest she should take it wrong, there was nothing she could do. Still, with so much coming and going these days there was little time to think. Mr Potterville's few visits had been pleasant while they lasted, but there were still many others, even if they weren't handsome men with bottles of sherry.

As Mrs Willoughby said one evening to Tina, testing her leg for a small skip, 'I'm happy as a lark.'

Two weeks passed in which neighbours dropped in three or four times a day. Then a district nurse came and took off the bandages. She declared Mrs Willoughby fit enough to go out now, provided she took care. She found herself strangely disappointed at the news. Eileen had got into the way of doing her shopping, bought just the right brand of soup without being told. With some reluctance she explained to Eileen she had to get back to normal now : there was no need to carry on with her kindness. Eileen appeared quite huffy, and in the following week only dropped by once for a few moments.

It took Mrs Willoughby a week or so to realise that visits from her new friends, as soon as her health was back, were dropping off. They still smiled at her slightly should she see them in the lift, but it seemed as if the sudden flare of their interest had been eaten up. They needed her no more : as a target of their transitory benevolence, or curiosity, she was a spent thing. Gradually, the small flat returned to its former quietness : only Tina chirruped on, without cease. 'Funny what a fall does for you,' Mrs Willoughby said to her one evening. 'They're all round you, to help, then they're gone. We're back on our own again, Tina, but very fortunate, all things considering. Very fortunate indeed.' And for the first time for several weeks she took down the photograph album of her wedding. This reversion to her old ways, her old reliance on the past, took a little getting used to, but it wasn't long before she accepted the inevitable pattern of things once more. Though just occasionally she had to exert a little extra self-control, like the morning she went shopping and found it was a windy day, very much the same kind of weather as the day of the fall. She stood at the edge of the kerb, for an irresistible moment, where it had all happened. Holding on to her hat, she remembered. And a wicked thought suddenly came to her.

Wouldn't it be nice if . . .? She wouldn't really be sorry if . . .

Quickly, she cocked her chin in the air, ashamed of herself. Then, she raised her stick defiantly, stepped off the pavement, and crossed the street without misadventure.

Azaleas for Sale

The *Azaleas for Sale* notice was nailed outside the fence, uneven letters painted in tar on a piece of board, and immediately you entered the gate you saw them : plantations of azaleas, frail bushes not more than a couple of feet high, and here and there the first spotted flower.

The house itself, a great slab of a house, grey stone, defied the daylight to make it sparkle. Its heavy portico was supported by plain thick pillars, and one of those shrubs that clings to stone grew thickly round the windows, its blackish leaves gloomy as funeral gloves. In the cold January day of Marina's visit, dull sky, it was a forbidding place : difficult to imagine that fifty years ago a butler flashed instantly in the door at the sound of wheels and, according to Colonel Adlington, gay young things tripped across the lawns to pluck azaleas for buttonholes and hair.

No one heard Marina arrive. She pushed open the huge front door, stood shivering for a moment in the flagstone hall. She could feel the bite of salt in the dank air, though the coast was a mile away. High on the walls stuffed things in glass boxes began to register – fish and birds. There were footsteps, squeaks, the muffled thump of doors. Then the husky bray of Mrs Adlington's voice which had, as late as 1940, she claimed, thrilled audiences all over the country.

'Marina !'

'Isabella !' The names small bells in the semi-darkness.

'What a morning ! Bloody dank, gets into you. You arrived? Marvellous, marvellous. Come on in and have a drink. Gerald can't wait to see you.'

They kissed. Isabella's breath, staled by years of gin, was superficially refreshed by the drink she carried in one hand. She swilled the liquid around.

'Hope you don't mind I didn't wait? Got to have something

to keep out the cold. Should keep your coat on for a bit, if I were you. Gerald, you know, has been hopping up and down all morning waiting for you. Filthy old thing.' She pulled her cardigan more tightly round her large bosom which once, too, no doubt, had thrilled audiences. The cardigan was an aged, matt thing, dullest ever navy, which must have been pulled from years of slumber in a drawer earlier this morning, and was still clumsy with lack of use. 'You look marvellous, darling,' croaked Isabella, 'you really do. Gerald'll have a seizure.'

Marina followed her through tall dark passages past doors that smelt faintly of cloak-rooms and kitchens. Isabella finally flung open the door of the drawing-room, with a theatrical sense of timing.

'We're in here in honour of you,' she said. 'Your first visit. It'll warm up soon, the fire. Gerald! She's here.'

Gerald stood at the window – huge panes, eighteen inches high – surveying all he could of his land through the mist that rolled in from the sea. He turned towards them, his nose bigger than Marina remembered, his cheeks one tone deeper than the old rose of the walls. If in reality he had been hopping up and down all morning in anticipation of Marina's arrival, the exercise had exhausted him: for now his very stance was tired. His tweed shoulders sagged. Lustreless eyes revealed nothing of the wicked desires that his wife warned were raging within him.

'Look at him waiting for you, Marina, you see! What did I tell you? Gerald, come along! Open the bottle. What are you dithering for?'

Gerald shuffled towards Marina, greeted her politely.

'Like to come and see the pantry?' he asked. 'We've turned one of the old kitchens into a pantry, makes it much nearer.'

'For heaven's sake, darling!' Isabella clutched at Marina's arm. 'For God's sake, *don't*! He'd pounce on you before you can say knife, wouldn't you, Gerald?'

Ignoring the question with a dignified tilt of his head, Gerald moved towards the door.

'I'll go alone, then,' he said.

Marina huddled on a stool by the fire. The flames crouched

pathetically low over the three damp logs, overawed by the size of the chimney into which they were expected to rise. They gave no heat. Isabella thumped down on to a sofa, spreading her legs. She had fat knees and good ankles.

'We're keeping body and soul together,' she said, 'skin of our teeth. Economising like crazy, just the odd nip to keep ourselves going, and we see a lot of the grandchildren, which is nice.' Her voice was a bandaged rattle, the sound of an old steamboat grinding sluggish water. With it, once, she had lured an international film star to love her. And, for a time, to marry her. 'We're having oysters, as I promised on the telephone. Oyster pasties and a bit of lamb. Now, tell me your news.'

A long time later Gerald returned, a champagne-shaped bottle in his hand.

'Pushing out the boat,' said Isabella. 'I told you, darling, the old boy's nutty about you.'

'Don't worry, it's not the real thing. Just something sparkling.' Gerald opened the bottle with difficulty, poured two glasses. Isabella heaved herself up.

'Don't try to give *me* any of that rubbish, now. I'm off to have a decko at the pasties. For Lord's sake scream, darling, if the old sod gets too fresh.' On the way out of the room she filled her glass from the bottle of Gordon's Gin which stood beside a small vase of pale dried flowers on the mantelpiece.

Gerald chose an armchair as far as possible from Marina's seat by the fire. Due to his deafness, conversation had to be a series of barked shouts. Marina enquired about the progress of the azalea farm.

'Very good, really,' Gerald replied, 'considering Admin, isn't all it might be, but we're seeing to that. It'll all fall into place, gradually. But we get a lot of orders, you know. We get orders from all over the place. People seem to like azaleas.' His slow eyes flitted among the damp patches that bruised the old pink walls. ''Course, when it all takes off, we'll be made. No more worries. Be able to get it all done up a bit.'

'I'd like to buy about a dozen bushes, if I could,' said Marina. 'They make such good presents.'

'Really? Want to buy a couple, do you?' Gerald sounded surprised. 'Ah, well. We could see about that after lunch, perhaps.'

'Didn't Isabella tell you that's what I'd come for? I wrote you several letters asking you to send them. In the end I thought it best to come myself and collect them.'

'Don't think she did,' said Gerald, 'but then we don't look at the post much these days. Think she just said you were coming all this way for lunch, wasn't that nice? She thinks the world of you, of course. Wish the bloody mist would clear, and I could show you the view.'

Isabella returned to announce that lunch was ready. She was unable to resist enquiring how their five minutes alone had passed.

'Kept his hands off you, sly old fox, has he? I only have to turn my back, you know. Any pretty face. You'd never think he'd had two heart attacks in the last eighteen months, would you?'

'Never,' said Marina, watching Gerald totter to the door, one arm weighed down with the half-empty bottle of sparkling white wine. They made their way through a series of high ceilinged rooms: faded walls, curtains drained of colour, left only with the skeletal print of patterns: the odd dark portrait clenched in a gilded frame. There was no heating in any of the rooms, but each one was furnished with a single bottle of gin. To keep out the cold as you passed through, Marina supposed.

Lunch was in the kitchen. Here, any risk of disturbing ancient planning by modernisation had been avoided. No bright formica noises – sounds redolent of the past: drip of tap into an enamel sink, splutter of kettle on top of ungainly black Aga. Smells of coal and sprouts and steam: tenebrous light through the one small window, designed in the days when it was not considered that staff required much light to work by.

Isabella had laid the lunch with care. Small silver knives and forks – the last of the Georgian stuff, she said – were arranged on the pitted wood of the table. Real linen napkins, unaired, so limp they dipped into the shape of the Crown Derby side plates. Fine-stemmed wine glasses, home-made mint relish in a crystal bowl.

'Got to keep things going,' said Isabella, and Gerald uncorked a bottle of dusty claret.

Lunch, it was evident, was the high spot of the Adlingtons' day. After their morning chores, checking the wood store, pottering among the azaleas, peeling potatoes, stretching up to dust some of the high fireplaces, it was there to reinvigorate them, to give them strength for the lesser delights of the afternoon (shuffling bills) and the long, cold evenings. Besides, the kitchen was warm : only warm room in the whole bloody house, for God's sake, said Isabella : and the two high-backed benches each side of the table made an agreeable feeling of enclosure. This was the vantage point of their fortress against worrying conditions. Here, armed with the knowledge that they could flog the remaining silver as a last resort, they allowed the warmth of possibilities to cocoon them for a while. In the First War, shoulders braced, Gerald had received the VC for bravery. He had been taught to face the enemy without flinching. In old age, a new kind of enemy, he did not find it hard to adapt. Same tactics, really. Take each blow as it comes, and plan to fight the next one. But don't let them shoot you out. Stick to your territory. Be cunning in your strategies. (Azaleas turned into a business.) Gerald would happily die starving in his house, but while he lived he would protect it from being sold for institutional purposes – and who, these days, would want it for anything else?

Fired by the mixture of gin, claret, and oyster pasties, the courage of the Adlingtons grew. It took diverse turns, but Marina recognised it in all its disguises, and admired. Isabella, in a vitriolic attack on paper napkins, showed the strength of her own determination. She banged a speckled hand on the table. The English upper classes would never allow *all* their standards to slip, no matter what happened to the pound, she said. We had all reduced our living standards, of course, but who cared about that? We had probably had it too good for too long. Besides, the war had trained us to regard hard times as a challenge. Well, they were a challenge. And we should face them. But paper napkins – no, never. Paper napkins would be like . . . the Blues giving up horses in favour of Japanese cars.

Gerald said she had gone too far, as usual. Isabella shook her head, agreeing. She poured her husband more wine with a merry lack of reverence for its age, making it swirl in the glass like her own gin. Gerald averted his eyes from the swaying liquid.

'I'm off to the South of France for a short break in March,' he said.

'By himself,' explained Isabella. 'I never want to go further than the village these days, you know. Had my travelling. Bloody South of France every year when I was young. Grew out of it. Bloody mean Frogs.'

'You didn't see many of *them* in the Negresco,' said Gerald.

'Don't like to imagine what he gets up to down there by himself, anyway.' Isabella bent towards Marina. 'He comes back looking a wreck, I can tell you.' She turned to Gerald. 'Anyway, unless the azaleas take off whizz, bang, ducky, what about the fare?'

'Marina's come to *buy*,' explained Gerald. He smiled. Suddenly, the idea of selling her two plants seemed like his whole salvation. 'Didn't you know?'

Isabella's mouth fell open in surprise.

'Hadn't a clue. That's lovely, darling. Awfully generous idea. But of course we'll give you some, can't let you pay.'

Marina was firm.

'No, really,' she said, 'business is most especially business among friends.' She felt her strength to be ineffectual in the wash of their generosity.

'Well, we'll throw in some extras,' conceded Isabella.

'We might go down after lunch, what about that?' asked Gerald. 'Choose some good ones. Then I better ring the travel agent, confirm my ticket. March nearly upon us . . .'

'Sleep, for me,' said Isabella, cutting into a beautiful apple pie. 'We have very regular lives, you know. We like being old. Nothing much changes. My energy runs out a bit quicker, perhaps. But Gerald's the same as ever, the old dog . . .'

'God Almighty,' interrupted Gerald, looking deeply into his wine, nose quite blue now.

'Yes, I sleep. Only go to the village when I have to,' went on Isabella.

'You should come to Monte this year. Give you a break.' Gerald nodded at his wife with the optimism of one who knows his own suggestion will be rejected.

'Never! Me, risk an aeroplane just to see you hobbling after starlets, making a fool of yourself? Never. Besides, someone's got to stay at home and look after the flowers.'

Her voice had ground incredibly low. The claret was finished. Gerald blinked at his own drowsiness. Marina judged it time to go. They protested at her leaving, but could find no reason to urge her to stay.

'Just the plants,' said Marina. 'Could we put them in the car? So sorry for the trouble.'

Azaleas! The very thought of them caused the Adlingtons a sudden, mutual exhaustion. They struggled against it.

'Tell you what,' said Gerald. 'I've got to get on about the wretched tickets before three, but we could send them to you. Trust me to pick out the best ones.'

'Or better still, you could come *back*!' Isabella was clinging to Marina's arm in the hall. Echoes of their footsteps overlapped. 'Just write and give us a little warning and we'll have them ready, won't we, Gerald?'

'Of course, of course.'

'And it's been so *lovely* having you, darling. Someone young about. I'll see Gerald doesn't go too far next time, sexy beast.'

They were steering her across the gravel, through the cold, grey, salt air. They were waving goodbye, shouting at her to promise to come again. Azaleas . . . good excuse, what?

She drove away along the drive, past the acres of thriving plants, wonderfully protected from audacious buyers. They stretched into the distance, finally to be lost in mist now coming more thickly from the sea: mist which by tea-time would quite obscure the Adlingtons' afternoon, blot out their view entirely, so that the azaleas would only exist in their imagination again, a brave idea with which to defend themselves against alternatives too terrible to contemplate.

Up-State New Jersey

She thought they were going somewhere Up-State New Jersey, wherever that was. Later, when someone told her no such place existed, she laughed. Its non-existence was appropriate.

But it had taken place somewhere, that strange weekend, an hour or so from New York. Although as the years passed – what was it now? – five? – and still none of those involved ever referred to it, bound by some unspoken bond of silence, Imogen often found herself wondering at its reality. At the time, she remembered, she had thought of herself as the comi-tragic heroine. But in retrospect she could see that each one of them had been heroes or heroines in their own eyes. Even today she did not know precisely what had happened to anyone except herself. From off-stage screams and cries and wild laughter she had come to various conclusions, but had no way of knowing if she was right. It was not possible to ask any of the others. It never would be, perhaps, until they were very old and the memory had become a light tracing of the facts in their minds. Besides, they were all scattered now : Olivia and Giles divorced, Piero and his wife living in Denmark, Imogen herself back in England. It was unlikely there would be a reunion.

Imogen vowed she would write about it when enough time had passed to clear the obscurities. She waited, but those obscurities never cleared. Equally, her own part in the spontaneous charade never dimmed. She still laughed at the thought of her blustering vanity, and the way it had been felled in one swipe. In the cool reason of retrospect she still stuck to the declaration she had made at the time, out loud, colourless dawn blasting into her sleepless eyes; it was a moment of growing up, at the age of thirty. A time to be remembered with some of the same awe as first communion, first sex, wedding day, divorce day, death. Yes : in a way it had been a kind of dying – that is, if you believe in the deathliness of self-disillusion.

148

Up-State New Jersey

Imogen had long been of the opinion that if only one could explain to the person one was meeting the circumstances one had arrived from, and they could do the same, then moods and behaviour would be much easier to understand. Contact would be altogether more simple : fewer mistakes would be made, fewer confusions entered. But in the frenzy of social communication there is no time for such niceties. Besides, explanations have little appeal. Best to keep your silence, and to put on a face that betrays nothing of ordeals past. Thus, when Imogen met Giles in the Algonquin lobby that Friday afternoon, and he asked how she was, she replied quite convincingly that she was fine.

In truth, this was far from the case. She was more exhausted than she could ever remember : waxy-limbed and light-headed. Five days of ruthless New York summer had flayed her. The temperate breezes of Hyde Park are no training for the enervating humidity of Manhattan, and as Imogen hurried from showroom to showroom, from the blasts of icy, indoor air to the cloying stuff that lapped randily against her outside, she was increasingly irritated by her own inability to beat the weather. The heat had made her unattractive, too : curling hair and shining face. But by now, Friday, she no longer cared. She wished only to arrive at Giles and Olivia's country house, and to sleep.

In the midday semi-darkness of the Algonquin's Rose Room Giles ate his lunch : prawns big as handcuffs gripping the edge of a glass full of lettuce. Imogen sipped at chilled orange juice. She thought she probably smelt quite bad, after a terrible morning spending the last of her backers' money – no time to change her clothes. But Giles made no comment. He did not even avert his nose. They spoke of England. They spoke of the American liking for English muffins. They watched the lobby door. Each time a new arrival swung through, the brown light was sparked by icicles of sun, horrible reminder of the gaudy light outside. Imogen dreaded the journey to the country : they were to travel by bus.

Then Piero arrived. Giles had not warned that he was coming. He shook a cool hand with Imogen. Too weary to entertain any real form of vanity, Imogen cursed her appearance : even in the poor light, she thought, she could not have made a memorable first impression.

Piero, by contrast, dazzled in the awareness of his own good looks. (In retrospect, for all its handsomeness, she could remember nothing of his face.) He wore an old silk shirt, forget-me-not blue, unquestionably Turnbull & Asser. Gucci shoes, Gucci belt. International shit stamped all over him. And yet his fluent English, with its Italian lilt, was instantly appealing. Any other time, Imogen felt, she would have been inclined towards him, knowing that such men are the merest weekend visitors; but often a weekend is all that is required.

She sat beside him on the bus. He read extracts from a magazine article on how to be a good weekend guest. They weren't very funny, but they both laughed. Giles, leaning over from his seat behind them, said, 'What's up, you two?' and in reply they laughed again. Through the windows Imogen noticed that Up-State New Jersey, or wherever, was becoming quite rural: wooden houses with unfenced gardens, the pillared terraces of middle-class O'Hara land.

Olivia and Giles had rented a white clapboard house more deeply hidden from its neighbours than most. There was a real field to one side. The garden was untidy as an English cottage garden: a muddle of lavender and roses, longish grass, bush honeysuckle that had outgrown its strength and trailed long wisps of curling yellow flowers.

Olivia neglected the garden in favour of the house. The table was already beautifully set for dinner on the terrace: matching cloth and napkins strewn with poppies, scarlet candles protected from the breeze by globes of smoked glass. Baskets of pink geraniums hung from every pillar. A warm sweet smell of roasting apples came from the kitchen. But Imogen felt too weak for appreciation. She asked if she might sleep for an hour before dinner. Olivia showed her to a room from a Disney film – painted floorboards, ruffled curtains, and frilled cushions scattered over the white bed. Imogen paused only to look for a bluebird on the window sill, then fell asleep.

Later, having had a bath, feeling and looking better, Imogen

returned to the terrace. Two other English guests, David and
Camilla, lay on cushioned chairs. Piero gave his seat to Imogen
and sat beside her on the floor. Everybody drank Daiquiris. They
talked quietly, aware of the prickling noise of crickets in the
garden beyond them. In the pale darkness, fireflies skittered
about, restless as fireworks.

'Are there still fireflies in England?' someone asked.

They ate iced green soup and chicken in a lemon sauce.
There was much wine and the candle flames bent about in their
glass globes, twisting faces into fluid shadows. Imogen, opposite
Piero, noticed the gravity of his eyes whenever he looked at her,
which was often. She laughed to herself, thinking that such
seriousness must come from nefarious intent rather than pro-
bity of character. A young student came from the kitchen bearing yet more wine. Fat knees sprouted beneath sawn-off jeans, and
pebble glasses magnified her eyes. Huge breasts sprawled beneath
her tee-shirt and her hair hung in greasy locks. She was unsmil-
ing, protected by her own thoughts from the hilarity at the
table. Olivia said she was called Di and was marvellous with
the children, better than many *au pairs* from Europe. Imogen
thought : thank God I'm not sixteen. Giles said,

'Now for the grass. Believe it or not, it's grown by the local
policeman.'

A joint was passed round. Olivia was the only one to refuse
it. She smiled at them all, a tolerant hostess. David told a
long story about some experience with the BBC. His wife interrupted to dispute every fact. There seemed to be constant
laughter and the former neatness of the table slipped into disarray. Then everyone but Imogen and Piero got up : it was
midnight. Music came from the house. There were cries of
'Let's dance!' Piero leant across the table to light Imogen's
cigarette.

'Later I will come,' he said, and seemed put out by Imogen's
giggling response.

'You're like something out of a third-rate drawing-room
comedy,' she said. But she thought that any other time she
would have been pleased. Not flattered – she was, after all, the

only single woman, and in such conditions she had learned that men are hopelessly indiscriminate. No, not flattered, but amenable. As it was they gazed into each other's eyes, full of differing intentions. Then, in what she supposed was a resolute manner, Imogen wished Piero good night and went to bed. She did not disturb the other two couples who were dancing with each other's husbands and wives. As her frilly white room spun about her, and the floorboards turned to liquid, Imogen realised that apart from being exhausted she was both a little drunk and very stoned. She did not remember getting into bed.

Piero joined her some time later. Two, he said it was. He'd had to wait so long, bored, until the others came upstairs. Imogen was too dazed to comment. Or to resist. They lay together with the peculiar closeness of strangers who have no desire to analyse their nakedness. Then they made love. Piero prised Imogen from her state of drowsiness. She was awake, alert, uncaring. They made love many times, till dawn blanched the frilly curtains, and for decorum Piero had to return to his own room.

When Imogen came down at midday she found the others on the terrace, pristine again, the table re-set for lunch. Giles handed her a drink, iced vodka and orange. Olivia asked – was that a suppressed smile at the corner of her mouth? – if she had slept well. Piero kissed her on the cheek and sat on the ground beside her chair. She noticed looks pass between Camilla and David. Could escapades, she wondered, in a house of that size, go undetected? Not that she really cared. No one, surely, would be foolish enough to convey their suspicions to Piero's wife.

Imogen noticed, in the speckled shade of the terrace, that everyone looked pale. They talked with vivacity. Giles complained of a hangover. At lunch, beneath the jokes, Imogen sensed a tension between them all she could not define. She decided to take a risk, investigate.

'Did you all go to bed very late?' she asked.

'Terribly,' said Olivia with a smile, then a frown.

'You shouldn't have missed the dancing,' said David, glancing at Imogen then back to Olivia. 'Oh, it was wild.'

'As far as I can remember, we were almost asleep on our

feet,' said Giles. Camilla looked at him. 'Christ! Sleep, this afternoon. That's what I'm going to do.'

'But I thought we'd go down to the river,' said Olivia. 'We can swim. It won't be that icy in this heat.' Giles nodded, his head too painful to argue.

They drove to a deserted valley and spread rugs on the flat rocks that banked the river. The heat came down upon them in great fat gusts, making them feeble. There was some discussion about how you could tell the place was American – how, for all its similarities, it could never be confused with a Scottish valley, or a Somerset one. But the argument, half-hearted in the first place, soon petered out. Giles fell asleep. Piero indicated to Imogen that they should explore a little.

She walked beside him in the blaring sun. He was bare-foot, wore faded jeans. Tanned body. She was able to look at him properly for the first time, and remembered the energies of the night.

'They're all so uptight,' he said, petulantly, but his accent gave some charm to the observation.

'Oh, I don't know. They're just tired and bored and fancy-ing each other.'

Piero laughed.

He found them a triangle of soft grass shaded by silver birches and pillowed with bushes of wild honeysuckle. They could no longer see the river, but could hear its shallow waters jumping from one level to another, filling rock pools, spilling over and gurgling on its way. There were butterflies, the sound of insects. The heat was almost tangible, oppressive. They lay on the grass and talked of Swann's Way. Piero rolled a joint. Its effects worked quickly. Imogen was convinced they spoke with great erudition. Her thoughts danced along in time with the river. Piero agreed with everything she said. He kissed her. She pushed him away only for a moment.

'Proust said one should always show great indulgence for platonic love,' she said.

'Of course one should.'

Piero the stranger was all over her, smelling of hash and

sweat and warm grass, telling her to shut up about Proust and to open her eyes.

Later they all swam in the river and lay spread-eagled on the rocks to dry. Back at the house Di the student was giving tea to two small children on the terrace. She frowned at them through her thick glasses.

'Hope *you've* enjoyed yourselves,' she said, sullenly.

That evening a slight breeze shifted the heat from place to place, scattering the fireflies, making small showers of them brush against the insect screen. Whisky-sour in her hand, candle flames trembling among the flowers, Imogen lay back in a bank of cushions and delighted in a feeling of total irresponsibility. The weekend had by now become quite misted, a mirror in which reflections were beautifully distorted. Through it she saw that Olivia remained with a straight back and neat smile, efficiently organising, symbol of weekday reality. The rest of them – though she could have been mistaken, judgement impaired by joints and alcohol – seemed to flicker dangerously towards each other, as if to test how near they could come to some sort of explosion before withdrawing.

At dinner, Imogen found herself very gay. Centre of attention. Funny. She made them laugh so much. She could say almost anything and they would respond with laughter. They urged her to wilder anecdotes and, with the pressure of Piero's leg against hers under the table, she became unusually histrionic.

Then, music again.

'Piero, dance with me,' said Olivia. He politely did so, then led Imogen into the small dark room where the music played. Camilla and Giles followed. Olivia and David. There was no pretence of wanting to change partners. A pale moon lit fragments of a fluttering skirt, a decorous smile. Ruth Etting sang *Bye-Bye Blackbird*.

'Such antics,' Imogen whispered to Piero.

'*Perché non?*'

'Why not, indeed? Imogen felt his hands cradle her neck. He gently pushed back her head to expose her mouth. The others, equally involved, did not seem to notice. Imogen wished that she was in love with Piero, not merely full of silly elation and insatiable desire.

In bed, very late again, Piero explained how very happy he was with his wife. Had he not been so happy, he would not be here, now, would he? Of course not, conceded Imogen. They had two small children, he went on, and wanted two more. That would be nice, agreed Imogen. But he didn't feel guilty, somehow, because his wife would never know, would she? And what was a man supposed to do, alone?

Quite. Imogen allowed herself to be pulled closer. She liked the thought of tomorrow : the last day of sleepy pleasure, the last night. She would try to keep Piero off the subject of his children – his wife she didn't care about. Then, Monday – New York. London. Over. Sated?

'You are funny,' Piero was saying. 'You make me laugh. *Sei molto simpatica.*'

'*Ma non!*' She felt she was only very tired, melting, but infinitely wanting.

'*Vieni qua, e qua.*'

Speaking Italian, somehow, increased their desire.

It always surprised Imogen how two days in the same place, so close to each other, could be so very different. Sunday morning was outwardly no different from Saturday : same sun, same sitting about on the terrace with drinks and papers. And yet there was a sense of unease. Indefinable but strong. Imogen felt it as soon as she took a chair. This morning Piero did not kiss her, or look up from his paper. Camilla asked her husband some question and he didn't bother to reply. Giles, behind his dark glasses, rolled his eyes towards Camilla.

As usual Olivia was the only one to be bustling about. Much to everyone's annoyance she had asked eight for dinner that night, and was arranging two tables. Imogen asked if she might help. No, said Olivia, sharply. She requested instead that Piero should open some white wine for lunch. He followed her into the kitchen.

It began to occur to Imogen, through the liquid, light-headed state caused by lack of sleep, love-making, hash and drink, that she had done something to offend Olivia. Perhaps Olivia did not approve of whatever it was she may have suspected between Imogen and Piero. Imogen sighed, still unable to care very much. The weekend was nearly over : she might never see any of these people again. Besides, Olivia and David had seemed very happy dancing together the night before. Perhaps she was imagining the whole thing, and Olivia was merely irritable because she had so much to do, and was not feeling up to it after two very late nights.

After lunch both married couples went to bed. Imogen and Piero lay in the shade in the garden.

'Olivia's giving me some funny looks,' he said.

'So you noticed, too ? Jealousy.'

'She's a great friend of my wife.'

'Ah. Surely she wouldn't say anything ?'

'Women often believe it the kindest thing to do, to tell a friend who her husband is screwing.'

'*Screwing?*' said Imogen. She hadn't thought of it like that before.

'Not that I'm *just* screwing,' Piero went on, in a kindly voice. 'I love listening to you talk, as well. If my wife knew that it would make it worse, of course.'

'Well, our time is almost up.'

'I wish it wasn't. I'd like to spend a week with you in New York.'

His funny accent made such banalities almost endearing.

'Nonsense. We're too old to confuse a weekend adventure with anything more lasting. Everything has its allotted time. We should recognise that and not try to change it.'

'You're horribly practical. Kiss me.'

She kissed him.

'Are you incurably unfaithful?'

'Incurably. It doesn't stop me loving my wife. And you – how is the expression? – have swept me off my rocker.'

Imogen laughed and fell asleep in his arms.

Olivia had invited the neighbours for dinner. Pretty boring, she said, apologetically, but she would be grateful if an effort could be made. Imogen put on her prettiest dress – for Piero, not for them. Demure Liberty print cotton. She pinned a skein of honeysuckle in her hair. Alone with him for a moment on the stairs, she let Piero compliment her with the inimicable gallantry of the Italian race.

As the English were to be outnumbered by Americans tonight, it was American habits they had politely to adhere to. Drinking began early : the guests arrived very late, eager for Martinis. They did not sit down to dinner till after ten. Olivia had put Imogen on a different table from Piero. His back was towards her and she could see he was flanked by two large women. Pity it had to be like this, the last night, she thought. She made an effort to concentrate on the lawyer on her left and the chairman of a cement firm on her right. She was of the belief that if there is one other person in a room with whom you exist in private harmony, that is good protection from the tedium of all the others. All the same, conversation was not inspired.

The avocado mousse was finished. Imogen noticed Piero was no longer at his table. She looked about. She had not seen him leave. His neighbours were speaking to each other across the canyon of his empty chair : politeness no disguise to the kind of indignation which always strikes women who are left talking together at a party. Piero took a long time to return. When he did, it was with a huge bowl of spaghetti. He was followed by the student, in her ubiquitous sawn-off jeans, carrying jugs of sauce.

Imogen's glass was constantly full. The talking of cementing problems became a drone in her ears. She was suddenly aware of empty plates, everyone moving. Piero had disappeared again.

Disinclined to join the general babble – they had moved to the comfortable chairs at the end of the terrace – Imogen began to clear the table. For all the heat of the night she felt a coldness about her skin. In retrospect, she thought that it was probably then, stacking plates, that she knew : though the knowledge had not yet hardened into absolute conviction. Then she had piled everything into the unruly kitchen – only the winteriness of her limbs stopped her from the ultimate gesture of washing up – and moved back to the terrace, looking for Piero.

He was not among the guests.

'Looking for me, little girl lost?'

The cement man swung her into the dark room where couples were rasping together, hoping for some flame of romance. Imogen felt her partner's fat lips nibble at her cheek, and the wedge of his thigh fought to prise its way between her knees. Suddenly near to unaccountable tears, she broke away from him with no explanation and went upstairs. There, on the landing, she found Di the student brushing small dry leaves from her hair. Imogen hesitated.

'You haven't seen Piero, Di, have you?' she asked.

The brushing stopped.

'Why, no. Well, yes. I have, as a matter of fact. He just came back from taking a walk. He must be on the terrace.'

'Thank you.'

Imogen turned to go back downstairs. She paused when Di called to her.

'Say, Mrs . . .? If you don't mind my saying . . .' she was brushing her hair again. 'You look awful pretty.'

'Thank you, Di.'

Imogen hurried back to the terrace. Her heart was beating very fast. She saw Piero sitting between Camilla and Olivia, drink in hand, a small leaf on his shoulder. He smiled at her.

'Where've you been?'

She managed to smile back.

'Where've *you* been?'

'That's what we've all been asking,' said Camilla.

'I've been sitting out in the garden, not two yards from here, watching you all through the screen. Listening. Hearing terrible things about myself.'

'Nonsense,' said Olivia. She got up to say goodbye to departing guests. Imogen took her seat. Piero patted her hand.

'Serves her right for asking in the neighbours,' he said.

The neighbours were emerging from the darkened room where their dancing had left them in various states of disarray. The women patted at their hair while the men, hands deep in their pockets, made what they hoped were inconspicuous arrangements to their private parts.

'Sex maniacs, the lot of them,' said Piero. 'I wish they'd go.'

Imogen wished the same. It was already two o'clock: not much of the last night left. Giles, rather drunk, opened more bottles of wine. They could hear cars driving away too fast. Olivia returned to the terrace, for the first time careless of her deportment, hair blowing into her eyes.

'Thank God they've gone,' she said. 'I'm sorry. You were all marvellous. Now we can play the truth game.'

She looked round the table, provocative. Her four guests remained silent. Her husband scratched his neck slowly, savagely.

'That's a silly idea, darling,' he said. 'Always ends in disaster.'

'I'm for it. Anyone else?' Olivia's eyes circled the table again.

'One round,' said Piero. 'Then bed.'

Imogen closed her eyes, watched spinning particles of gold beneath the lids. Her hands, round a glass of icy wine, felt too far away to raise the glass to her lips. She heard them asking each other innocent questions. She heard desultory answers. No one's heart seemed to be in the game.

'Your turn, Imo.'

She opened her eyes, fixed them on Piero. He had the look of a victim, hunched.

'Is it true,' she said, 'you spent some time earlier this evening sitting in the garden, just beyond the screen, listening to what we were saying?'

'No,' he said, at once, and although she did not take her eyes from him, Imogen felt the shift of the others' glances, one to another. The question, which she had tried to resist, exhausted her. The answer, a mere confirmation, flayed her. She managed to stand, with some dignity, and announce she was going to bed. If her smile looked as grim as it felt, the others were in no condition to notice it.

She went to her room, and let her clothes drop to the floor. She got into bed. For a summer night, the sheets were icy.

Two hours passed. During that time, propped up against a

bank of ruffled pillows, Imogen watched the square of sky in the window change from dark to pale. There was no colour : a blanched dawn.

She listened to occasional noises, signals she could not understand. Muffled talk on the stairs, a sob. Camilla's voice, she thought. Then a single step, Piero's, going past her door. She waited for him to return. She imagined it might be a long time : he would have to wait till the others were all upstairs.

Much later there was sudden laughter from the terrace. Then the sound of two people heavily creeping. Doors shutting softly. Long, long silence. Piero didn't come.

Imogen looked at herself in a small mirror. She had had no energy to remove her make-up, so in the opalescent light her face was a clown's : thick eyelashes and shining lips. Considering the energies of the weekend she thought she looked quite good. Beautiful, Piero had said earlier. *Piero!* What was he *doing*?

With no conscious plan in mind Imogen got out of bed and crept to the door. She paused, opened it. Listened. Silence. She tiptoed down two passages, winced at every creaking board. Piero's room was at the opposite end of the house. Reaching it, at last, she found the door shut. If he was asleep, she thought, she would wake him gently, slip in beside him, lightly chiding.

Not the sort of thing she was in the habit of doing, she reminded herself : but it was the last night, and she was in America. Liberation seemed in place.

Quietly she opened his door. The bed was empty. Untouched. Imogen listened to the thudding of her own heart for a while, and felt the chill of dawn, from some passage window, about her shoulders. Then, from the room next to Piero's, she heard a low moaning, a laugh, a pleading voice.

'Please don't go back to her, not again, not tonight. Please stay with me.' It was almost a cry.

Imogen crept back to her room. Cold, she sat upright in bed again and regarded once more the empty sky that filled the window.

A couple more hours went by, this time filled with pantomime. Imogen watched, glassy-eyed as the characters played out their parts in her mind. A familiar figure she recognised as herself seemed to be the heroine : attractive, confident, swooshing about, watching the smiles of admirers, never still, eyes always on some further horizon. Men followed, men returned, and on she strode, this figure, strong in the belief of her own power. Piero was in the queue, in his blue shirt, undone to the waist for some reason. When it came to his turn he danced with her : they spun off their feet then earthed again. And back on the ground he stretched out his arm towards something, a bundle of rags in the corner. He touched the bundle and it stood up, an ugly girl. He put his arm about her and they walked away. The heroine was left standing, mists swirling about her feet, shouting after Piero, but the shouts were silent. After a while, words came, quietly. 'For the first time,' Imogen heard herself saying, out loud. And then came the laughter. She laughed herself to scorn. She laughed wildly, her body churning among the frilled pillows and cold sheets. The humour of the situation, suddenly clear to her, gave great strength. She knew as she laughed like a maddened creature, stifling the noise with the bedclothes, that she had passed some kind of crisis. Total vulnerability would never exist again. A protection against caring, and trusting, and believing, and assuming, would take its place. Perhaps even those mean stabs of jealousy would return no more. Ah, strength. The tiredness of her body and mind were nothing to her strength. But there was just one, last, important thing to complete the night : the hunting of the truth.

At six Imogen heard the cry of a child, and the heavy clump of Di the student going down to the kitchen. Swiftly she left her room again, ran to Piero's, careless of creaking boards this time. He was asleep in bed. She climbed in beside him, stirring him.

'Oh, it's you . . . I'm so sorry. I was so tired last night.' He opened his eyes. Imogen, resting on her elbow, looked down at him.

'Listen,' she said, 'I know what happened last night. No — please don't deny it. And please believe – I can't ever explain why, but something odd happened to me in the night, too. Anyhow, whatever it was, I don't mind. Do you understand – *I don't mind.* In fact, I think it's all rather funny.' She began to laugh. Piero joined her.

'Oh my Christ, what was I thinking of? She seduced me in the kitchen, you know. Just lifted up her tee-shirt, stirring the spaghetti, and said how about it, and she loved me and all that crap. Then, in the garden, I don't know, all that dope . . . I got quite turned on, her dreadful spectacles. After, in bed, of course it was a disaster, all her proclamations and worries about getting pregnant. She was a virgin, poor thing, out of her mind with jealousy of you.'

'What about the others?'

'Goodness knows who was doing what to whom. There were terrible noises. I saw Olivia and David out of the window walking towards the graveyard.' Imogen laughed again. Piero pulled her towards him.

'Here, it's so early, and our last day.'

They made love. From the kitchen beneath them came the noises of Di the student as she set about the dreadful task of washing up.

In what was left of the morning everyone was subdued, drank nothing but fresh orange juice. Di the student, emboldened by her experience, emerged from the kitchen terrace where she fed the children and cleared the tables in a dreamlike manner. Imogen could see she tried to hear what Piero was saying: leaning in his usual position by Imogen's chair, he soliloquised about his work, seemed unaware of Di's presence. Then he broke into Italian, explaining she had caught him for a moment in the kitchen to ask him to write to her, and not to forget her, and to send her some money if she got pregnant. '*Che pazza,*' he said, and sounded quite hostile.

For a moment, refilling jugs of orange in the kitchen, Imogen too was caught by Di.

'I just wanted to say I'm so sorry, Mrs . . . about last night. If I snatched him from you.'

'That's all right. He's nothing to do with me. Just a week-end friend.'

'But you're going back to New York with him?'

'Yes, but I go home to England tomorrow.'

'You're lucky, you'll see him again. I wonder if . . .'

'Look here, Di, don't wonder: don't hope, don't think, don't remember.' She knew she sounded tired and old. 'He'll never come back. It was just another night for him.'

'Yes. But it was terrible, you know, those first two nights, hearing you. My God, I thought, I can't bear it. This is the first man I want. I must have him, I thought. What can I do? You, there, having him, and not really caring. It wasn't fair, I thought. So I showed him my breasts, bigger than yours by lots.' Imogen smiled. 'It worked, didn't it? It worked. And then you must have heard us, so you knew how it felt for me.' Imogen smiled again. There was no point in explaining that part of it Di the student had miscalculated. They said goodbye, then, shaking hands, suddenly formal.

Later, everybody but Olivia left. Piero, Imogen noticed, did not bother to find Di and say farewell: he left five dollars for her on the kitchen table.

That night in New York she and Piero ate quantities of raw fish in a Japanese restaurant and drank too much saki. Near to exhaustion by now, some adrenalin kept them going. There was no sleep that night: much speculation about what the others had been up to. Imogen felt half inclined to tell Piero what had really happened to her on Sunday night. Then, in her new wisdom, she kept silent. Traumatic experiences that end well, she decided, are even more private than those that end badly. Next day in the darkness of the Algonquin bar, mid-morning, she drank a whisky-sour for final strength, and felt quite grateful to Piero. All women should learn to take advantage of such monsters, then minor adventures would be happier. She was quite impatient to go, even: when the porter announced her taxi was ready Piero said he wouldn't come to the door, he didn't want to say goodbye. Had it not been for Sunday night, Imogen realised she would have minded such a juvenile decision. As it was, with genuine glee she left him without a word.

And in the aeroplane, glancing at the distant land for a last look at Up-State New Jersey, she bought champagne to celebrate the first of many happy endings. Piero's face and voice and feel and smell wonderfully extinguished themselves from her tired mind, and in all her new wisdom she slept.

The Outing

Mrs Christopher Radcliffe, as the wife of an M.P., was a practised speaker. Since she had married she had made dozens of speeches, opened numerous shows, shops and fêtes. Nevertheless, she still felt slight unease before a public occasion, however small, and this nervous tension always seemed to mar her judgement about precisely how long it would take to reach her destination.

On the Saturday afternoon of the local fête, which was held every year in early summer, Mrs Radcliffe drove her car very slowly along the narrow road that twisted over the moors. She was a good ten minutes early. Just before entering the village she stopped the car in a gateway to check her appearance. Navy straw stetson at a nice angle; neat belted coat; navy gloves; sensible shoes for tramping from stall to stall. Not too ostentatious for the country. She should do, she thought.

Miss Warburton, head of the local branch of the Country Women's Guild, was looking out for Mrs Radcliffe as she drove up to the village green.

'Oh, Mrs Radcliffe. How kind of you to come.'

'Hello.' Mrs Radcliffe brandishing her practised smile. 'How nice to see you again. All right if I park here?'

She was aware of a small flutter among the onlookers as she got out of the car.

'I hope we'll be lucky with the weather.' Miss Warburton was a little nervous. She led Mrs Radcliffe across the village green. The grass was a sour yellow : the colour grass goes before a storm. Huge oak trees surrounded the green, towering into the thunderous sky, their leaves an ominous colour, too. Behind the trees stood the small village houses : built of West Country grey stone, the deep-set windows in their gaunt façades showing glimpses of snug rooms lit with flowers.

'It looks as if it might hold out,' said Mrs Radcliffe. 'Let's hope it does.'

They reached a trestle table that had been set with a cloth and a long, narrow vase of carnations stuck into a ruffle of fern. Mrs Radcliffe took her place behind the flowers and nodded at a few familiar faces. She looked about her: the stalls weren't up to much, at a glance, but she would make straight for the home-made cakes. It was easy genuinely to appreciate *them*. There wasn't a bad crowd, for a dull day. But they were a bit scattered. With no microphone, she'd have to raise her voice. She could be away, she calculated, in just under an hour.

'I am so pleased to be able to welcome today,' Miss Warburton was saying, 'Mrs Christopher Radcliffe – wife, of course, of our local M.P.' A smattering of claps from the listeners. Mrs Radcliffe smiled in response and turned to take an interest in the introduction. She would keep on smiling, now, till the end of the welcome, which Miss Warburton was having some trouble in reading from a small piece of paper that fluttered nervously in her hand.

A couple of hours previously Miss Pears had been told it was time to get ready for the outing. This news, like almost any news that involved action on her part, put her mind into a considerable flurry. What should she take with her? Her lunch, for one thing. That was sure. She had it beside her on the bed, in a scrumpled up paper bag. Two hard boiled eggs, a piece of cold fried bacon and a buttered roll. That would be nice, later on.

She glanced out of the high windows to the dull sky. Scarf, she thought. My pink or my blue? It might come on to rain, but then again it might not. But when in doubt wear a scarf, had always been her motto. Mrs Grace had only set her hair yesterday. It would be a pity to have it all come out in a sudden shower. Money – how much money should she take? They'd been told it would be a nice outing, to a garden party or a fête or something – she had forgotten exactly – up on the moors. There would be a chance to spend.

Miss Pears scrambled about her locker for her purse. It was

a worn old leather purse appliquéd with a giraffe that was coming unstuck, but somehow there was never any glue handy. Janet, her only niece had sent it to her, Christmas '68, before she'd married and become too busy to send more than a card. The purse contained exactly forty new pence – eight shillings to Miss Pears. She'd die before they got her round to decimals.

She tied her blue scarf round her head, pushing it well forward so that her fringe, should it rain, would at least be partially protected. There was no mirror, but the hefty knot she tied felt secure : it felt as if it gave her chin a good lift.

She set off down the dormitory. There was no one else there. She was the last, as usual, but then she'd never been quick on her feet. She laughed out loud a little to herself, anticipating the chiding she'd get from the others on the bus. 'Good old Apples,' they'd say, 'late as usual.'

'Buck up, Apples, we haven't got all night,' one or two of them did shout, as they climbed the steep bus steps. But by this time the laugh had died in her throat and she knew her face looked quite stern. Funny how she wanted to laugh with them, just as she'd done a few moments ago alone in the dormitory. But when it came to the time that they actually teased her the laugh always vanished, and some of them, the grumpier ones, said she was stuck up.

Miss Pears found an empty seat next to Mrs Grace. She sat down beside her. Mrs Grace was almost her friend. She didn't say much, Mrs Grace, but she'd made her mark by doing things. Little things, like setting your hair or giving you a cigarette or a chocolate, all for nothing in return. She had a temper, of course. Sometimes, she went wild. Semolina all over the place, for no apparent reason, more times than Miss Pears could remember. And then Mrs Grace would be taken away for a few days, and come back sleepy, and start doing things for you again. Miss Pears liked Mrs Grace. She would have shown her the Valentine card she got this year, had some sudden intuition not told her that it was Mrs Grace herself who had sent it.

Miss Pears looked down at her hands. They were indeed shaking, so that the bag made quite a noise.

'I'm all nerves, going out,' said Miss Pears, quietly, so that no one else should hear. She envied Mrs Grace her composure. Nothing seemed to shake *her* – outings, medical check-ups, anything. But then of course she'd lived in villages, she'd worked for the nobility, she'd probably experienced many a garden fête.

The first thing Miss Pears noticed when they arrived at the village green was the brass band. The musicians sat in a semicircle, legs apart, shaking spit from their instruments and flipping through their sheet music. In her excitement Miss Pears tightened her grip on her lunch bag and tore it at the corner.

Then, as she dithered down the steps, causing a lot of complaints from those behind her, the musicians struck up with *Whenever you feel afraid.*

'Well I never,' said Miss Pears to Mrs Grace. But Mrs Grace was thinking about something else and only answered, 'Nasty sky.' Then she turned away and waddled off in the direction of the church. Miss Pears considered shouting after her that she was going the wrong way, and to mind the road : but then she thought it wasn't worth it.

She was left standing on her own, her mouth slightly open, looking up at the giant trees – terrible thing if one of them crashed down – and listening to the music. Then she noticed most of the people seemed to be herding towards something, past the band. She set off to follow them – something must be going on. Mrs Grace would miss it, but perhaps Mrs Grace had been to too many of these sort of things to mind.

Mrs Radcliffe wetted her lips as the applause died down at the end of Miss Warburton's speech, and reset her smile. After a suitable pause, she began :

'Ladies and gentlemen, I find it a great honour and pleasure to have been asked here today. As you know, I myself am a firm supporter and indeed a *member* of the Country Women's Guilds, and I honestly believe that the day we open membership to men, your first new member will be my husband.' (Small laugh. That line always went down well with women's institutions.) 'As you know, although he's a very busy man, he takes a great interest in all our activities, and he has asked me to tell you how very sorry he is not to be able to be here today. But you know what a politician's life is . . .'

Her eyes trailed round the listeners. A Miss Burrows, the district nurse, she recognised; the farmer, she forgot his name, from whom she used to buy free range eggs; a few strange mothers and children. And then a small woman with sloping shoulders and wide hips, hands lolling at her sides, a detached expression on her square face. Mrs Radcliffe found her eyes paused when they came upon this woman. There was something odd about her. Mrs Radcliffe hesitated, then returned to her speech with a jolt she hoped no one would notice.

'Looking round – ' (she gave another quick look round, this time determined not to stop at the woman with the odd face) – 'looking round there seems to be a most impressive display on the stalls, and I know how much trouble this means you must have all taken : what hard work behind the scenes it must have been.' Her voice was rising. People at the back of the crowd were beginning to fidget. Bloody stupid of Miss Warburton not to have arranged a microphone. It was difficult enough to hold their attention . . .

Her own attention was on her listeners again. This time she caught sight of a woman a little apart from the crowd – a woman standing alone looking up at the trees, solid legs planted wide, blue scarf round her pudding face, hands clutching at a small paper bag. – Of course.

It was then that Mrs Radcliffe remembered. Well, it would make a lovely afternoon for them, poor things. She renewed her smile and decided, with a spontaneity unusual to her, to cut her speech short. A quick word about all the good work the Country Women's Guilds do, and on with the opening.

'And so I ask you to give as generously as you can to this very good cause. And now, I won't keep you any longer from enjoying yourselves – and *spending*. And so it is, with great pleasure, I declare this fête open.'

Miss Pears heard the clapping – it sounded a little muted from where she stood – and gave a brief dab at her paper bag. She could see a small girl with a satin bow in her hair shuffling up to the lady in the big hat and smart red coat. The child curtsied and handed the lady a beautiful posy of carnations

and fern in a twist of silver paper. The lady laughed, and held
it up to her lapel. It was a pretty sight, thought Miss Pears. She
wondered if her niece Janet's little girl would be about that
age now.

The crowd round the table began to break up and make for
the stalls. Miss Pears noticed several of her lot seemed hesitant,
dithery, compared with the villagers. Well, she for one knew
where she was going. The home-made cakes.

She walked towards a stall under one of the largest trees,
the long thick grass tickling her ankles above her shoes. But
when she managed to reach the stall, pushing her way through
the nattering women, there were no cakes, but only second-hand
clothes. Hands were holding them up : a very large bathing suit
with boned breasts, and a tatty old scarf, no better than a duster,
blew in the breeze. Nothing that Miss Pears wanted. A lot of old
rubbish. She saw Mrs Grace nearby, sniffing at the stuff, not
touching anything – so she knew that she was right about that. It
was a lot of old rubbish.

She turned, and made her way to another stall. This time she
found the right one, a long trestle table covered with tantalising cakes. It was difficult to take them all in at a glance, with
people shoving and pushing and asking the price. But there was
a particular one which caught Miss Pears' fancy : chocolate-
iced and decorated with a swirl of pink sugar roses. It was hard
to tell, just looking, whether the icing was soft or hard. If it was
soft, she'd have it. She put out a finger to prod it, very gently
– she wouldn't harm it in any way, of course, just test the
icing, when a lady with a biting voice behind the table snapped :
'No touching please.'

Miss Pears' finger whipped back in fright. She'd meant no
harm. Oh well, have to risk the icing. She took out her purse.
The ticket on the chocolate cake said 35p. She tipped all her
coins into the palm of her hand, still holding her paper bag, all
very awkward. She began calculating in her head. Counting
the odd coins was difficult because the paper bag got in the
way, and yet if she didn't put her finger on them she forgot
which number she'd got up to. Very muddling. She realised,
though, if she bought the chocolate cake, and she could just

manage it, there'd be precious little over for tea. Though of course that didn't matter so much, seeing as she'd still got her lunch.

Miss Pears was about to ask the snappy lady if she could have the chocolate cake when the people around the stall suddenly began to drift apart, as if to make way for someone. Miss Pears turned round. There before her, so close she was almost touching, was the lady in the big hat and the red coat, the posy of carnations pinned to her lapel now. The lady gave a huge smile, her lips all glossy red. She seemed not to be looking at Miss Pears, though, but at the snappy lady behind the counter.

'What lovely cakes!' From under the big hat her voice brayed, close-to. 'I must take some home for the children. They're real fiends for cakes.'

'There's a good selection, isn't there?' A middle-aged woman in silk polka dots edged up to the lady in the red coat. She had a kind face under a shiny straw hat that danced with cherries.

'Which ones will you have, Mrs Radcliffe?'

The snappy woman's voice was all sweetness now. Miss Pears' hands tightened on her paper bag and her coins and her empty purse. Several people craned forward to get a good view of Mrs Radcliffe's decision.

'Well, I don't know, do you? It's so difficult to decide.' She put a navy blue finger to her chin then suddenly pointed it very fast at several different cakes. 'That, that, that, that, and er, that, I think.' She took a £5 note from her bag and handed it over the counter. 'Why don't you keep the change as my contribution to the afternoon?'

'Well, that's really very kind of you, Mrs Radcliffe,' the snappy woman glowed.

'Thank you so much, Mrs Radcliffe. We'll get Mrs Radcliffe's cakes boxed up, won't we, Mrs Leigh, and get someone to put them in her car?' The nice lady with the cherry hat sounded efficient. 'Would you care to come and look at the garden produce, now, Mrs Radcliffe?'

The two ladies, red coat and polka dots, moved away. Miss Pears stood by the stall and watched Miss Leigh snatch up the five chosen cakes, including the chocolate one, and put them under the table. Without them, it was almost bare. A couple of dull sponges left, sprinkled with icing sugar, and a weedy looking jam roll. Miss Pears began to put her coins back into her purse. Then she opened the paper bag to check on the bacon, shining pinkly through its piece of greaseproof paper. She might as well go and have her lunch.

Miss Warburton was privately disappointed by the bring-and-buy stall. There, not much imagination had been shown – tinned pears, dishcloths, a silver painted horseshoe, a baby's dummy. Mrs Radcliffe had had quite a difficult time choosing anything. Eventually, she had settled for a bottle of tomato ketchup.

Miss Warburton was also disappointed in the weather, as she kept repeating to Mrs Radcliffe.

'Just our luck, after so many good Saturdays.'

'Well, at least it isn't raining.' Mrs Radcliffe made it quite clear, by her determined step, there was no point in her stopping at the second-hand stall. Miss Warburton took the hint, and didn't suggest it. Instead she guided her guest of honour towards the village hall, where she could be certain a good tea had been laid on.

The band struck up again, this time *Getting to know you.* They seemed to have a particular liking for the music of the fifties. Mrs Radcliffe sprang a little on the balls of her feet, in time to the music.

'My husband and I used to dance to this before we were married,' she said. Anything to get off the weather.

'Really? How very interesting.' Miss Warburton herself hadn't danced for fifty years.

The village hall was a bare, lofty place which smelt of newly-scrubbed wood and warm scones. Mrs Radcliffe noticed that its high windows were edged with skimpy maroon curtains, and she wondered why it was that nine out of ten village halls she went to chose that particular colour for their curtains. She'd have to tell Christopher.

A couple of dozen tables were laid with white cloths and jam jars of cow-parsley and honeysuckle : someone had taken a lot of trouble. Extra chairs lined the walls of the hall, and on the stage a trestle table was stacked with thick white cups and home-made things. Miss Warburton introduced Mrs Radcliffe to the tea helpers, and pressed her to choose a lot to eat. But Mrs Radcliffe picked only one salmon fishpaste sandwich, besides her cup of tea. Miss Warburton laughed understandingly.

'We all have to think of our figures, don't we?' Then she waved her hands in a flurry as she saw Mrs Radcliffe beginning to open her bag. 'No, no, please! Tea on the house.' Mrs Radcliffe thought it wise to accept the offer with no fuss.

She and Miss Warburton wound their way through the tables, nodding at people, looking for a free seat. Mrs Radcliffe noticed that the woman who wouldn't budge out of her way at the cake stall sat at a table alone. But instead of eating the provided tea, she seemed to be having trouble cracking a hard-boiled egg on the table. Miss Warburton hurried past all the tables that were occupied by only one, drab woman, and finally asked Mrs Radcliffe if she would care to join the Bennet sisters at their table. They were the people responsible for the raffle. Miss Warburton knew they would be honoured if Mrs Radcliffe would be so kind as to call out the winning numbers. Mrs Radcliffe cheerfully agreed to do this. She calculated that could decently be her last duty. She could still be home by five-thirty. She began to nibble her sandwich.

Miss Pears had never come across such a tough-shelled egg. She banged it on the table, thwacked it on her knee, but it wouldn't break. In the end, with great patience, she lay it on her plate, waited till it stopped rolling about – till it was quite, quite still, then crashed her fist down upon it with all her force. This caused not just the shell to break, but also the white and even the hard boiled yolk. Miss Pears began picking at the shattered bits, peeling away small chunks of white from small pieces of shell.

She noticed, meanwhile, that quite a lot of her bus-load sat at tables by themselves, while the villagers chose tables with their friends and sat together. The child who had given the lady the flowers passed nearby Miss Pears' table. She held out a small chip of egg to her and the child smiled. But then a fat woman snatched at the child's arm and hurried her away to the other end of the hall.

Still, she was happy with her lunch, on her own. She liked to eat alone. That's why she always saved her meals till past the proper meal times. No one seemed to mind. Perhaps they didn't notice.

All the others seemed quite happy, too, as far as she could tell. There was Lily, at the next table, squinting over her pile of sausage rolls. She'd always been greedy as a pig, Lily, and her table manners were nothing to write home about, either. When the lady in the red coat passed her table, Lily looked up, still chewing, mouth still open, with no respect at all. Then her eyes watered – she couldn't take bright colours, they always hurt – and the tears trickled down her face.

Mrs Grace, Miss Pears noticed, had chosen one of the chairs at the edge of the hall. But then she wasn't eating anything, just sipping a cup of tea. Miss Pears looked at her quite hard. There was something up with Mrs Grace, she could tell. She had that look in her eye. She'd been obliging for so many days, too: perhaps the time was up. Miss Pears looked round for the Supervisor – not that she ever listened to anyone, stubborn old bitch, but it would be worth giving her a hint about Mrs Grace. However, the Supervisor was nowhere in sight, so Miss Pears began on her bacon.

As soon as she had finished her lunch she made her way to the stage to choose her tea. On the way she passed Mrs Grace.

'Coming up for something to eat?' she asked. Mrs Grace didn't answer, or didn't seem to have heard. 'There's some lovely gingerbread,' Miss Pears went on, 'and scones. Shall I treat you to something?'

Still Mrs Grace didn't answer. Instead she got up, as if Miss Pears didn't exist, put her unfinished tea on her seat, and left the hall. She'd always been unpredictable. Muttering to herself that there were some people who looked a gift horse in the mouth, Miss Pears climbed the stage. She decided to spend every penny she had on tea.

Half an hour later, feeling pleasantly full, she made her way back to the village green. She had no money left, so there was nothing else she could buy. She would sit on the grass beside the band and listen, until the Supervisor told them to get back into the bus.

Outside, the sky was darker, the green of the trees and hedges more vivid. Miss Pears shuddered. Sometimes, millions of pellets of sky, black as soot, streamed through her eyes, her mouth, her nose, till she could hardly breathe, and her hands and feet went icy cold. She hadn't had an attack like that, mind, for several weeks now : not since they'd been giving her those new red pills. But she didn't like anything black : it always reminded her.

She walked carefully back to the band, heavy with tea. It swayed and gurgled in her stomach, a comforting sound.

But the musicians weren't there : probably gone for tea themselves. They'd left their instruments propped up against their chairs, their peaked caps on the seats, their sheet music making little snapping noises as the breeze pecked at the pages.

Mrs Grace sat on one of the seats, in the front row. Her feet, not quite touching the ground, swung backwards and forwards, hitting a trombone. She stared into space, sulky looking. Still, Miss Pears thought, might as well have a go at her.

'Understand the music?' she asked. No answer from Mrs Grace. 'I used to be able to play a few notes, years ago.' She paused again. Mrs Grace just didn't seem to be interested in anything today.

Oh well. She'd tried. Nobody could say she hadn't. Anyhow, here was the band coming back. Now Mrs Grace would have to budge.

A dozen large men in silver-buttoned uniforms tramped back to their places. The one who should have occupied Mrs Grace's seat had a bristly red beard.

'Had a nice sit-down, have you?' he asked. 'Afraid I've got to shift you now. Back to work.'

Mrs Grace took no notice of him. She stared unblinking at his stand of music. The man touched her shoulder.

'Come on, now, love. Up you get.' The conductor was tapping his stick impatiently on his knee. Everyone was looking at Mrs

Grace, now. The man with the red beard tried again.

'I said come on, dear. Very sorry and all that. Up – you get.' He tried to lever her gently up from the chair.

But with startling speed Mrs Grace leapt to her feet herself, spun round, picked up the slatted chair, brandished it for a moment above in the air, then brought it crashing down upon his head.

'Bugger off, you fucking creep,' she screamed. 'No one's going to bloody turn me off a fucking chair if I bloody want to be on it.'

Her voice ripped the heavy air. At once every member of the band stood. The conductor edged forward to protect his trombonist, whose face was scattered with blood from his head : it streamed down into his beard. The conductor tapped Mrs Grace on the shoulder with his stick.

'Now, now, madam, we don't want any trouble – '

'And as for you, you toady old bit of bullshit – '

She lashed out at the conductor with hands tightened into claws, and kicked at his shins.

Miss Pears was aware that all at once everyone at the fête seemed to be crowding round Mrs Grace and the musicians. All her lot had appeared from nowhere, very fast it must have been : usually they moved quite slowly. There was Lily, eyes full of water, screaming abuse at the whole band : Wendy the Egg running round and round in small circles, cackling with laughter, her head quite bald : her wig must have fallen off somewhere. Barbara the Giant was standing on a chair, almost as tall as the oak trees, fists clenched, ready to punch someone : Annie and Mavis, hand in hand as usual, stamping their gym shoes – when it came to revolt against authority, they were a loyal lot, the girls.

Quickly, Miss Pears decided she must do her bit. Mrs Grace after all was her friend – well, more or less her friend. She'd done her hair so nicely yesterday, not pulling once. She'd every right to her seat. She deserved support.

Miss Pears ran faster than she'd run for years across the green, the screams and weird laughs pounding in her ears. The home-made cake stall was empty now except for the one dreary sponge. With a heave Miss Pears tipped over the table. The single cake rolled away like a coin into the grass, brushing it with icing sugar. And there, exposed by the tipped up table, lay Mrs Radcliffe's cakes in a box, waiting for arrangements to be made to get to her car.

With an almighty cry Miss Pears jumped into the box, and felt them squashing beneath her feet. She stamped on them with all her force, bashing the chocolate and pink roses to an ugly pulp : coffee icing, white icing, strawberry fillings, crushed almonds oozed over her shoes and ankles, warm and soft. She began to laugh, her mouth widening over the whole of her face. The strong knot of her scarf snapped and the scarf fell off, but she didn't care. She kept on stamping, mincing the cakes to a multi-coloured mud, and then the rain came. It fell into her mouth, turning black, and began to fill her eyes and nose and mouth till she cried out to breathe. She felt her feet turn to ice in the mess of cake, and her hands, icy too, rose like rags in the air, calling for help.

Miss Warburton and Mrs Radcliffe had just finished their tea when they heard the screams. With everybody else left in the hall, they hurried out to see what had happened. Mrs Radcliffe shoved her bottle of tomato ketchup into her pocket so that she could run. Miss Warburton held on to her hat.

As soon as she turned the corner and saw the fight, Mrs Radcliffe hissed out loud : 'You can *never* rely on those people. They should be properly supervised.' But Miss Warburton was far behind her, so her observations went unheard.

Mrs Radcliffe quickly made up her mind that there was nothing she could usefully do to help the situation. A fat policeman was blowing his whistle and grappling with a woman who appeared to be having hysterics by the bandstand. The district nurse was leading away a bloody man with a red beard. A thick-set woman in a navy uniform and stocking seams all askew was running about shouting unheeded orders, and a monster woman, standing on a chair, fists thrust into the sky, screamed obscenities. And there was Miss Warburton, suddenly very fast on her feet, chasing a woman with a completely bald head, dabbing at her with her straw hat, as if she was trying to catch a butterfly.

I hope to God the local reporter has gone home, thought Mrs Radcliffe. This sort of publicity wouldn't help the next election. For Christopher's sake, in fact, it would probably be better to make a discreet exit and write a letter explaining to Miss War- burton – who was in no way fit to say goodbye to at the moment.

She threw away the bottle of ketchup, which was digging into her hip bone, cursed the rain, and began to tiptoe as incon- spicuously as possible round behind the trees. At one moment a man crossed her path – he looked like a bus driver – dragging a crying woman, the one who'd had the blue scarf, and whose feet were now covered in some kind of revolting mess. The woman's cries, and ugly twisted face made Mrs Radcliffe feel sick : she had never been any good at coping with scenes, as she was the first to admit.

Unnoticed, she got into her car. Quickly she closed the window, which half shut out the hysterical yells of fear, hatred, abuse and despair. She switched on the wipers. The water on the windscreen blurred the writhing people among the upturned tables, and scattered brass instruments of the band. She shut her eyes for a moment as the bald-headed woman ran quite close by, still screaming – Miss Warburton still chasing her, her wet polka- dotted dress now clinging to her thick body.

Mrs Radcliffe switched on the engine, glanced at her watch, very calm. If she put her foot down, she reckoned, she could still be home by half past five.

Deception is so Easy

'My wife,' said Angus, 'has been getting up at a ridiculously early hour ever since we've been married. Over the years she's instilled in me an unnecessary feeling of guilt. I wish she hadn't.'

Angus lay naked on the bed, the sheets a crumpled foam round his ankles, smoking. By day – on the infrequent occasions he and Sarah met for lunch now, he called his wife by name, Lorna. In bed, he always referred to her as his wife.

Beside him, Sarah sighed. They had had a happy night. Happy nights always inspired Angus to remember his wife with particular affection in the morning. Sarah wondered which recollections would come to him today.

'She has this old dressing gown,' he was saying. 'Filthy thing. She says she has it cleaned twice a year, but you'd never know. You never know what to believe. Anyhow, she wears it till about eleven o'clock in the morning.' Love in his voice. Sarah gave him a moment.

'And where does she think you were last night?' she asked. Angus's deceptions gave her the temporary pleasure of false security.

'Sheffield.' He felt safer if he named a town north of the Home Counties. 'Conference.'

'Common Market again?'

Angus nodded.

'God knows what'll happen once my particular negotiations are settled,' he said, and they both laughed. 'We'll think of something. My wife's the most trusting woman on earth. I love her for it.' He slapped Sarah's thigh affectionately.

You can't win, thought Sarah, if you're mistress to a man who needs no one to console him about his wife. Aloud she said :

'You realise it's been seven years now?'

'What has?'

179

'Us.'

'Oh. Us.' Angus stubbed out his cigarette. 'Eleven years married. Seven years – us.' He scratched his chest, a sign that he would be getting up in a moment, his mind on other things. Sarah took her chance.

'Why don't we meet for lunch today?'

'Lunch?' He stopped scratching, quite surprised.

'All our meetings seem to be in bed, these days. I practically never see you dressed.'

'Nonsense, darling. Nonsense.' He patted her hand.

'It's true. Why can't we have lunch?'

'Absolutely out, I'm afraid.'

'Why?'

'Lorna's mother's birthday.' He paused.

'Is that true?' Sarah asked.

'Of course it's true. She's eighty-six and wants to go to the Post Office Tower. Awful idea. I hate heights. It's been arranged for weeks.'

Sarah frowned.

'I don't mind your putting me off for business reasons, but putting me off for your mother-in-law is a bit hard to bear.' She heard herself sounding petulant. Angus sighed.

'I'm not putting you off if I didn't ask you in the first place, am I? Silly one. Hell, you made the suggestion. I merely said it wasn't possible. I'm sorry.'

'All right, all right. I understand. It doesn't matter.' Sarah smiled, her humour restored. 'You deserve to get giddy, whizzing around in that tower.'

'My mother-in-law will survive it better than me, I don't doubt,' said Angus. 'She doesn't drink. She's a remarkable woman, as a matter of fact. She climbed a considerable way up the Matterhorn at the age of seventy-three, and only last year I saw her dive off the second top board.'

'*My* mother-in-law,' said Sarah, rummaging in the packet of cigarettes on Angus's stomach, 'has just organised an exhibition of needlework which is going to be opened by the Queen Mother, and she's seventy-four.'

Angus swung his legs out of bed.

'Everything you have ever told me about your mother-in-law has always led me to imagine her as a woman of quite remarkable dullness,' he said. Again Sarah smiled. One of the things that she loved about Angus was that he made his bitchiest observations in a voice warm with benevolence.

Standing legs astride on the floral carpet, Angus screwed up his fists and punched himself gently on the chest. In the pale light from the window, strained through a net curtain, his body was grey white, a homogenised colour. These days, his ankles were still puffy in the mornings. When Sarah first knew him they swelled at night but would have returned to their normal trimness by breakfast time. His paunch was increasing, too. One day, she thought, he would die of a heart attack. What would she do without him? She needed a little comfort.

'Gus?'

'What?' He was getting a bit deaf, too.

'Kiss me.'

'What?' He leant over and kissed her on the forehead. 'I didn't mean that about your mother-in-law,' he said.

'That's all right.' Angus was moving away again, towards the bathroom. Briefly Sarah had felt like persuading him back into bed, delaying him for half an hour. Now she had lost her chance. Making love in the morning, like lunch with Angus, was a rare thing these days.

In the bathroom Angus turned on the bath taps, and the noisy hot water sent up a cloud of warm comforting steam. He had slight indigestion and a board meeting at ten, otherwise he might have obliged. Sarah, in accordance with the cliché, was getting randier with middle age. Randier and flabbier. He sometimes wondered how much longer he would be able to go on satisfying her the way that he could now – just. Perhaps the occasional lunch would make up for a slacking off on the sexual side of things, he thought. It was an idea.

'Gus?'

'What?' Stupid, she was, shouting against the taps. Irritated, he turned them off. The water wasn't half deep enough for real enjoyment. He got in.

'Can I come in and talk to you?'

'If you like.' That meant he wouldn't be able to turn on the water again. Something of the pleasure of his morning went from him.

Sarah, wrapped in a very white towel, curled herself up on the wide edge of the bath. Angus, peering at her through the steam, noticed that her eyes looked very small without mascara. When he first knew her she would get up early, before he was awake, and spend half an hour in front of the mirror. Then she would greet him with a face that was not visibly made-up, but burnished and glowing, eyelashes darkened, teeth fresh and shining. He had liked that very much. It had always roused him again.

'We're terribly lucky, you know,' she said, blowing smoke into the steam. 'Aren't we? Don't you think?'

'Why?'

'Well, our arrangement. We've never had any real trouble, I mean, have we? No nasty scenes or anything.'

'Ah.' Sarah tended to ruminate in the mornings upon subjects which Angus could only find stimulating after a few drinks late at night. At 9.00 a.m. he could find little to say about their relationship. He lifted one leg heavily out of the water and noticed, sadly, the huge ankle. It would be down by lunch time, with luck, though the central heating in that damned tower could bring it up again.

'Look at Sebastian and Jessica,' Sarah was saying. 'Jessica found out he was sleeping with Felicity only *three weeks* after they'd started their affair, and all hell was let loose. He had to give her up. It was too complicated. I mean, nothing like that has ever happened to us, has it?'

'No,' said Angus.

'And yet I suppose some people must know.' Angus shut his eyes against a flannel of soap. Like this, there was no need to answer. 'What always amazes me,' Sarah was going on, 'is how the person one *lives* with can go on for years without having a single clue. Even now, you know, Adrian has absolutely no idea about us, I swear. Not that he's very observant or inquisitive, so that makes life easier . . .' Angus, washing his ears, couldn't hear very well.

Later, Sarah followed him back to the bedroom and sat on the bed while he dressed. For some inexplicable reason she felt a little cheerless this morning, still in need of some small measure of comfort before Angus left her for the office and lunch with his mother-in-law.

'To go on with what I was saying,' she said, though they had spoken of no other subject in between, 'I mean, what does Laura think you *do* in Sheffield or Birmingham or wherever?'

Angus was easing himself into his braces. By mistake he let one snap down on to his shoulder. It hurt.

'Hell, Sarah, I don't know what she thinks.' Sarah's questioning about Lorna never failed to irritate him.

'She must have *some* suspicions. She's not unintelligent.' Sarah knew she had trodden on dangerous ground. She watched Angus's reactions carefully.

'My wife is no fool,' he agreed, struggling with the zip of his flies, aware he sounded pompous. He went over to the bedside table, picked up his glasses and fitted them into the permanent dent on the bridge of his nose. 'Perhaps she just turns a blind eye,' he added, and at once regretted having said it.

Sarah swivelled round, the towel drooping from her shoulder. 'Do you mean . . .' She spoke slowly, each word sonorous. 'Do you mean you think she might *know*?'

With his glasses on Angus could see her quite clearly now, her nosey little face, peeked with a macabre kind of interest and some fear, her hair stiff, greasy and unbrushed, the soft flesh of her underarms oozing on to the pristine fabric of the towel. He disliked her considerably at this moment.

'You little fool,' he said, 'of course she knows. Of course she's always known.' He paused. 'I think you would agree she's behaved with quite remarkable dignity. I admire her for it.'

There was a long silence. When Sarah spoke at last her head bobbed up and down, puppet-like. Her face, small anyhow, had shrunk : her tiny eyes were gauzed.

'How long has she known?' she asked.

Angus shrugged.

'Almost since the beginning, I should say.'

He had always dreaded a scene, a show down. He knew there would never be one with Lorna : she was much too intelligent. Now there was one with Sarah he was quite enjoying himself. Besides, you couldn't go on deceiving for ever. She had to know sometime. He was running out of places to tell her he had told Lorna he was going . . . With Lorna, he never had to lie. He simply said he'd be away for the night, and that was good enough for her.

'You *pig*,' hissed Sarah, finally. 'All these years you've been deceiving me.'

'Ah,' said Angus, fiddling with his tie.

'And to think, all those times we've laughed about how easy it was to fool *her* . . .' Sarah gave a great cry, suddenly, so that the towel slipped from her shoulders completely, revealing her small, yellowish breasts. Then she threw herself face down into the pillows and gave herself up to sobbing.

Angus looked at the clock. By the time he'd paid the bill and walked to the office it would be ten o'clock exactly. Sarah raised her head. Her face was red, and wet with tears. For a moment Angus thought she might break into her old smile, a smile she sometimes produced at the most awkward moments between them, and forgive him. Instead, she spluttered almost incoherently.

'You know what you've done, don't you? You've slashed up the last seven years, just like that. Slashed them all to pieces. You've taken all the fun out of it, ruined it all. Talking about *me* with *her* – is that what you did? Oh God, I can't believe it. Her, knowing . . .'

Angus was no longer enjoying himself. He had seen Sarah angry before, but never like this, wracked and bitter. He felt a trickle of sweat beneath his arms seep into the stiff clean silk of his shirt. Reluctantly, he went over to her, touched her shaking shoulder.

'Sarah . . . don't. I must go, I'm afraid.'

She seemed not to hear him, but continued to sob. He spoke a little louder.

'I tell you what, next week . . . I'm a bit tied up in the evenings as a matter of fact. Why don't we have lunch one day? Say Tuesday?'

Under the spread of his hand Sarah's small head moved in such a confused manner that he was unable to tell whether she meant to accept his invitation, or to refuse it.

Last Love

Beth Soper bent her head to avoid seeing the clouds in the sky and set off down the Bermondsey Street to St Michael's Church. There, Thomas Harrow was waiting for her and they were quietly married. Beth was seventy-eight and Thomas was eighty-two.

They had wanted no fuss, just a simple private ceremony. Their friends in the Sunset Home had asked permission to come to the church, eager for an outing. But when they had been refused, they understood. There was promise of some kind of celebration later, after the honeymoon.

Man and wife, Thomas and Beth returned to the street hand in hand. The vicar had offered them a lift in his car, but they said no, they would enjoy the walk. They hadn't gone far when it began to rain.

'Dratted weather,' said Thomas.

'My hat,' said Beth. With her free hand she patted at the pale blue feathers which were becoming clotted in the wet.

Thomas had not seen the flat furnished, and it seemed to please him. Beth had just managed to get it all ready in time, with the help of Madge and Eileen from the Sunset, and the lady from the Welfare. Beth pointed out every detail to Thomas lest he should miss something: green tiles in the bathroom, nice yellow kitchen curtains, velvet three-piece suite in the sitting-room, patchwork bedspread (one of the few things she had kept when Christopher died). Thomas said he thought it was all grand. He said their savings had been well spent.

When he had seen everything, and repeated his approving comments several times, Beth lit the gas fire and they sat side by side on the sofa, noting with pleasure its firm springs. It was only eleven-thirty, a good hour before Beth should heat up the tin of Swiss ravioli for lunch, but she suggested they should wait no longer to cut the cake. It was a rich fruit cake iced in pink and white. Kept in a tin, it would last for weeks. Beth's daughter Annie had sent it with best wishes from Plymouth.

They ate their slices slowly, to guard against indigestion. After a while Thomas said,

'Well, Mrs Harrow, we're married at last.'

Beth's head, which of late shook constantly, like a flower in a slight wind, nodded more strongly in agreement. She was thinking that tomorrow she would pay for the rum in Annie's cake, and how she would enjoy the afternoon sorting out their stores in the kitchen cupboard. Her own kitchen again. Strange thought, really, but a good one.

Thomas and Beth met in the Sunset Home. Thomas had been there several years before Beth arrived from a Home in the country. She was newly widowed, and very quiet. From his chair in the semi-circle round the television – a long way from the chair assigned to Beth – Thomas observed she was prettier than most of the old ladies who came. She had a kindly face and a lively eye, though of course this was veiled by present sadness, her husband having so recently died.

They did not have occasion to speak for several months. Then one Saturday afternoon, in the middle of Match of the Day, the old man in the chair next to Thomas shut his eyes and died. It gave them all a shock. They were used to their neighbours dying, but were upset by the witnessing of actual death. Going into tea that day, the bell ringing imperviously in his ears, Thomas found his mouth trembling and his eyes filled with tears. William Best and he had sat next to each other for seven years. They had not tried to know each other very well, but they enjoyed their mutual silence. They would nod at each other's occasional remarks, and sometimes share a bag of sweets.

In his upset state Thomas hardly noticed a tug at his elbow. It made him sway a little on his feet. Beth Soper it was : the pretty old lady who still looked sad. He struggled to regain his balance.

'Terrible thing, death in the afternoon,' she said quietly. 'I know how you felt about Mr Best.'

'Ah,' said Thomas. And then an inspiration came to him. Beth should take William's place. Beth should be his armchair neighbour. 'I would like it if you moved into his chair,' he said, 'otherwise they'll put in a new one. There's no accounting for who I'd get.'

Beth thought about it only for a moment. Then she said,

'Very well. I'll move my rug after tea.'

After that Thomas and Beth stuck closely together. Beth moved into Mr Best's place in the dining-room, too, and by the second meal Thomas knew she liked two spoons of sugar in her tea and put them in without asking. Beth was impressed. He was a good, quiet man, Thomas, but uncared for. It wasn't long before she was darning his socks and reminding him to tie his laces. On Sunday, if it was fine, they would go for a drink together in the local pub. Wednesdays they would walk to the post box: Beth wrote to Annie every Tuesday evening, and Thomas wrote to his son Allan, in Australia, once a month. Neither of them received much news in return, but their mutual reminiscences were some compensation for lack of letters or visitors.

Thomas and Beth's association did not go unobserved by the others, for all its quietness. 'The young lovers' they came to be known as, and sometimes blushed at the public ragging. If they left the television room together to repair to the small lounge for a few moments' peace, they would cause much speculation and merriment at supper.

'Young lovers at it again?' Alice, the spinster ringleader would croak. 'You'll be dead before your time, this rate.'

Laughter all round, threads of soup wavering down chins. Beth privately thought Alice was coarse – she had been in the fish market all her life, after all – and was uncertain how to react to her jibes. Thomas, sensing the difficulty of Beth's smile, would move his wiry thigh to touch hers under the table, and she would be comforted.

On Christmas Eve Thomas proposed to Beth in the small sink room where they filled their hot water bottles each night. There was no one about. Drip of the tap and growl of the kettle the only noises. Night sky through the curtainless window, milky with reflections from the neon city outside.

'I was thinking it might be more sensible, Beth, if we lived out the rest of our years together as man and wife.' He was calm and firm, sure as he had been all those years ago when he had proposed to Josephine O'Reilly on Westminster Bridge.

'Well, that would be nice, I think,' said Beth, unscrewing the cap of her hot water bottle.

'Seeing as we're both in such good health we could leave this place, find ourselves a little flat. Be independent.'

'So we could,' said Beth, and the idea of her own home again made her hand tremble. She returned the kettle to the table for fear of spilling the scalding water.

'We could discuss it more in the morning, when you've had time to sleep on it,' went on Thomas, with his usual consideration.

'Oh, I'll say yes all right. There won't be any changing my mind in the night.' Beth smiled shyly at him.

'There! You sound like a girl.' Thomas handed her a filled bottle, screwed tightly as he could manage with his arthritic hands, and kissed her on the forehead. Then they went their separate ways down the corridor.

Thomas gave Beth a cameo brooch for Christmas; she gave him the pair of red socks she had sworn she was knitting for her son-in-law.

'And what about a ring?' Thomas asked. 'An engagement isn't right without a ring.'

Beth looked down at the wedding band Christopher Randolph Crest had slipped on her finger in a Dorset church in the spring of 1915, promising to have her and to hold till death parted them, and he had kept that promise. She wouldn't like to take his ring off now, for all that he would be pleased she was to marry again and be happy (a different sort of happy, of course). Besides, it wouldn't be possible to get it off, over her swollen knuckles. Beth felt the brush of one of the small awkwardnesses of second marriage. She fingered her new brooch.

'Oh, not a ring, Thomas,' she said. 'This is quite enough, what you've given me already. Very like one my mother had. And anyhow . . .'

189

She held out her hands. They looked at the lumpy joints on what had once been long and thin fingers.

'Very well, on this occasion,' said Thomas, and lapsed into an understanding silence. Beth was grateful to him.

Their engagement was not a secret for long. Everyone approved of the idea and rejoiced. They sent small presents wrapped in tissue paper: soap and tobacco, writing paper, a potted hyacinth. Madge and Eileen efficiently set about finding a Council flat, and on fine days Beth went shopping for things they would need, most of her savings, added to Thomas's, in her bag.

In early spring Beth fell ill. Perhaps it was a chill: a nasty wind unexpectedly had savaged her on one of her shopping expeditions. Perhaps it was all the excitement – no one could tell. The doctor said she would soon recover if she took things quietly for a while. But the wedding, planned for March, had to be postponed.

Beth, in bed, cameo brooch on a velvet ribbon round her neck, cried a little. Thomas sat by her, dabbing her handkerchief with eau de cologne.

'Don't worry yourself,' he said.

'But I do, Thomas.'

'You just gather your strength.'

'I never had more than a day's illness in my life. Christopher said I was strong as an ox.'

'We'll be married soon as you're on your feet.'

Beth cheered a little. They could hear Alice's penetrating voice in the corridor.

'Expect she's come to see what we're doing,' said Beth. 'Whatever will she be thinking?'

They both smiled.

It took Beth longer than she had supposed to recover completely. But with the warmth of summer strength returned to her, and a new date was set for the wedding in October. By then, the Council flat was acquired, the furniture in, the carpets down. The day of the wedding there was early sun. The rain that came later was disappointing, but neither of them really cared.

They had too much else to think about : so much to plan for the years ahead.

The first day as Mrs Harrow passed very quickly : there was all the enjoyment of sorting out the kitchen cupboards, of seeing Thomas dozing in an armchair (which soon would lose its new look) in front of his own gas fire – of making mince in a parsley sauce for supper. The sauce was a little lumpy, but Beth felt soon she would be back in practice.

They did not stay up late. When the nine o'clock news was over they took it in turns to undress in the bathroom. Then they lay in the new bed, just touching, the patchwork quilt drawn up high across their chests.

'I think this was a very good idea of mine,' said Thomas.

'It was, too.' Beth smiled.

'My first honeymoon wasn't half as damn comfortable as this.'

'Nor mine,' said Beth.

Thomas sighed.

'Ah, Beth, if it was years ago . . . a few years ago.'

'Put all that out of your mind,' said Beth, touching her hair-net.

'You can't help thinking,' said Thomas. 'Still, I should be grateful for a lively mind, even if the old bones can't keep up with it.'

'I should say so,' said Beth.

Thomas took her hand.

'Believe me, I was quite . . . a devil in my time.'

'Of course you were,' said Beth. 'Now, I'm going to put out the light.'

They kissed, briefly, each smelling an echo of parsley sauce and wedding cake on the other's breath. In the dark, their legs intertwined.

For a while they were silent, listening for signals of sleep in the other's breathing : pondering upon the extraordinary sensation of someone new, however much loved, beside them in bed. Then Thomas said,

'Beth, I can't manage to sleep with . . . I mean if you don't mind I'd like to take out – '

'There's a glass of water beside your bed, love,' said Beth.

'You're a good and thoughtful woman, you know.' Beth felt him move, stretch his arm about in the darkness. She heard two small splashes in the water. 'Happy marriage doesn't mean changing all one's ways, does it, Beth? That's what Josephine and I agreed.'

Then suddenly he was definitely asleep, on his back, snoring a more rattling snore than Christopher Randolph Crest's; but she would get used to it. Beth turned on to her side. Living into old age with someone you scarcely noticed the changes, could not be sure of the precise time when your habits changed, more milk puddings by day, bedsocks and bare gums by night. There was no unease. With a new person the small private acts of an ageing body could cause awkwardness close to shame unless there was much understanding. With Thomas, Beth could not imagine feeling more happily herself, but all the same she was glad that it was dark and he was asleep when she dropped her own teeth into the glass of water at her side of the bed. Then, at once, she joined her husband in sleep.

When she thought about it later Beth could not recall exactly when it was that she began to find running the flat more difficult than she had supposed. Accustomed to the sedentary life in the Sunset, no worries about food and shopping and washing up, she had felt full of energy – indeed fed up, sometimes, that there was not more she could do. Now, with everything to think about again, to be responsible for, she felt curiously tired. Thomas helped as much as he could, of course : he carried the shopping bag and laid the table, but it had always been Beth's belief that it was a wife's duty to look after her husband once he had retired, and she would not allow him to assist her as much as he would have liked. Besides, he was older than her.

Gradually, the punctilious rhythm of the day, which Beth had adhered to all her life, and had expected would continue in her new married life, began to disintegrate. It occurred to her that she and Thomas were still in their dressing gowns at eleven o'clock one morning, and last night's supper things were unwashed in the sink. The pile of clothes to be ironed had grown dauntingly high, and winter sun exposed the dusty tops of furniture. On shopping expeditions the cold bit through their gloves, and made their arthritic hands to ache, and to open a tin, to turn on a tap or do up a button became a struggle. Some days, when it rained and a vicious wind blew, neither Beth nor Thomas had the heart to go out and buy something for supper. They made do with bread and jam, and suffered indigestion the next morning.

Madge and Eileen visited them every now and then: Beth made them tea and bought iced buns with wings of angelica, and listened with interest to news of the Sunset. Madge and Eileen seemed concerned: but Beth and Thomas assured them independent married life was very nice: no troubles, they could not be happier. And indeed this was true: to have your own home, rather than to be part of an institution, however comfortable, was an achievement in old age: and although neither ever mentioned it, both Thomas and Beth both privately intended to die at home.

They bought a budgerigar and a collection of cacti for their window, and sometimes they treated themselves to the luxury of a small glass of sherry, or brandy, which they preferred now to drink on their sofa rather than in the pub. They spoke often of their children, and their past, and of the odd characters in the Sunset, and felt quietly content, while all about them gathered signs of Beth's fatigue. Sometimes, she worried so much about what to give Thomas for his lunch or supper that she could not sleep. She was stricken with headaches in the morning. She could no longer make pastry, she discovered, because of her arthritis, and for so long she had been telling Thomas what a good pastry maker she was. He believed her, of course, even though she could produce no proof: but the disappointment depressed her.

Then one morning, the first snow of the year smudging their window, Beth knew she could not get up. A great weakness gripped her, making her too feeble to explain how she felt. Thomas made her a cup of tea, and brought her biscuits for lunch, and she stayed in bed all day.

That night a terrible pain spread over her chest and she

moaned out loud. Thomas woke. He took one look at her, dragged on his heavy coat over his pyjamas, and went downstairs to the call box to ring for an ambulance. Beth was taken to hospital. Heart attack, they said.

Madge and Eileen were very good about it all. They assured Thomas that when Beth was better there would be room for the two of them back at the Sunset. Thomas protested. He wanted so much to return to their own flat : he would insist on doing more of the housework, he said, and perhaps a home help could be found. But the doctor was adamant. Beth needed professional care.

And so Thomas moved back to the Sunset, to a new, light room with twin beds. He left it to Madge and Eileen to organise the selling of their new furniture and carpets and curtains. They gave him quite a large cheque, but it gave him no pleasure. He bought roses for Beth, and a pretty shawl, her favourite blue, and a picture of a country village which he hoped would remind her of Dorset. He visited the hospital each day, almost an hour's journey on the bus, and in between visits the hours passed slowly.

Beth returned within ten days, seemingly recovered. But, once again, she had instructions to take things quietly. So they spent most of the day in their room, away from the others with their sympathetic looks. They had their television and their budgerigar, and received much kindness. But for all that, they missed their own flat.

One evening Thomas noticed that Beth's complexion had deepened to the colour of a stormy sky, and her eyes were sad as they had been when he first saw her. She began to talk about their time in the flat, and Thomas realised Beth was a little confused : she thought they had spent many years there. In reality it had been scarcely six weeks.

But Thomas did not contradict her. She seemed happy to talk about their past. In some way it seemed to have replaced the greater stretch of time she had spent with Christopher Randolph Crest, and she wanted Thomas to assure her that when she was quite better they could return to the flat and continue their independent lives.

'It will all be waiting for us, just as we left it,' she said. 'Just a few weeks' time. A good dust, and there we'll be.'

Thomas broke the news to her gently.

'Not that flat, won't,' he said. 'You see, you being ill, it had to be given up, now we're back here. But we can get another one, just the same. Easy. Same block, probably.'

'Oh, good,' said Beth. 'That will be nice.'

'Just a little patience, that's all we need.' Thomas found his own mind confused, now : perhaps another flat was a real possibility. Beth, with all her spirit, even after the heart attack, seemed so sure she could manage it. He had faith in her. He was sure she could. He pulled a small package out of his pocket.

'Here,' he said.

'Oh, Thomas, you shouldn't.' Beth opened it with trembling hands. It was a small porcelain pot encrusted with roses.

'For your hairpins,' Thomas said. Beth smiled. She looked beautiful in the evening light, in spite of the glowering colour of her skin.

'You spoil me, you know,' she said. 'It's just like you're courting me all over again, isn't it?'

Thomas scratched his head.

'Seems to me when we were courting before we were making plans. We got a lot more plans to make again.' He could not quite think what they were, but felt a strange certainty that in the days to come, with the return of Beth's health, they would sort themselves out.

Beth pulled her blue shawl more closely round her shoulders. She touched the cameo brooch at her neck, given to her by Thomas Harrow, and the wedding ring on her finger, given to her by Christopher Randolph Crest, and it seemed to her that everybody was together again in the room. They were all rejoined for the future.

'A few days and I'll be out in the shops, looking,' she said. 'Wait till you see.' Her head nodded at the darkening sky. 'I'm a little tired tonight, I think, but tomorrow we'll make a list of what we'll need ... Thomas Christopher,' she added, 'you're good to me.'

Thomas patted her hand. He was glad that she had put his name first, and that she agreed with him about what they should do, and that they were married. He heard the supper bell, but Beth was sleeping now. Not wanting to disturb her, Thomas remained motionless where he was, his hand in hers, waiting for her to wake, restored, and to smile at him again with her pretty eyes.

Printed in the United Kingdom
by Lightning Source UK Ltd.
131214UK00001B/2/P